A MOST TEMPTING OFFER

"I am very impressed with the way you handle these vexing affairs, and it seems to me, Miranda, I would never find a bride with such beauty, intelligence, and capability in handling a crisis. They are incredible and rare assets in one so young."

Miranda, not entirely sure whether he was funning or not, tossed her head. "Don't try to gammon me, Rupert. You don't want a wife. You want to be free of designing women, which makes me think of your Mrs. Castleton, a cast-off mistress and a dangerous one at that, don't you think?"

Rupert roared with laughter, then drew Miranda close to him. "What can I do to persuade you I am not some evil ogre with an unsavory past and a reputation for treating women badly? You may be making a grave mistake, my dear, in turning down my proposal so abruptly. I might make a most agreeable husband. Think about it."

And before she could collect her disordered thoughts, he gathered her into a close embrace, pinioning her hands so she could not resist, and began to kiss her. . .

A Reluctant Proposal
Violet Hamilton

ZEBRA BOOKS
KENSINGTON PUBLISHING CORP.

ZEBRA BOOKS are published by

Kensington Publishing Corp.
475 Park Avenue South
New York, NY 10016

Zebra and the Z logo are trademarks of Kensington Publishing Corp.

First Printing: July, 1993

Printed in the United States of America

Chapter One

"Your father has been asking for you, miss," the Houghton's parlor maid greeted Miranda in a worried tone as she entered the house.

"Thank you, Jessie," Miranda smiled at the maid, not too concerned. Jessie, whose wispy brown hair straggled beneath her cap, was usually flustered and frightened. Not that the Houghtons were unkind to her, but life in general seemed a continual struggle for the poor girl. Miranda herself, a tempestuous beauty with wayward auburn curls, a *retroussé* nose, and large, heavily lashed green eyes, found little in life to depress her volatile spirits and could not conceive of behaving like a scared mouse. But then, she admitted, with some compunction, her lines lay along far more pleasant paths than Jessie, the support of a drunken father and a slattern mother.

Before obeying Jessie's message, Miranda swept up the narrow staircase of the Houghton house, to repair the damages to her appearance. Her father was apt to deplore her disregard for propriety, and she did look somewhat disheveled. She had been out on the river with Peter Worthington, and the wind had played havoc with her curls. Giving a tug to her faded blue muslin gown, she grimaced at her image in the mirror of her small bedroom. She did look rather hoydenish, she admitted, running a brush quickly over the offending hair and then washing her hands in the basin. Deciding that this sketchy toilette would have to do, she skipped down the stairs again, prepared to face her parent.

Without ceremony she entered her father's study to be faced by both her mother and father, who indeed looked grave. Now what had she done? Casting her mind back over her latest transgressions, she could not think of any one misdeed which would earn her a reprimand.

"Good afternoon, Father, Mama," she greeted them cheerily, rather daunted by their expressions. Her father, at the best of times, was not given to conviviality. A lecturer in English literature at the university, he looked the part: a tall, brown-haired man of some forty five years, with piercing green eyes and stern demeanor, whose normal mien impressed his students but had never subdued Miranda. Her mother, on the other hand, lived in some awe of her husband—quailing when even a slight frown darkened his brow—and studied to please him in all matters. Miranda often wondered what her father had found so attractive in his meek wife, whose faded elegance hinted at a youthful beauty quenched by a domineering husband. But on the whole Miranda was not an introspective girl and took her parents as she found them with little thought of their relationship to each other or to her.

"You wanted me, Father?" she asked, seating herself before his desk and gazing up with cheerful candor.

"Yes, Miranda. Your mother and I have a matter of serious urgency to discuss with you." He spoke pompously. Professor Houghton usually talked as if delivering a lecture, even when dealing with his family.

"Nothing wrong with Robbie, I hope," Miranda asked, wondering if her young brother, a student at Harrow, had suffered some mishap or even been sent down from school. Robbie, five years younger than his sister, shared her volatile spirits. Who knew what he might have done?

"Robert is fine, as far as we know, although his last reports

6

were not what I had hoped," Professor Houghton said with some uneasiness. "No, this matter concerns you, Miranda. You are nineteen years old, certainly more than ready for marriage, and I have received an offer for you."

Miranda, startled, turned to her mother, who appeared more than normally distraught. Evidently Eleanor Houghton did not share her husband's pleasure in this offer. Who could it be? Most of Miranda's beaux were young Oxford students who were not eager to enter the parson's mousetrap and were neither emotionally nor financially able to do so.

"Horace Howland, a distinguished colleague of mine, has indicated he wishes to make you his wife. As he has considerable private means and is a man of great respectability as well as a brilliant scholar, you are a most fortunate girl that his choice has fallen upon you," her father said in measured tones.

"Old Howland. You must be joking. I would never marry him. Why, he is almost as old as you, Father! And a prosy bore and quite repulsive," Miranda replied in disgust.

"You must marry him, Miranda," her mother intervened, almost in tears.

"Why?" Miranda asked reasonably. She realized that her father was serious and wondered why her parents were so determined to force her into marriage with such an unacceptable man. Looking at her father's flushed face, she realized he was embarrassed as well as adamant. There was a mystery here and she would uncover it, for she would not be coerced into such a wretched union.

"I do not care for Mr. Howland and, in fact, cannot understand why he would make such an outrageous suggestion," Miranda insisted firmly. She thought of Horace Howland with a shudder. Her was a balding, corpulent man, a classics professor who had never paid her the slightest attention and seemed thoroughly preoccupied with Socrates and Plato. He lived in the ancient world with little heed to the delights of the modern one. "Why would you even consider such an idea, Father?"

"Horace has indicated that he has watched you with growing affection for some years. He has decided he needs a wife and believes you would make a delightful one," her father explained solemnly, as if this horrid idea were not in the least exceptional.

"Nonsense. He must know I would never consent," Miranda scoffed, almost laughing at the notion but quickly sobering as she saw her father's expression. Turning to her mother, she said, "Why must I marry him, Mama? I don't want to marry anyone, and, if I did, Horace Howland would not be a man I would consider. There is some reason you are pressing his suit, and I want to know it."

"Don't be impertinent, Miranda," her father reproved. "I am your guardian, and you will do as I say. I have accepted Horace's kind offer on your behalf."

"Well, you can just unaccept it," Miranda protested boldly. "I won't have him, and I am ashamed to think you would press such a dessicated old fogy on me."

"He is five years younger than I am, Miranda," her father commented—as if that had any relevance!

"If he were twenty years younger, I would not have him. What can you be thinking of?"

Eleanor Houghton, turning with despair to her husband, wailed. "You will have to tell her, Adrian."

"Yes, I suppose so." Miranda was surprised to see that her father looked both contrite and angry, as if he dreaded explaining. He loathed admission of guilt. Possessed of an overweening pride, he insisted on his family's utmost obedience. Now he could not hide behind his usual facade of omnipotence; he had to admit his fallibility.

"Unfortunately I owe Horace an impossible sum of money, a debt of honor incurred at some rather disastrous runs of cards. I cannot pay off the notes, but he has suggested he would forgive the obligation if you married him." Adrian Houghton's reserve crumpled, and Miranda realized that he was pleading with her, something she would never have thought possible. She had always respected her father; and if he did not inspire great affection, she had at least always been impressed by his integrity and intelligence. She did not expect human failings in her formidable father.

"Well, you must borrow the money or ask him to allow you time to pay it off gradually. I will not marry him to satisfy your debt," she said with more resolve than she felt. Suddenly apprehensive, she knew with certainty that her father would not consider her refusal. His stubborn frown boded ill in the face of her defiance. Could he force her to the altar with the hateful Horace?

"Do you want to see your father disgraced and possibly dismissed from his post?" her mother asked with surprising spirit.

"No, of course not. But there must be another way. You are asking me to sacrifice my life to pay a gambling debt? Is that fair?"

An uneasy expression crossed Adrian Houghton's face but was at once repressed. It was obvious he was not going to justify his conduct to his daughter. "Surely you are not so naive as to expect justice in life? Or could it be you have conceived some unsuitable fondness for a callow Oxford student?" he sneered.

Despite herself, Mrs. Houghton intervened. "Sometimes parents know best about a daughter's choice of a husband."

Miranda wondered fleetingly if her mother were referring to her own lack of wisdom in defying Miranda's grandparents to marry Adrian Houghton. For the first time, she saw that her mother's life had not justified such rebellion. But her own miserable future concerned her to the exclusion of all else. If she gave a passing warm thought to the devotion of young Peter Worthington, she was wise enough not to voice it.

Studying her father's implacable visage, she decided that apparent compliance might serve her better for the moment. She had no intention of wedding Horace Howland, but she needed time to determine how best to effect her disobedience. Outright defiance would avail her nothing.

"Howland is coming to dinner tonight to put forth his proposal. I expect you to receive it with proper gratitude, Miranda," her father instructed, his dignity—and authority—restored. If he doubted her response, he did not show it. His bearing made it clear that he would permit no opposition.

Fixing an obstinate stare upon him, Miranda did not confirm or deny his assumption that she would obey.

"In that case I had best prepare myself for this momentous occasion," she agreed. If her father disliked her tone, he chose not to challenge her. Nodding instead, he turned to the papers on his desk, signifying the interview was over.

Miranda, without more ado, left the room, trailed by her mother. Unwilling to show any sign of weakness, Miranda squared her shoulders and marched upstairs to her bedroom, her mother on her heels. When the door closed behind them, she turned to face Eleanor Houghton.

"Did your family object strongly to your marrying father?" she asked gently. She was taken aback by her mother's fierce expression.

"Very much. They wanted me to marry a neighbor's son, a young man in every way a desirable *parti*, but I was young and foolish and insisted on following my heart."

"And you have regretted not acceding to their wishes?" Miranda asked, her own dilemma somewhat softened by this amazing disclosure. She had always believed her mother adored her father despite his indifferent treatment of her.

"I have never regretted it for one moment. I realize you think your father difficult, demanding, and egotistical; and that may be true in some respects. But in any marriage an onlooker, even a daughter, only sees some of the relationship.

10

Your father is really quite insecure. He feels the difference in our birth. And he needs me, my love and respect, to bolster his image of himself. Sometimes, I know, he thinks I regret my choice; but, believe me, that is not so." Mrs. Houghton offered her explanation awkwardly, twisting her hands in her effort to persuade. She dreaded, too, that her forthright daughter might use her confession against her.

Miranda, surprised by her mother's unusual honesty and this new perception of her father, wanted to argue that Adrian Houghton showed more exasperation than affection toward his wife; but she could not bring herself to behave so meanly when her mother had behaved so bravely. She knew it had cost her a great deal to expose her true feelings.

Watching the expressions at war on her daughter's face, Eleanor pursued her case. "Usually, Miranda, parents know best in these matters. I don't believe mine did, but our situations are not parallel. Since you are not in love with anyone, why is Horace so unacceptable? You have to marry some-time; there is no other life for a respectable woman. We do care about your welfare." The older woman came to an abrupt finish, realizing that her argument was specious and that she could be accused of favoring her husband at the expense of her daughter.

"So it is father's welfare that is at risk, not mine? Never mind, Mama, there is little you can do," Miranda soothed, knowing her mother was incapable of defying her husband. Rejecting any signs of comfort from her mother, she tugged at her dress. "Well, I must dress, I suppose." Not entirely trusting her daughter's compliance, Mrs. Houghton would have pressed Miranda about her intentions, but the girl's closed face indicated without question her unwillingness to discuss the situation further. Eleanor retreated helplessly into her usual, inadequate fluttering.

"Well, I will leave you then. But, Miranda, don't do anything foolish. You cannot thwart your father," she warned ominously and made her exit.

Miranda sat down heavily on her bed. What recourse did she have? If she refused Horace Howland, she had no doubt that her father would see that she suffered. And where could she turn for relief? She had few options; respectable girls had little choice. She actually could run away and go on the stage: Her repertoire of Shakespearean plays was immense. She had been well tutored by her father. But did she have the courage? She knew too well the pitfalls of flight. Without a reference, she could not secure a position as a governess or companion in a well-regulated household. Discouraged but not daunted, she convinced herself she would find an avenue of escape. Marriage with any of the young Oxford students who enjoyed her company was not unthinkable, but she needed time to devise a plan—and select a bearable union. For the moment, she had no option but to appear to consent to her father's dictum. If she refused Horace, she would be confined to her room, watched and guarded, badgered constantly. But she would find a way. For now her best policy was acquiescence; that would give her the necessary respite. Her father, lulled by her submission, would be off his guard.

Later that evening as she faced Horace Howland across the dinner table, her determination to escape this unthinkable marriage hardened. What a self-satisfied prig the man was. She disliked exceedingly the leering complacency that implied he had bestowed a great honor upon her. His smooth bland face, protuberant light-blue eyes, and stubby fingers repulsed her. And he had an annoying habit of cracking his knuckles when he made a conversational point. The thought of being with such a specimen disgusted her, but she displayed none of her aversion and smiled demurely, as if pleased by his proprietal glances. She forced herself to eat and in no way indicated that the interview which would follow this difficult dinner would not meet with her approval.

Her parents, wary and ready to counter any hint of rebellion, did not allow the conversation to turn on personal matters. Her father, as usual, dominated the talk, discoursing heavily upon a colleague's paper on Ben Johnson which met with his scorn. Howland agreed affably, sublimating his own scholarly perspectives in deference to his anticipated relationship with his colleague. Mrs. Houghton said little. She was not as convinced as her husband that when the moment approached Miranda would do her duty, but Eleanor had long since learned to keep her own counsel.

Miranda and her mother at last left the gentlemen to their port and retired to the drawing room.

"You are in good looks this evening, Miranda. I like that new *eau de nile* silk very much. It well repays its high price, and Mrs. Colton has done it up nicely," Mrs. Houghton placated as she settled behind her embroidery frame.

"Yes, it does quite well, I think," Miranda replied briefly, dreading the inevitable confrontation. Although she was determined she would never wed Horace Howland, she was apprehensive. He would make offensive demands, she feared, once she had accepted his proposal. But she would have to submit, at least for a few days, to his insistence on a fiancé's rights.

In any event she was spared such indignities. When the gentlemen entered the room, her father lost no time in getting down to the matter at hand.

"Horace has something he wishes to ask you, Miranda. Perhaps it would be best if you heard him in my study where you can be private," he suggested gingerly, determined to put as good a face as possible on the occasion.

Miranda, disguising her distaste, rose unhurriedly and drifted from the room, the eager Horace in tow. In the study, she turned and faced the man she now thought of as her adversary.

"I understand from Father you have a proposal to make to

me, Mr. Howland," she dared him, intent on settling matters without maidenly shrinkings.

Nervous, he grasped the nettle and plunged into his offer. "It may come as a surprise to you, Miss Houghton, but I have long admired you, your spirit, your beauty, and your utter suitability for the position I am pleased to offer you." Beads of sweat appeared on his forehead.

Surely he must know that she would not entertain his suggestion for a moment if her father had not incurred this dreadful debt. Obviously he thought it would be ill-bred to refer to it and wanted to assume this was an honorable proposal. Well, she would play his game.

"What can that be, Mr. Howland?" she asked with wide-eyed wonder.

"I want to make you my wife, and your father has consented. I know there is some disparity in our ages; but often an older husband is more understanding, more patient with a wife than a young, untried, demanding fellow," he stammered. Really, Miranda thought, she could almost pity him if her were not so ridiculous and so unattractive. She surveyed his stocky figure, the broad pale face, and an emerging embonpoint not successfully concealed by an excellent tailor's efforts.

"I do hope you will be patient with me," Miranda simpered.

"Then you accept. You will become my wife." He seemed overwhelmed, as though he had anticipated a refusal. Certainly this calm acceptance from a rather exuberant young woman was a surprise.

"Yes, indeed, Mr. Howland. I accept your offer. It is most kind of you," Miranda said with a composure that astonished him. She waited, bracing herself for some sign of affection, but he did not presume to make any overtures, contenting himself with raising her hand to his lips and kissing it fer-

14

vently. Even the feel of his wet lips on her hand was loathsome, but she steeled herself not to flinch.

"Let us tell your parents that celebrations are in order," he preened, comfortable now that the interview had concluded to his satisfaction. Not that he had ever doubted the outcome, he persuaded himself. After all, Adrian was in a precarious position. Horace had the power to disgrace his colleague, and he would have availed himself of that prerogative if Miranda had proved recalcitrant. If he wondered what threat Adrian had held over his daughter, he refused to entertain such an uncomfortable idea. She was a sensible girl and understood her duty, which promised well for their married life. He would not frighten her with the depths of his feelings now; but once they were wed, he would master her, of that he had no doubt. Still, it would behoove him to go warily for the present. Young women were so easily offended by the passions of mature men, and rightly so. He glowed with righteousness and the secret musings on a delectable future as he followed Miranda back to the drawing room, not suspecting for a moment that she intended to deceive her parents and him in the near future.

15

Chapter Two

After a restless night during which she hatched several wild schemes and regretfully abandoned each of them, Miranda awoke all the more determined to make her escape without arousing her parents' suspicions. She doubted she could play the role of complaisant fiancée for an extended length of time, and Horace, anxious for their nuptials, had set a wedding date within the month. Her father had prudently taken himself off to his lecture before Miranda breakfasted; and her mother, beyond casting Miranda a worried glance, was reluctant to discuss the engagement. Eager to get out of the house, Miranda gratefully accepted a commission to exchange some embroidery silks for her mother and hurried down the High Street to the shop as soon as she had finished her chocolate.

She completed her errand with dispatch and was wondering what she could do, and where she could go to find a peaceful spot to contemplate her next move. But on emerging from the shop she was surprised to find Peter Worthington lounging against the stone wall.

"Good morning, Miranda. I spied you through the window and waited, hoping to catch you." His eagerness to see her warmed Miranda's heart. What a nice young man he was, with his shock of heavy brown hair, his candid brown eyes, and tall gangling stature. A university student, of course, and still engagingly naive, Miranda thought even as she felt the weight of her own dilemma. But she needed a confidant, and Peter was both trustworthy and caring.

"We had such a nice day on the river, yesterday," she remarked as they strolled through the busy street crowded with students in their gowns and housewives and maids caught up in their shopping chores. It was a damp misty morning but not at all cold, and there was the promise of sunshine later on.

"Yes, we must do it again soon if the weather holds," he agreed cheerfully. Then, glancing at her somber face, he asked tentatively, "Is something bothering you, Miranda? You seem uncommonly gloomy, not your style at all."

"I am gloomy. And when I tell you the reason you may laugh, but believe me it is a serious matter. My whole life is at stake," Miranda informed him dramatically, directing their steps toward Cornmarket Street.

"Oh, come now, Miranda. It cannot be that dreadful," Peter said, taking her arm and skillfully steering her from the path of a beladened matron, who struggled ahead of them.

"It is worse," Miranda confessed. "Come, let us go into St. Michael's Church out of the wind and I will tell you all about it." She wondered briefly if she were wise to confide in Peter. Would he be put off by her circumstances? No matter, she had to discuss her plight with someone, and Peter could supply a fresh outlook and—perhaps—a ready solution. Might he not have a relative, an aged aunt, who needed a companion? Or a cousin with children, searching for a governess? She cast about madly for an alternative to the miserable fate which awaited her. She *had* to take action.

St. Michael's, with one of England's few Saxon towers, had been a refuge for centuries, and its massive walls offered a suitable sanctuary, Miranda thought. They slipped into the deserted church and perched on the chairs placed for worshippers just inside the narthex.

"This is the deepest secret, Peter, and you must not breathe a word to a soul," Miranda appealed, laying an urgent hand on his arm and gazing at him in supplication.

By now, thoroughly alarmed, Peter nodded assent, wondering what could be causing the normally ebullient Miranda such unhappiness. He would have promised anything, for he was entranced by this charming girl who was so different from the customary meek misses of London society.

"My father has forced me to accept an offer from Horace Howland. He insists I marry him because he owes the horrid man an immense amount of money and Horace will disgrace him if I do not consent. Yet I cannot wed that old windbag," Miranda blurted out in desperation.

Peter, appalled, grabbed her hands, "Of course you cannot. Your father must be mad."

"No, only worried about his livelihood and reputation." With a sense of loyalty and fairness, Miranda defended Adrian Houghton.

"You have not agreed," Peter protested, echoing her distress. He was willing to offer whatever solace he could, but Miranda needed more than comfort: She needed a plan of action.

"Only to buy time," she explained, "but I've got to escape." She felt foolish. How could Peter possibly be of help?

But he did not let her down. With a gulp, he rushed to her aid. "There is only one thing for it. You must marry me. We will elope to Gretna Green," he said masterfully, barely aware of what such a solution to Miranda's problem entailed.

"Oh, Peter, that is so kind of you, but you cannot think what you are saying."

"Yes, I can. I do. I am frightfully fond of you, Miranda. And surely you would rather wed me than that frightful Howland. He's old enough to be your father—and a tedious

18

bore besides. I would be good to you, you know, do everything in my power to make you happy." He reached for her hand and urged his own suit with a passion he had not known he possessed. The thought of Miranda in the bed of old Howland infuriated him, and a romantic notion of himself as her saviour took root in his mind.

"But your parents. They would never accept me. And you would have to leave the university. You are a dear, Peter, to want to rescue me, but it would never do. And you are not of age." Miranda was touched by his offer, yet she could see the impediments to such a rash resolution. And she really did not want to marry anyone. All she wanted was to regain her carefree existence, her independence. She thought of Peter as a lighthearted young companion to her days of freedom, not as a husband to whom she would be tied forever.

"Oxford is so stuffy. Real life is in London. And I am not doing well, you know. No doubt I will be sent down anyway for some transgression or other. I would not miss it, and when we are married we can have such a good time," he insisted with a careless disregard of obstacles. "I have my allowance, and thus quite enough money to hire a post chaise to speed us to Gretna Green before anyone knows we are gone. Once wed, what can our parents do? They will have to accept the *fait accompli,*" he said grandly, impressed with his own argument.

Miranda hesitated. She knew it was disgraceful to even consider such a plan, desperate as she was. No respectable girl eloped to Gretna Green. They would create a scandal; and sensibly, she realized that it would not be as easy as Peter believed. She doubted that either set of parents would hail their marriage with any enthusiasm, and how would it solve her father's problem with Horace Howland? In his fury at the defection of his fiancée, the man was perfectly capable of seeking his revenge on Adrian Houghton. Was she selfish enough to gain her own freedom at the expense of her father's dire fate? Perhaps, once wed, she could prevail upon Peter to find the money to pay off Howland. She did not even know the full extent of the debt, but she doubted Peter had the funds. One day he would come into his inheritance, but she dimly remembered that a high-toned uncle managed his affairs. He would never agree to pay off Horace. Oh, dear, what should she do?

Peter watched the myriad emotions—hope, doubt, despair—cross Miranda's mobile face, undeterred. "It will be a great lark, Miranda. Surely you would rather wed me than suffer the attentions of that old man. It's not to be thought of for a moment." Peter shuddered for, unlike Miranda, he knew exactly what the marriage bed entailed.

"Oh, Peter, I should not consent. It is not fair to you." Miranda weakened at Peter's insinuation. She was not so innocent that she did not realize what marriage with Horace meant, and she shunned the idea. Peter, at least, was appealing, with his eager winning ways, his strong body, and his cheerful temperament. If only he were a few years older and in a position to claim a wife!

"No, no, not at all, Miranda. It is you who would be making the sacrifice. Oxford is filled with fellows who would want to make you their wife if they had the chance. You should be making your come-out in London." He studied her wistfully. "You would be a stunner."

Fond as he was of Miranda and appalled at the idea of her being pushed into marriage with horrid Horace, he had no illusions that the match would be hailed with enthusiasm by either of their families. And he doubted that Miranda would have accepted his remedy of an elopement to Gretna Green if she had not been desperate. Peter frowned and ran a hand through his brown hair. What a damnable situation for Miranda.

Then his brow cleared and he smiled. It would be a great adventure, cocking a snook at Horace, old Houghton, and his mother, who was always after him to remember his station in life and his duties and not disgrace her with intemperate action. Well, here he was, contemplating the most intemperate of actions. Serve her right. Now he must wrack his brain to come up with a clever plan. He must manage this affair well. Nothing could be more disastrous than for the elopement not to succeed, for Miranda to be dragged back to Oxford in disgrace, and for his mother to ring a peal over him, even enlist the services of his Uncle Rupert.

For a moment Peter's stout heart quailed at the thought of Lord Rupert St. Cloud Hastings, that notable man-about-town, Corinthian, member of the Four-in-Hand, and arbiter of manners. He only hoped that Rupert was hunting in the shires or away on a house party where he was fully occupied in seducing a willing matron and much too busy to concern himself with Peter's affairs. Rupert's interference might prove disastrous. Unwilling to let Miranda see any of his doubts or allow them to prevent him from acting in a dashing heroic manner, Peter said in a no-nonsense voice, "Now we must make a sensible plan, Miranda. No use in going off higgledy-piggledy and ruining the thing. Here is what I suggest." He then presented a credible outline of how they were to proceed, impressing Miranda and quelling her final doubts about the wisdom of Peter's drastic solution to her problem.

Contrary to his nephew's hopes, Lord Rupert St. Cloud Hastings was not pursuing his various interests in the country but at the moment that Peter and Miranda were conspiring was presenting himself at the Worthington mansion in Mount Street. His sister, Lady Worthington, had demanded his presence, and he knew from long experience that he might as well accede to her request sooner rather than later.

Charlotte had never accepted that Rupert, younger by some ten years, once under her thumb in the nursery, had graduated from her dominance. Her late husband had warned her many a time. "Don't try ordering Rupert about, old lady," Sir William had advised. "He won't have it and will do just the opposite of what you want out of sheer obstinance."

But neither Sir William nor Rupert himself had ever managed to stanch Charlotte Worthington's efforts to manage her family to her satisfaction no matter what obstacles she faced. For years she had been urging her brother to behave in a more seemly fashion due to his rank. She despaired of ever arranging a proper marriage for him, but at the same time was not eager to see him wed since her son, Peter, was his heir. Not that she would have complained if Rupert had proposed to an eligible, well-dowered young woman. Peter was suitably provided for by his late father, although he would not come into control of his tidy little fortune until he reached his majority. No, Lady Worthington was not so mean-spirited or grasping that she would deny her brother a proper marriage and children—*if* his choice fell upon a girl who satisfied her own standards. But there seemed little chance of such an event occurring. Lady Worthington felt Rupert was in danger of becoming a scandal. His style of life was disreputable, licentious, and hedonistic in the extreme. And it was not just a question of his sowing his wild oats as young men were prone to do when they first came on the town. Rupert had inherited his title at seventeen, managed to win a creditable degree at Oxford, but then descended on London determined to enjoy himself. And so he had for the past ten years. It was high time he settled down and, more importantly, assumed his duty toward his heir. Lady Worthington believed her brother must be coerced into taking some interest in his heir, guiding him toward the right connections, putting him up for membership in White's, and generally seeing to Peter's welfare. Until now he had showed a lamentable lack of desire to take Peter under his wing and she was about to chide him for his attitude, among other matters.

Rupert, who had no illusions that the coming interview would be enjoyable, had decided it would be best to endure it now so that he might escape Charlotte's strictures for several more weeks. These attempts of hers to manage his life were tedious, yet they rarely affected his good humor. He had a certain tepid affection for his sister and found her amusing in small doses, so he was quite willing to expose himself to her lectures occasionally, while paying no heed to her demands.

Throwing the reins of his glossy black horses to his tiger, he walked up the marble steps of the Worthington house, hoping that his visit with Charlotte would take little more than an hour. There were some great goers promised for sale at Tattersall's, two lively grays he had been eyeing for some time, and he would not want to miss the chance to buy them because he had to endure Charlotte's complaints.

He gave his hat and gloves to Radleigh, the Worthington butler, and inquired after the butler's sciatica. Rupert was always very punctilious about these pleasantries, which earned him the respect and affection of servants wherever he went.

"Quite well, my lord. This warmer weather has effected an improvement." Radleigh, a stately man with an impressive mien, relaxed his usual austere gaze to smile warmly on Rupert. He certainly was a figure to evoke admiration: Above average height, with a firmly muscled, broad-shouldered figure and long legs which appeared to good effect in the fawn pantaloons set off by black Hessians and an admirable single-breasted black coat fashioned by Stultz. He would not have committed the solecism of calling upon his sister in riding clothes, no matter how convenient. Although his clothes were fashionable, a tribute to both his tailor and his valet, Rupert Hastings did not need their enhancement. With dark piercing eyes under strongly marked brows, a decided chin, an aquiline nose, his black hair closely cropped in the Stanhope mode, he was not strictly handsome, his features were too harsh for that description; but he was arresting and a man of considerable consequence.

His sister was apt to believe he exerted that consequence too often in her presence. She received him, standing before a cheerful fire in her morning room.

"Well, Rupert, you took your time in answering my summons. I wrote you three days ago," she reproved him.

"Alas, dear Char, I was out of town; but when I returned, I hastened to obey your wishes. You are looking in fine fig, my dear. Hardly know you were ten years the elder. You know, you might marry again. I am sure Carter-Welles would pop the question if you gave him the slightest encouragement. He's a viscount, too, quite helpful, wouldn't you say?" Rupert teased outrageously, on the one hand complimenting her and on the other distracting her from whatever criticism she was about to level with respect to his own conduct.

"Don't be ridiculous, Rupert, and I will not be fobbed off by your nonsense," she said, but a slight smile accompanied this admonition and she indicated that he should be seated. But Rupert was not to be caught by this ploy. He had no intention of entering into a long catechism from his sister. Propping himself against the mantel, and thus depriving her of the major warmth of the fire, he asked pleasantly, "And how may I serve you, Char?"

"By moving away from the fire, and stop glaring down at me. It gives you an unneeded advantage," his sister complained. Lady Worthington had inherited the family's dark looks as well as the stubbornness and a certain arrogance which were Hastings' characteristics. She had been clever enough to mask these traits when she was on the hunt for a husband; and, as she had an undeniable handsomeness, William Worthington had thought himself most fortunate to win her. He had been an easy-going man, and her determination and managing ways had not disturbed his peace. The marriage had been a happy one, blessed with two children—Peter

24

and his sister, Louise—and Charlotte truly missed her husband, who had succumbed in his forty-second year to a virulent fever.

"I need all the advantages I can summon when dealing with you, my dear Char," Rupert admitted, moving a bit away from the hearth but refusing to settle in a chair.

"Don't call me that," she complained automatically. "I want to speak to you about Peter," she said then, determined not to waste any time, knowing that her brother was perfectly capable of distracting her and then leaving before she had made her intentions clear.

"Is the boy in some trouble?" Rupert asked, disguising his complete lack of interest in Peter's exploits. In his experience, young men at Oxford were always up to some sort of jape, and the better for it. He recalled some dashing deeds of his own when up at Balliol, but he doubted that Peter had the mettle to emulate them. He had always found his nephew a stolid amiable boy lacking the imagination or style to commit any really disreputable acts.

"That's just it. I don't know, but I suspect he has become involved with some vulgar female," Lady Charlotte confessed.

"Probably has. Those are the only kinds of women to be found in Oxford, but he will come to little harm," Rupert replied carelessly. If Peter had formed some unsuitable liaison, Rupert was more apt to encourage him than take him to task.

"Yes, but Peter has such gothic notions. He might just be inveigled into marriage through some foolish notions of chivalry. I want you to go to Oxford and find out what he is up to. I wrote and asked him to come down for the Lansdowne Ball this weekend and have received no reply. That's not like Peter, who is usually so good about keeping in touch."

Seeing that his sister was really worried, Rupert decided he must calm her fears. "I doubt the boy is in any danger of proposing to some chit, but if it will make you feel easier, I will stop by to see him this weekend on my way to Gloucester-shire," he soothed her. It was a damn nusiance, but he sup-posed he could spare the time. Sir William would have settled her down, but in the absence of any support, she needed re-assurance from some male. Rupert had little faith in the good sense of women, especially when their sons were in question.

"Oh, thank you, Rupert. I do appreciate it, and I know you will sort him out. He does admire you so." Charlotte smiled happily, now that she had achieved her aim. Rupert might be a trial, but he did have some vestiges of family duty. They parted soon after with mutual esteem, each convinced that the other had behaved with admirable restraint.

Chapter Three

Rupert did not have a very high opinion of his nephew's spirit of adventure, and he would have been surprised at Peter's practical command of events leading to his elopement.

Once convinced that the answer to Miranda's predicament could only be solved by a trip to Gretna Green, Peter put the matter in train with great efficiency. He managed to provide himself with sufficient money, reserved changes of horses along the way, mapped out a strategic route which would avoid the obvious stops along the Great North Road, and fobbed off his tutor and friends with excuses for his absence during the next week. He instructed Miranda to behave with forbearance, act as if she were willing to go along with Howland's request for an early wedding, and deceive her parents as to her real feelings about this unwanted match. Caught up in the excitement and intrigue, he gave little thought to the consequences and persuaded Miranda that they would emerge from the affair commendably.

Three days after their meeting in St. Michael's, they set off. Miranda had managed to smuggle a small case from home without her parents knowledge and escaped with the excuse that she must consult a dressmaker about her trousseau. Arriving at Mrs. Colton's establishment in Beaumont Street, she had left Eleanor Houghton inspecting silks and muslins on the pretext of returning her mother's library books on the High Street. Mrs. Houghton, unhappy and distracted, eager to accede to any request of Miranda's, agreed, and promised to have several selections ready for her daughter's inspection when she returned. Miranda scurried from the shop and met Peter with the post chaise at the entrance to Balliol College. Within moments they were cantering up St. Giles on their way north.

Mrs. Houghton waited almost an hour before realizing that Miranda was not returning. Flustered and afraid, for, unlike her husband, she had not been entirely deceived by Miranda's compliance in the coming marriage, she immediately suspected her daughter had concocted some outrageous plan to thwart their wishes. What should she do? Her husband was immured in the Bodleian Library and could not be reached. Where could Miranda have gone? She understood what her husband refused to face, that Miranda loathed the idea of marrying Horace Howland and held her parents in contempt for forcing the match upon her. Adrian, with his usual indifference to anyone's comfort and desire but his own, had accepted Miranda's atypical assent. But Eleanor Houghton, knowing more of her daughter's character, had expected defiance and now was certain that Miranda had taken steps to see that she never became Mrs. Howland. What danger her refusal would expose her to in a world beyond the sheltered confines of Oxford drove her mother to extreme agitation. Hurrying home she wrote an urgent request to her husband to come immediately and cope with Miranda's flight. As she waited for his arrival, horrible visions of her daughter's situation brought her to the verge of nervous collapse. So when Adrian Houghton finally appeared, annoyed by the summons, she was in no condition to give a sensible explanation of what might have happened. Of course, he was furious and blamed her.

"Really, Eleanor. It behooved you to keep a strict eye on

Miranda. You should not allow her to roam the streets on some spurious errand," he fumed, seeing his hopes of disentangling himself from the disaster his gambling had brought about rapidly fade. He had little faith that Horace Howland would view Miranda's flight with any charity. The selfish chit, allowing her father to be disgraced and dishonored just because of a few shrinking scruples. She had to marry sometime, so why not take Horace and rescue her father? That was her duty, and she had failed to assume it.

"Where could she have gone, Adrian? Is there anyone to whom she could have appealed for help?" Eleanor asked, pacing the small sitting room, for once too afraid of what might have befallen their daughter to care about Adrian's dilemma.

"I have no idea. I trusted Miranda to your guidance, and see how you have abandoned your responsibility," he responded angrily, loathe to admit his own role in Miranda's desperate flight. "We must get her back before Horace discovers the ungrateful girl has disobeyed us."

They might have continued in this manner for some time, accomplishing little but mutual recriminations, if they had not been interrupted by Jessie sidling into the room with the announcement they had a caller.

Rupert Hastings had arrived in Oxford a few hours before, just moments after Peter and Miranda had rode off to the North. On applying to Peter's rooms and discovering him gone, he had lost no time in questioning Peter's friends and tutor. Their information had led him in short order to the Houghtons' cottage, where he intended to quiz them about their daughter's relationship with his nephew. He rapidly had come to the conclusion that Miranda Houghton had inveigled Peter into some shocking scheme which would cause Lady Worthington palpitations, if not worse.

He entered the sitting room on Jessie's heels in a towering rage, paying no mind to the civilities.

"Good afternoon. I am Rupert Hastings and have come to see your daughter, Miranda, who I understand is involved with my nephew, Peter Worthington," he explained brusquely, barely acknowledging the Houghtons' greeting.

"I don't know what you mean, sir. And I deeply resent your barging into our home demanding assurances," Adrian blustered, for one look at Rupert's card, timidly offered by Jessie, had roused his deepest forebodings.

"Resent away, I still want some answers. I suspect your wanton daughter has lured my nephew into some escapade which will rebound on your heads if you do not give me the information I seek," Rupert responded, not at all impressed with Professor Houghton's manner. Turning to Eleanor Houghton he continued, "Where is your daughter, ma'am?"

Unable any longer to repress her fears, Eleanor Houghton burst into tears, sobbing, "I have no idea, sir. She has vanished."

"With my nephew, no doubt. This is a damnable coil. How long have they been absent?"

"About three hours. And I doubt very much if your nephew is with her. She is engaged to a colleague of mine, and her wedding is just a few weeks away," Horace explained, prepared to quell this indignant peer with his own dignity.

But Rupert paid no attention, ignoring Adrian, and giving his full attention to the distraught Mrs. Houghton. "Do you think they have eloped?" he asked quietly, for he sensed that Mrs. Houghton was the weaker reed and could be compelled to tell the truth.

"Surely Miranda was not that desperate?" Eleanor Houghton offered, her tears magically disappearing as the thought took hold.

Rupert's suspicions confirmed, he had the story of the afternoon's aborted errand out of Mrs. Houghton in a moment. No mention was made of her father's attempts to blackmail

30

his daughter into a distasteful marriage. Rupert was led to believe that Miranda had thought Peter a better *parti* and persuaded the gullible young man into an elopement.

He stormed out of the house, determined to catch up with them. Opportunists like the missing Miss Houghton seized the chance to improve their status, and he had little doubt that she was the instigator of this plot. Well, she would not be successful, he decided and called up his horses, intent on apprehending the pair before nightfall.

Determined to put as much distance as possible between possible pursuers and their post chaise, Peter had insisted on making all speed to Cheltenham, not the direct route north, but westward some forty miles. They drew into The George as dusk was settling and Peter escorted Miranda into the coaching inn.

"We will stop here for the night and hope to get beyond Birmingham tomorrow. That city is so large, so busy, and so equipped with inns, it would be hard for anyone to find us there. And no doubt the pursuit would be confined to the Great North Road, which we have avoided," he reassured her. "I have bespoke a room for you and a private parlor where you will be most comfortable and out of the way of the general travelers. I have said you are my sister," he confided shyly.

Miranda, exhausted and troubled, could only be grateful for Peter's tact and gentleness. He had no intention of pressing his claims until they were truly wed over the anvil at Gretna, for which she could only be thankful. Not that she was prey to missish feelings, but she was in no mood to seal their new relationship on this, the first night of their elopement. She retreated to the bedroom prepared for her and made what adjustments to her toilette were necessary after their hectic ride. Now that the decision had been taken, she was determined to

31

put as cheerful a face as possible on this dramatic escape from Horace Howland's clutches. Peter's generosity and thoughtfulness only inclined her further to accept whatever plans he had made. She found she was quite hungry and met Peter in the private parlor a bit later, eager to partake of her supper.

"Peter, I had no idea you were so practical. You have really surpassed yourself," Miranda approved, settling down to some good York ham with relish.

Peter, dazed by Miranda's matter-of-fact acceptance of events, smiled encouragingly. "I must say Miranda you are a great gun. Most girls would be weeping and wavering, full of reproaches and doubts, but you have taken this whole thing with such sensibility."

"You mean I am not romantic. Are you disappointed? I confess that my chief emotion right now is relief. Until we actually were underway, I could scarcely believe I would avoid the miserable alternative facing me. I suppose I should feel some compunction for my father, but I am afraid I am not a dutiful daughter. Mostly I am angry that he should have driven me to such a pass," she admitted, feeling somewhat selfish, but unable to pretend a guilt she did not possess. She did wonder how her father would pay Horace the debt he owed but felt little remorse for what faced her parent.

"No regrets, then?" Peter asked, spurred by her frankness.

"Only for you, Peter. I do hope you realize what a sacrifice you are making," she replied seriously. She suspected that this elopement would cause Peter some uneasiness. She knew she was using him for her own ends. He could not really want to surrender his freedom, incur the anger of his relations, and find himself tied to a wife whose affection for him was founded on friendship and gratitude. Was that a basis for a successful union?

He flushed, lowering his eyes. The secrecy and chivalric impulse which had led him to risk his future on this adventure had carried him with enthusiasm to this point, but he was not without knowledge that he had indeed put them both in an uncomfortable position. He cared deeply for Miranda, admired her spirit, hated the thought of her allied to Horace Howland, but did he love her? Could such a marriage of expediency have a chance of success? Young and untried as he was, Peter still had a trace of common sense. He knew how this rash step would be viewed by his mother and his formidable uncle as well as Miranda's parents and Horace Howland. But he could not fail Miranda now.

"Not really a sacrifice, Miranda. Any man would be proud to claim you as his wife. But I cannot deny we face some rather sticky times ahead if we make it to Gretna safely," he said honestly.

Touched by his forthright admission, Miranda smiled. "Well, no point in regretting what we have done. We will just have to suffer the slings and arrows of misfortune if that is our lot."

Putting her doubts behind her, she turned to the realities of their situation. "How long will it take us to reach Scotland, do you think?"

"If all goes well, not more than four days. Depends on the horses, of course. But we will do it," he assured her stoutly, aware that he must act the efficient master of events no matter what fears he had. "But now it is getting late, and we must make an early start tomorrow. If there is any pursuit we are well ahead of it, I believe."

Miranda, relieved to have brushed through this first evening with a minimum of embarrassment, rose, agreeable to his suggestion. "I will say good night then and not prose on about the wisdom of our decision."

"Yes, and, Miranda, just let me say how much I admire your attitude. It augurs well for any difficulties ahead. We will come about, I am sure," Peter said stoutly as he stood up. "I will just finish this bottle and then go to bed myself. Have you everything you need?" he concluded with tentative concern.

"Of course, and thank you again, Peter." Miranda gave him a bracing smile. Then, feeling that perhaps a stronger evidence of her gratitude was needed, she crossed to him and put her arms around his neck, kissing him with fervor. Peter, responding to this surprising sign of affection, clasped her comfortingly and returned the kiss.

At that moment the door flew open, and Rupert Hastings, taking in the scene, looked at the couple with disgust. "Just as I suspected. What a fool you are, Peter."

Springing apart, the young couple faced the intruder, aghast and confused. Miranda had no idea who this forbidding man could be, but one look at Peter's expression convinced her that he meant trouble.

"Uncle Rupert!" Peter stammered, overcome with shock.

"Yes, my poor nodcock, and just in time, I think, to prevent you from disaster," Rupert drawled, looking Miranda up and down with an insulting stare which left her in little doubt that he blamed her for the whole sorry business. She stiffened, prepared to take issue with Peter's arrogant relative. She would not give ground to this haughty peer, nor allow Peter to suffer his recriminations. Nor would she make any explanations. She looked him over coolly, noting the dusty boots and many-caped coat, for Rupert had not stopped to divest himself of his outer garments. Beneath the tall hat, his face was hard and closed, his lips drawn into a sneer and his expression intimidating. Well, she would not be cowed.

"Perhaps you will tell me just what idiocy brought you to this pass? I have no doubt you think of yourself as a dashing knight, rescuing this wanton hoyden from penury or disgrace. Well, your escapade is at an end. Leave us, madame, while I sort out this young jackanapes," Rupert ordered scornfully, fully expecting Miranda to obey his command.

"No, sir, I will not. Whatever peal you intend to ring over

34

Peter, I will stay. You must feel you have some control over his actions; but let me tell you, you have none over mine," she objected with force and calmly sat down in the nearest chair, prepared to do battle with this odious disruption.

Chapter Four

If Rupert was taken aback by this unforeseen rebellion, he gave no sign of it. Throwing his hat, coat, gloves, and whip on the supper table, he stood, legs apart, regarding Miranda with evident dislike.

"You are a bold hussy, miss. But if you need to be coerced to see the folly of your actions, I am quite prepared to indulge you. As I am sure you are aware, Peter is a minor, my heir, and subject to the dominion of his mother and—more importantly—to me. I control his funds." He spoke tersely, as if expecting this news to alter her decision.

"I say, Uncle Rupert, there is no need to behave in such a barbaric fashion. I am the one who must be called to account. This elopement was my idea, to rescue Miranda from a horrid situation," Peter interposed bravely. Appalled as he was by his uncle's arrival, he had enough bottom to defend Miranda.

"Don't explain, Peter. I would prefer your officious relative not know any of the reasons for your kind intervention." Miranda quelled any possible mitigation Peter might offer. "Please keep my confidence," she begged giving him a stern look.

"Well, if you insist, Miranda, but I cannot have Uncle Rupert insulting you."

"And just how do you hope to prevent me, halfling?"

Rupert continued to regard Miranda with disdain, barely giving Peter any heed. His scorn was turned on the Oxford light skirt who had almost succeeded in luring his nephew into a most deplorable mess.

"I am quite willing to accept the full responsibility for this elopement, Lord Rupert," Miranda said boldly. If he intended to treat her like a trollop, she would do nothing to disabuse him.

When Peter had casually referred to his Uncle Rupert, she had pictured an antiquated peer with little sympathy for his young heir. She had never expected this boorish and insulting man, whose low opinion of women was obviously based on long experience. He could not yet be thirty, despite his hard swarthy face and the cynical dark eyes which raked over her as if she were an object of shoddy goods available for his inspection. She could see why Peter faced him with trepidation, but she had no such fear. She gave him back stare for stare.

"I see you have no shame, miss," Rupert accused her with a sneer.

"Come now, Uncle Rupert. You must not speak to Miranda in that nasty way. She is not the instigator of this elopement. It was all my idea, and you do not know the whole story," Peter challenged bravely.

"No, but I intend to find it out." Rupert ignored his nephew, but he recognized a worthy adversary in Miranda. She was certainly an attractive piece, although he disliked auburn hair and bold manners.

"Peter, there is no need to justify ourselves to your uncle. He may have the right to give you his opinion, but he cannot rule your actions," Miranda protested. "We have no intention of apologizing or excusing our plan, sir. If explanations are necessary, Peter will give them to his mother, who has the right to hear them."

"I am here as her deputy, not that that is any business of yours." He turned for the first time to his nephew, who stood between them. "Oh, for heavens sake, Peter," he exclaimed impatiently, "sit down and stop glowering at me. No doubt you would like to land me a facer for interfering, but it's not my choice, you fool. Your mother sent me after you." Peter recoiled in surprise, and Rupert continued in exasperation. "She suspected you had become entangled with some grasping female. I have better things to do than chase you across the country, you know." Having fully recovered his aplomb and his temper, he decided that contempt would serve him better than anger. "Striplings have a history of such follies when they come up to Oxford, but usually they do not go so far as marriage."

"These are special circumstances, sir, and I do not like your tone. Miranda is a very respectable girl, not the doxy or barmaid you imply." Peter, refusing to be cowed, gave his uncle a straight look.

"My apologies, miss." Rupert bowed although his voice mocked her. He was beginning to consider that he might have misread the situation. Her diction and dress indicated that she was not a common female, and it was with that observation that an outrageous suggestion came to his mind. Rupert Hastings had vast experience with women, and all of it confirmed his sense that they wanted one thing: Security in the form of a protector with well-filled pockets. Since coming on the town as a boy younger than Peter he had been the target of such women—the respectable ones eager to wed; the others just as avid for jewels, horses, a lavish establishment, and whatever else he could provide outside the legal bond. He was reminded that if he had been as naive as Peter he could have been entrapped by Chloe Castleton, his current mistress, a dashing brunette on the edges of society who believed their relationship could be parlayed into a wedding ring. She was wrong and all too exigent, so much so that he had been considering for some time how to dispose of her. Perhaps this Oxford miss might serve his purpose.

"You would not deny, miss, that one of your reasons for this dramatic rush to Gretna Green is that you need money," Rupert drawled, turning to Miranda and giving her a raking stare from beneath his heavy-lidded eyes.

"No, I will not deny that, but I refuse to tell you why," Miranda admitted curtly.

"Well, I might be prepared to offer you a sum, in return for certain favors." Rupert put forth his insinuating suggestion coolly, gauging her reaction.

"I say, Uncle Rupert, you cannot mean that," Peter interposed, realizing that his uncle might be offering Miranda carte blanche.

"Not at all, nodcock. You mistake my meaning. Miss Miranda here appears to be in sorry straits. She will not insist, I think, that this elopement is the result of an undying passion for you."

"I love Miranda and will not let you ride roughshod over her, attributing to her such disgusting motives." Peter's eyes blazed, his chivalry aroused by his uncle's derision.

"Charming, and I do not doubt your sincerity although I doubt Miranda's. I have seen no signs that she suffers a like fervor."

"I am very fond of Peter. We understand one another." Miranda heard the weakness in her declaration. Was this obnoxious man trying to buy her off? If he offered her enough money—five hundred pounds—to satisfy her father's obligation, she would accept his insults. Certainly Adrian Houghton would not insist on her marriage to Horace Howland if he had the means to pay his debt. She waited, not without a tremor, for whatever this brute had in mind.

"You might understand Peter, but do you realize that I control his money until he comes of age?"

"You have made that quite clear, sir. I do not envy you your suspicions and belief that money is the sole impetus for any action. It is true that my family situation dictates a pressing need for a certain amount without delay, but there is a limit to what I will do for money." Miranda spoke with sincerity but little hope that Lord Rupert would accept her claim. He was clearly prepared to think the worst of her.

As the interview continued, her initial anger and dislike for this man hardened into scorn. He represented a world and a set of values she found repugnant. Charity toward the less fortunate, respect for women, faith in the essential honesty of his fellows were not qualities that Lord Rupert entertained or even respected. He expected the worst of mankind and behaved accordingly, a philosophy Miranda deemed hateful. He might have tried to understand why she and Peter had taken this drastic step, even assisted them to solve their dilemma.

She admitted there was validity in the man's objection to their elopement: The disruption of Peter's Oxford career, the youth of the participants, the scandal which would surely follow. And Lord Rupert's scathing indictment, his sneering treatment of Peter, and his insulting attitude toward her had conveyed his feelings quite accurately. She owed him no explanation. Let him think what he liked. And if she could parlay his disgust into money, she would not be averse to accepting it. Serve him right, the haughty devil.

Rupert, who had learned to read more complicated people than Miranda, pondered how to turn her insecurities and dislike to his advantage. The bare outlines of a shocking idea which would rescue him from a personal crisis had now settled into a bold decision. If Peter objected, he could handle that young man. He had every reason to believe that Miranda's deepest emotions were not centered on his nephew, and the boy would recover from this unsuitable infatuation given time. Yes, this whole affair could be manipulated to relieve him of an uncomfortable burden. It would cost money, but then most things in life did, he concluded cynically.

Rupert appraised his nephew. Peter returned his uncle's stare with defiance and an ill-considered speech. "You do not intimidate me, Uncle Rupert," he threatened boldly. "I will protect Miranda from your salacious schemes."

Miranda, watching this byplay, was not impressed. Peter was a dear to champion her cause, but she was perfectly capable of meeting any challenge this supercilious lord mounted. "Thank you, Peter," she said, staying his anger with a gentle hand on his arm. "But your uncle has no power to coerce me into any action."

"You both wound me with your undeserved attacks. I have no intention of forcing you into anything, Miss Houghton," Rupert replied silkily, lowering his quizzing glass and giving Miranda a look she could not interpret, yet nevertheless did not like. Damn the man. If he thought he could control her, he was wrong. But she had a niggling doubt that she and Peter would emerge from this encounter the winners.

Rupert stood up and walked about the room, meditating upon his next move. Then he turned to face his nephew. "I have a proposition to put to Miss Houghton. You are free to listen and give her your advice, but I warn you I will brook no stupid histrionics. This is purely a business proposition and in no way endangers the lady's virtue."

"I suppose I cannot stop you from insulting Miranda, but take care. You will answer to me," Peter objected sulkily. He felt matters were rapidly going beyond the bounds of propriety, but he did not have the means to stop his suave uncle. He had tilted with him before and found himself the loser.

"No insult is intended, my boy. Here is what I think will serve us all. Miranda, I may call you that, I hope," he asked, turning to her and regarding her with a cool but amicable smile which she did not trust for a moment.

"Yes, of course," she murmured without relinquishing her suspicions.

"Well, Miranda." He leaned toward her, his hands resting tautly on the back of a chair. "If I have inferred correctly, the overriding motive for this elopement is your need to escape an unwanted marriage and amass funds for reasons you have not revealed." He continued on as she was about to interrupt. "No, I need not know what desperation led you to this romantic sham. However, I am willing to assist you with whatever amount you need in return for a trifling favor." He paused, prepared for objections, but none came forth. Miranda remained silent, her face closed and unreceptive; Peter adopted a sullen, wary expression—he knew his uncle.

"I find myself in a somewhat awkward situation. A very attractive lady believes she can blackmail me into a marriage which holds no enticement for me. The only way I can extricate myself from this annoying quandary is to announce my imminent nuptials to another lady. While there are some respectable females who would no doubt be willing to assist me, they might prove difficult to dislodge when the danger was past. Since Miss Miranda unmistakably holds me in some dislike, she would not, I think, want to legitimize any arrangement we might make. I would pay you, miss, whatever money you demand, within reason, if you agree to become my fiancée for the coming season. I will also pay for any gowns and incidental expenses of your debut into society as my intended bride and will establish you with a proper chaperone. You will be in no danger, I assure you, from my unwanted advances. Perhaps during the season you will meet a *parti* who is more suited to you than my nephew, who, alas, is in no position to afford a bride, especially one of your undeniable strength of character. If this meets with your approval, I will convey you to London forthwith and Peter can return to his studies in the post chaise he had hired." He laid out his complicated and outrageous plan with the bland assurance that no one could find it exceptional, as if such a shocking ploy was a practical solution to their difficulties.

Peter opened his mouth to object, but Miranda stilled him, turning to face Lord Rupert with her head high. "I need five hundred pounds immediately, before I leave this room," she demanded with a courage she had not realized she possessed.

"You shall have it if you consent to my plan. And believe me, Miranda, I do not press unwanted attentions on unfledged virtuous females." Rupert raised an eyebrow as if to question whether or not she was the adventeress he had thought.

"Miranda," Peter intervened, "don't even consider his proposal. Uncle Rupert has a nasty reputation with women."

"I am sure he has, Peter, but that is not my concern. I find him most unappealing, and would not encourage or allow any approaches from such a man." Carefully, Miranda examined Rupert's proposition for flaws. "I have never wanted you to get into trouble because of your chivalrous championship of me," she continued slowly, thoughtfully. "Your uncle is right in this matter. You *are* too young to marry, and I would not want you to suffer because you wished to save me from Horace Howland. Granted I would do almost anything to avoid marriage to him, but I would not sacrifice my virtue to a man like your uncle." The repugnance that she felt came through in the tone of her voice, but she was neither speaking to Rupert nor being kind. "However," she mused, "I don't believe he would jeopardize his own freedom by offering me carte blanche. And marriage to such a rake is out of the question." She smiled at Peter, ignoring Rupert, who merely looked amused at her indictment of his morals and manners.

"I won't have you treated shabbily," Peter deplored, but both Rupert and Miranda heard the concession behind the bravado.

"How perceptive of you, Miranda. You have realized that you have nothing to fear from me as long as you play your part convincingly. You can tell your parents that you have received an invitation from a respected member of the *ton* to enjoy a season. You need not tell them where you secured the money. They can believe a kind benefactor has come to your aid. And if you desire, you may return to Oxford at the end of the season, your virtue intact and safe from the meretricious Howland. He must be quite repulsive, for many young ladies would not be so determined to avoid a fate which in the end comes to most of them. Husbands, on the whole, are predictable and usually managed by a clever wife, which I have no doubt you would be. He must be, indeed, an ogre." Rupert's jeers proclaimed her scruples naive and foolish, but what the odious uncle thought of her was of little concern to Miranda.

"I prefer not to marry Mr. Howland. That is all you need to know, sir. And I must see the five hundred pounds before I will consent to your vulgar suggestion," she demanded brazenly.

"Vulgar? Really, I have always thought money quite pleasant. It is only vulgar when it is lacking. But rest assured, here are the notes." At that, Rupert pulled from his coat a wallet from which he took a bundle of pounds.

"Miranda, you cannot consider this," Peter fumed, losing whatever control he might have exerted until now when he saw that she would go ahead with his uncle's scheme. "And who is this respectable woman who will chaperone Miranda, sir? I did not think you knew any such females."

"Why, your mother, Peter. She will be delighted to assist me in this matter, I am sure. And she need not know the details of our bargain. Miranda will be perfectly safe with your mother." Rupert spoke fluidly as if this arrangement would undoubtedly be acceptable to all parties.

"She will not like the idea of championing an unknown girl who was about to elope with her son," Miranda said baldly.

"There is that objection," Rupert concurred. "But on the other hand, she will be relieved that Peter has been plucked from an unsuitable alliance. And she has told me many a time she hoped I would one day fall madly in love with some female who would lead me a dance, a fate I am certain you will do your best to insure."

He had cleverly cut the ground from under their feet, assuring them of Miranda's safety from his lascivious appetite and tempting her with a tidy solution to all her difficulties. "Well, what is your answer, Miranda? It is getting late, and I am fatigued by all this discussion." Miranda was certain that if she refused he would merely nod, dispatch Peter, and abandon her in this inn where she had no money to pay her shot. She really had little choice.

She held out her hand for the money which he promptly surrendered. "I have few options, so I consent, sir. Now, if you will excuse me, I, too, am weary. I wish to retire." And before either gentleman could demur, she whisked herself out of the room, tucking the money into her bodice.

As the door closed behind her, Rupert drawled, "A cool customer, your Miranda, Peter. You are well out of that coil. If you had wed her, she would have had you under her thumb in moments. You are not up to her weight, halfling."

"And you are, I suppose, Uncle Rupert. Well, remember, I dislike this arrangement and I intend to see that you observe your nefarious bargain. Do not try to get around Miranda with your insinuating ways. She has no idea how a libertine like you goes on," Peter growled, thoroughly disturbed by the course of events, but powerless to alter them.

"I shall heed your warning, but do not fear, Peter. The lady is too wanton, too blatant for me. She will serve her purpose and then whatever becomes of her will not involve me," Rupert promised, almost angrily. He had not liked Miranda's description of his morals or manners, and seldom had he encountered a female who had been so little impressed with his title or his purse. It should prove to be a distinctly unusual season.

Chapter Five

As the coach which Lord Rupert had hired to transport Miranda to London entered the outskirts of the city, she could barely suppress her excitement. She had never been farther from home than a few villages in the Cotswolds; and the noise, color, and confusion of the capital fascinated her, helping her forget for the moment the uncomfortable interview she faced. Up to now she had little complaint to make of Lord Rupert. He had prevailed upon a serving maid at the inn to accompany her in the chaise, lending a spurious respectability to her journey. More importantly, she had bundled up the money for her father with a brief explanatory note as to her intentions. Peter, after a rather painful argument about the wisdom of her acquiescence to Rupert's plan, had agreed to deliver the missive when he returned, reluctantly, to Oxford. He had continued to object to Rupert's improper proposal, but Miranda was adamant. He had at last consented to return to Oxford, promising to come up to London soon to see how she was getting on.

Miranda, touched by his concern and hiding her own fears, managed to bid him goodbye with an insouciant air that deceived him into thinking she was quite able to manage the affair. She might have deceived Peter, but she doubted that the formidable Lord Rupert found her manner convincing. Not that she cared a pin what he thought. He had decided she was a brazen chit with an eye to the main chance and, she conceded ruefully, he was correct.

"Oh, miss, isn't it grand?" Polly, the servant girl, exclaimed, her pale blue eyes popping as she gazed with wonder at the busy streets, the impressive houses, and the crush of carriages.

"Yes, indeed, Polly, but dirty and crowded, too full of beggars and poor, hungry-looking children. A mixture of progress and poverty, I suspect," Miranda answered abstractedly, relieved that Lord Rupert had not deigned to ride with them but was tooling his own curricle up ahead. He would ridicule their innocent appraisal of the metropolis. She must try to assume a blasé attitude no matter how inadequate she felt. But when the coach drew up to the Worthington mansion, a greystone, four-storied house on Mount Street, she was hard pressed to retain her vow. Goodness, what a splendid edifice! As the coach came to a stop, a footman descended the marble steps and opened the door.

"Good afternoon, miss. Is this all your luggage? Lord Rupert is awaiting you," he said in a lofty tone.

"Thank you, and will you please see that my maid receives some refreshment?" Miranda asked politely. She would not be cowed by a manservant. Lord Rupert took her arm and glanced at her frozen face as they mounted the steps.

"Come now. You can be excused a little apprehension at arrival, but you must show some affection for me or my sister will not believe our tale," he twitted her.

"Do not concern yourself, my lord. I will play my part to perfection," Miranda responded, a flush coming to her cheeks. She wished she looked more the part and, as they entered the entrance hall, could only feel ashamed that her cloak and dress were so dowdy. Surely Lady Worthington would fear that her fashionable brother, a noted connoisseur of women, had taken leave of his senses, proposing to such a drab female.

Actually, Rupert thought she looked quite fetching. There was no denying the chit would pay for dressing. She had lovely hair and an exceptional figure; if her ways were as flattering as her appearance, she would do. Of course Charlotte might wonder at his choice, but then she always expected the outrageous from him. He smiled grimly when he thought of Chloe Castleton's reaction to the girl who had supplanted her. Relieving Miranda of her cloak and straw bonnet and tossing his own cape, gloves, and hat to the footman, he asked to be taken to Lady Worthington.

"She is expecting you, my lord," the man replied, repressing his own curiosity. He was soon supplanted by a most august butler, who greeted Lord Rupert with license.

"Lady Worthington received your letter and will receive you in the drawing room, my lord," Radleigh announced in portentous tones. If he shared the footman's curiosity as to the young woman accompanying Lord Rupert, he was too well-trained to express it.

"Well, Radleigh, I know you will wish me happy. This is Miss Miranda Houghton, my fiancée. Radleigh, my dear, is an old friend, and I know you can rely on him during your stay." Rupert unbent, to Miranda's surprise, giving the retainer a winning smile.

Certainly the rogue had charm when he wished to use it, Miranda allowed. Turning to the butler, she smiled in answer to his murmured good wishes and told him how glad she was to meet him. Then without further ado she was swept by her fiancé *faux* into the drawing room.

She had great difficulty in repressing a gasp at its magnificence. The whole first storey of her parents' Oxford cottage could easily be accommodated in the great high-ceilinged room with its wide windows draped in cerise velvet. But she was denied a more thorough inspection as she became aware of the woman rising from a brocaded settee before the fireplace. At first glance Lady Worthington appeared even more imposing than the room and easily as formidable as her brother.

Possessing in full measure the dark haughty look of her brother, she was obviously a matron of middle years, accustomed to deference. Dressed in a fashionable gown of pearl gray merino lightened by Alençon lace at the low neckline and sleeves, she looked well able to challenge any pretensions Miranda might entertain.

"So here you are at last, Rupert, and with the young woman you intend to make your wife." She greeted them with raised eyebrows, giving Miranda a look that implied she did not think much of his choice. Before Miranda could say a word, Rupert took charge.

"Now, none of your airs, Charlotte. I will not have you take that condescending tone to Miss Houghton. Lord knows you have been after me to wed these many years; and, now that I have obeyed, I expect you to welcome Miranda with some show of enthusiasm." He had assumed that mocking hateful tone Miranda disliked. But she had no need for his championship. She would not suffer condescension from either Lord Rupert or his imposing sister. With great difficulty she bit back an angry retort.

"I am pleased to make your acquaintance, Lady Worthington, and I must thank you for offering me your hospitality," Miranda said in a dulcet voice belied by a stormy expression in her mobile face which Rupert had no difficulty in reading.

"Come now, Miranda, do not take offense. Charlotte can be a bit starchy, but she will do her best for you, I am sure. No reason to look down your nose in that platter-faced way, Charlotte. Miranda's antecedents are impeccable. She is the daughter of an Oxford professor and the granddaughter of an earl," he concluded slyly, knowing his sister could not quarrel with such a background.

Charlotte, who had no wish to antagonize her brother, suspected she had better assume at least an appearance of compliance to this *outré* alliance. "Yes, well, let us sit down and get to know one another, and I must wish you both happy. You understand, Miranda, it is just the shock of the engagement which has rather overset me," she excused herself, smiling grimly as she waved them to seats before the fireplace.

Rupert sprawled negligently in a brocaded chair and contemplated his two victims with what Miranda considered unseemly enjoyment. He was not fooled by his sister's reluctant welcome, nor by Miranda's facade of meekness.

"I am sure you would both enjoy some refreshment after your taxing journey," Charlotte said, now recalled to her duty as a hostess.

"A glass of madeira, perhaps. And Miranda might like some ratafia," he suggested blandly. Charlotte nodded and rose to ring the bell.

"We are exceedingly grateful that you will take Miranda under your wing, arrange for vouchers to Almack's, rig her out suitably. Of course, I will stand all the doings. Just send me the bills," Rupert advised.

"Isn't that rather unusual, brother?" Charlotte reseated herself and offered this criticism with thinly veiled contempt. She hoped she was not sheltering a light skirt under her roof.

Miranda had no doubt what she was thinking and was about to reply with a bitter denunciation of this slur on her morals, but Rupert had no intention of letting his sister get the upper hand.

"Not at all, Charlotte. Miranda's parents are unfortunately not in a position to underwrite a season for her, and I would not wish her to appear at a disadvantage when she is introduced to society," he explained suavely.

"Yes, of course. And you will pay for dressing and a more

fashionable coiffeur," Charlotte agreed looking Miranda over in a rather patronizing way.

"That is very kind of you, Lady Worthington, but I do not want to cut my hair," Miranda objected.

"Now, my dear, do not thwart Charlotte's kind intentions. Although I find you charming as you are, a little town gloss cannot hurt; and you will like a new wardrobe, I know," he soothed in a way which made Miranda long to give him a facer, as her brother Robbie would say. Suddenly she wished she were safely back in Oxford despite the wretched Horace. Why had she ever allowed herself to be enticed into this bogus engagement? Then she remembered the money and bit her tongue, casting a murderous glance at Rupert that did not go unnoticed by Charlotte.

"Your fiance does not appear to be besotted with you, Rupert. I find this alliance rather unbelievable, as I know you are incapable of a *coup de foudre*. You have never been one to be bowled over by a demure miss with a pretty face," Charlotte said sharply. There was a great deal here she didn't understand and she was determined to discover the reason for this engagement. She did not think it was impelled by love or even passion on either side. Still, it was of little use to quiz Rupert. He would tell her only what he wanted her to know; he was not one for confidences. Perhaps she might be more successful with the girl if she played her cards right.

"And how did you meet?" she asked with what she hoped would be mistaken for a kindly smile.

"Why, in Oxford. Peter introduced us some time ago. And you need not fear for your son, Charlotte. He is behaving with the greatest compunction," Rupert confided, looking smug.

"I am delighted to hear it, and I must thank you for paying him a visit," she answered equally insincere. If Peter had some responsibility for this engagement, she would get the whole affair out of him at their next meeting. "And is Peter planning to visit me soon?"

"Well, I imagine he will be up for some of the gaities of the season," Rupert said in a bored tone. Thankfully they were interrupted by the entrance of Radleigh with the wine. The butler deposited the tray, taking in the scene at a glance and feeling a bit sorry for the young lady for he understood his mistress very well.

After the servant's departure, Rupert drank his wine in a gulp and stood, preparing to make his escape. He thought he had done his best for Miranda, although he rather feared leaving her to the mercy of his sister. Perhaps a cautionary word might be in order.

"Before I leave, Charlotte, I would like a moment alone with Miranda. Surely now that we are formally engaged that would not be out of order."

"Of course not. I will just check with Mrs. Smedley to see that your fiancées room is in order and allow you a few minutes," she agreed briskly and sailed out of the room.

"What a tartar," Miranda complained after the door had closed on Lady Worthington.

"True, she can be, but I am sure you can handle her. You are not deficient in spirit yourself, my dear," Rupert conceded. "And I must say, she will never believe we are madly in love if you continue to glare at me so savagely whenever we meet. Could you not pretend to a modicum of affection?"

"It will try my histrionic abilities, I assure you, but in view of our bargain, I suppose I must make an effort to look on you with some favor," she granted, frowning as if the idea were repugnant in the extreme.

"Thank you. I appreciate your forbearance. But perhaps a little rehearsal might help," he suggest wryly; and, before she knew what he intended, he had jerked her roughly from her chair and, holding her in a tight embrace, kissed her with practised skill. His passion caused her blood to course

52

through her body, evoking a response she despised herself for afterwards. Before she could protest or slap his face, which she yearned to do, he had moved away. "Already I have dishonored our agreement, but I do not regret it," he excused himself and might have said more, but Lady Worthington returned.

"If you have concluded your leave-taking, I will show you to your room, Miranda. And Rupert, do I understand you will be joining us for supper?" she asked.

"Yes, indeed. We have plans to make." he said smoothly. "I will bid you both *adieu* till later. Thank you, Charlotte, you have vastly relieved my mind with your kind chaperonage of Miranda." There was no mistaking his readiness to be gone.

"Until this evening, Miranda." He faced her with a sardonic smile and, raising her hand to his lips, kissed it with lingering affection. Then, before either lady could demur, he took himself off.

Conscious of the heightened color in her cheeks and her barely repressed fury at his effrontery, Miranda made a strong effort to compose herself. Obviously he meant to play their game before his sister as well as the world. But if he thought that entitled him to unwonted liberties, she would soon disabuse him.

Lady Charlotte, aware that some effort to appear obliging was necessary, interrupted her turbulent thoughts.

"I do hope you will be comfortable here, Miranda. And we shall soon have a long cose: I want to hear all about Oxford and your acquaintance with Rupert. But I know you must be anxious to get rid of your travel dirt and have a rest before this evening," she clucked, sweeping Miranda before her.

Not loathe to attaining some privacy to control her unruly mood, Miranda thanked her prettily, and the two left the drawing room, having established a tenuous truce.

Chapter Six

Miranda viewed herself with satisfaction in the long mirror in her bedroom. She was not vain, but she could not help but be pleased with the results obtained by Alberts—Lady Worthington's maid—and the new gown provided by Mme. Berthe. Alberts had a deft touch with the scissors and had managed to trim Miranda's flyaway curls into a fashionable style which gave her an unmistakable sophistication and yet had retained most of the glowing auburn tresses which were Miranda's pride. Mme. Berthe, after much protesting, had managed to finish a gown that would ensure success at Almack's tonight. A fine white tulle over a satin slip trimmed with Brussels lace and *crêpe lisse,* the gown flattered Miranda's slim figure, although she found the low-cut bodice a trifle shocking. Alberts had assured it was all the rage and not the least bit out of the way. Whatever Lady Worthington's drawbacks as a hostess, she had a real gift for assessing fashion and had entered into the provision of Miranda's wardrobe with more enthusiasm than she had in making the girl comfortable in her new home.

Miranda sensed she disliked the engagement but was too accustomed to her brother's temper to offer more than a token objection. The announcement had duly appeared in the *Gazette*. Miranda only hoped her parents had not yet heard of it.

She had received a letter from her mother, thanking her profusely for the money that rescued her father and congratulating her on her good fortune in obtaining a London season. Nothing was said of Horace Howland's reaction to the disappearance of his fiancée, and no reference made to Lord Rupert, for which Miranda was exceedingly grateful. She had been installed in the Worthington household a week now and was on guarded if not intimate terms with her hostess. She could not fault Lady Worthington's hospitality.

Peter's mother, making cautious inquiries as to her guest's relationship with her son, had concluded shrewdly that she would welcome Miranda more complaisantly as her sister-in-law than a daughter-in-law. Lady Worthington had not been told of the aborted elopement, but she was not an unperceptive woman and suspected that Peter had some interest in her reluctantly received house guest, particularly since her son had rushed up to London to attend a few routs and tonight's debut at Almack's.

Oxford had let out for the spring holiday which offered a good excuse, but Miranda suspected Peter would have made other arrangements if she had not been staying at his Mount Street home. He had dragged her away upon his arrival with all the secrecy of a deep-dyed conspirator to inform her that he had delivered the money to Adrian Houghton and undergone a sticky interview. But he proudly disclaimed revealing any hint of the improper proposal she had accepted from Rupert. He reminded her again that his uncle was a dodgy customer and paid for watching, a warning Miranda did not need.

As for Rupert himself, she had seen little of him. Tonight's introduction to society within the sacred portals of Almack's would mark only the third time she had seen him since her arrival. He had paid two duty calls and had joined them once at dinner, but she had barely been alone with him. That was no doubt by his contrivance. Miranda had every intention of taking him to task for his unwanted embrace. She did not want to suffer a repeat performance, for his kiss had left her disturbed and embarrassed. He might have certain rights, but they did not include making careless love to her when the mood struck him. She meant to remind him that he had promised not to extend unwanted advances.

The problem was she was not sure that the advances were unwanted. Could she be the wanton he accused her of being, willing to endure his lovemaking without feeling anything but disgust and aversion to the man himself? Miranda had to admit, for she was an honest girl, she had not shown herself as adverse to his kiss as she should have. Well, she would soon disabuse him of any inclinations he had to dally with her just because they had this shocking bargain. She wondered if the announcement in the *Gazette* had quelled the hopes of his mistress, Chloe Castleton.

The man was a rake and a libertine and not a suitable object for her attention, but she must pretend to hold him in affection tonight. He was escorting Lady Worthington and Miranda to Almack's under protest, for he disliked what the more knowledgeable members of the *ton* called the Marriage Mart. He did recognize that he must play the part of a devoted suitor and had insisted at their last brief meeting that Miranda show some signs of an equal ardor. She wondered how he had handled Chloe Castleton and if she would appear at Almack's. She would dearly love a glimpse of Lord Hastings' mistress, but somehow she doubted that the respectable hall would welcome the lady. It was no business of hers how Rupert conducted his affairs, she conceded, but she did have an unholy curiosity as to the outcome. Well, she concluded, she certainly looked her best to brave the lady patronesses of Almack's, and she determined to enjoy herself no matter how the arrogant Rupert behaved.

She might have relished the interview Rupert was experiencing that very moment at Chloe Castleton's bijou house on

Wimpole Street. The lady had read of the engagement the day before when the *Gazette* had appeared with her morning chocolate. Even her maid, who was accustomed to her outbursts, had been surprised at the scream of outrage and the tantrum which followed her perusal of the announcement.

"How dare he become affianced to some little chit from the country! He will not get away with this insult," Chloe stormed, throwing her tray aside and staining the contents of her lavishly bedecked bed. Even in anger she was a luscious creature, with coal-black hair spilling over a bountiful bosom lightly draped in diaphanous peach chiffon. Pacing up and down the room, throwing whatever crossed her pass in an orgy of destruction, she looked all the more a beauty. Her fury spent, she called for her pen and paper and wrote a scented plea to Rupert to come and see her. She was not foolish enough to upbraid him in the letter and was nothing but sweet patience and gentle reproach. As one of his dearest and oldest friends, she wrote, she was hurt that he had not told her his news himself and hoped he would call that very day to tell her all about this surprising change in his circumstances.

Rupert, upon receiving this *billet doux,* laughed cynically. He would certainly see his mistress and deliver the *congé.* He suspected it would cost him heavily, but he had been exceedingly generous to her in the past and could not be expected to relieve himself of her without a suitable parting gift. He repaired in due course to Rundell, Bridge and Rundell, jewelers to the Prince Regent, in Ludgate, to select a stunning ruby necklace for the lady and, as an afterthought, a large emerald engagement ring for his betrothed. He only hoped she would not refuse to wear it.

Really, women were the very devil and often not worth the scenes they caused. He had little doubt that he would encounter more than his share of trouble from both the ladies before he was through with this masquerade. Miranda might be innocent, but she was a handful. He recalled with some pleasure the kiss in Charlotte's drawing room. Under her fierce facade she was a passionate creature. It might be interesting to educate her in the more exciting aspects of lovemaking. He regretted his pledge not to make approaches but then dismissed the promise. Her strictures were probably just a pretense of chastity, and he could get around them easily. He intended to enjoy this relationship and emerge without danger, just as he thought himself able to handle Chloe, who might rage a bit, cry, and plead, but must realize eventually that all between them was over. The ruby necklace should solace her.

So, before the Almack's introduction of his fiancée, he decided to clear the decks and grant Chloe's request for a visit. Dressed in the white-satin knee-britches which were *de rigeur* for this important evening, his black superfine waistcoat—a testimony to his tailor, and his cravat, a pristine and intricate Oriental arrangement, he arrived at Wimpole Street, bracing himself for the uncomfortable interview.

Chloe, having decided on her tactics, received him in her over-decorated drawing room, a maze of pink and cerise draperies and riotous, silk stuffed chairs, looking ravishing. She was wearing a low-cut ivory gown festooned with lace which revealed her abundant charms to a treat.

"Dear Rupert, I thought you had deserted me. It has been days since I saw you last," she pouted, rising at his entrance and gliding toward him with the expectation of an embrace.

"Good afternoon, Chloe. You are looking charming as always," he said, gently removing her outstretched arms. Positioning himself at the fireplace, he regarded her warily.

"So austere. I suppose now that you plan to enter parson's mousetrap, you must play the puritan. So unlike you, Rupert. I wonder how long it will last," she cooed spitefully.

"Long enough. At any rate, Chloe, I am engaged, and so our delightful relationship must end," he said sternly.

"I don't see that at all. Surely you do not intend to be faithful to this little nobody who has managed to entrap you?" she cried, losing any pretension to gentility in her anger.

"Actually, she was clever enough to allow me to do the entrapping. I had quite a time persuading her that we should suit," he explained amiably. He knew that Chloe would be furious at the innuendo, but he could not ignore the temptation to score. From the beginning Chloe had blatantly thrown herself at Rupert, a most eligible lord, but she had made the mistake of allowing him access to her bed before the vows were spoken.

"What can a simpering virgin offer you that I cannot?" she asked angrily. She eyed him with a smoldering gaze, a promise of delights he had only recently enjoyed to the full.

"Not an apt description of the lady, my dear, and she has—if nothing else—one virtue of special value," Rupert replied facilely, then directed his insult. "I know any child of this union will be my own, not an assurance you could give, I fear."

"You malign me, Rupert. I have been a pattern card of fidelity to you,' she pouted.

"Well, you will not be taxed any longer to restrain your natural ardor to attract gullible fools. No, Chloe, you must accept that what was between us is over. I have enjoyed our interlude, but it is done," he said with a decisiveness she knew would not be easily overset. "I never promised you marriage, you know."

"I expected it," she rejoined, prepared to challenge him, but realizing that she had little chance of changing his mind. Rupert Hastings was not to be coerced. That had always been one of his attractions. She had thought that passion might

59

drug his senses, but in that suspicion she had misread her man.

"Come now, Chloe, let us part amicably. I thought you might accept this trifling gift as a symbol of all we have shared." He smiled and tendered her the velvet case, watching cynically as she opened it and exclaimed with avaricious delight at its contents.

Taking the necklace, she sidled up to him, and purred, "Do put it on for me, won't you. The clasp looks difficult."

He placed the necklace around her neck and secured it then, patting her briskly on the backside, stood back. "Yes, charming. I was sure it would flatter you. Well, I must be off, Chloe. Good hunting," he advised outrageously as he walked toward the door. She pursued him, flinging herself upon his person. "You cannot mean this to be the end," she cried out dramatically.

"That is just what I mean, so you can turn off the histrionics, my dear. We have had a good time of it, but it is over. Goodbye." And he left unhurriedly, letting the door shut firmly behind him.

Surprisingly Chloe Castleton made no move to follow him, although her lovely face was flushed with rage and her dark eyes burned. She was not done with the noble lord yet. He would see he could not callously abandon her without paying a price.

Although Rupert felt he had brushed through the interview with Chloe fairly well, the episode had left an unpleasant taste and reinforced his tendency to think women created most of life's problems. So his mood upon arrival at the Mount Street house was not of the most sanguine.

He wondered, and not for the first time, whether the remedy he had chosen to rid himself of Chloe would not turn out to be more vexatious than the original problem. His reactions to Miranda were an annoying mixture of admiration for her mettlesome spirit and a dislike of that independence when it warred with his own desires. He had found her surprisingly passionate but also amazingly stubborn, and his pride was wounded by her obvious dislike of him. Not that he thought every woman should fall at his feet, but rarely had he encountered one who made her aversion so apparent. So he was prepared for any passages at arms they might enjoy when he arrived to dine and escort her to Almack's that evening, a venue he found boring and would have preferred to avoid.

However, he was taken aback at his first sight of her when he entered the Worthington drawing room to find her in animated conversation with Peter. She certainly repaid the considerable expense he had been put to in supplying a new wardrobe. She did him credit and he would not be the object of surprised or pitying stares from society when he introduced her as his future wife. For that he could only be grateful, but he did not like the intimacy with Peter and interrupted the couple brusquely.

"Good evening, Miranda. I must say you are a tribute to Mme. Berthe's art. That gown is delightful, and you appear in high alt," he greeted her, bowing over her hand and giving only the most cursory nod to his nephew.

"So glad you approve, my lord," Miranda replied, a certain sarcasm in her tone. The idea that fine feathers made the bird was one she did not endorse. She wished now she had worn a shabby muslin just to discomfit him, and much of her own pleasure in her new finery disappeared.

"Somehow I feel that my approval is not of overweening interest to you, my dear," he mocked, yet he was disappointed by her continued animosity. Really, they would have to get on a more friendly footing if the charade of this engagement were to convince anyone. He had not intended to offer her the ring before company, but her reception raised his hackles. Reaching into his pocket, he pulled out the token of their arrangement and extended it to her.

"Perhaps this will sweeten your disposition, my dear. Most

women enjoy jewels. A badge to seal our agreement," he added silkily, reminding her of their bargain. "May I be allowed to put it on you?"

"Yes, of course." Miranda extended her hand, feeling mean-spirited, which was exactly the effect Rupert had intended. He placed the ring on her finger, which he then kissed in a lingering manner. To her annoyance Miranda felt a blush rising to her cheeks.

"It's quite splendid, my lord. Thank you. I will return it when we have completed our masquerade," she said, knowing she was being ungracious, but Rupert Hastings had aroused her ire yet again, a talent he seemed to have.

Peter looked at the two protagonists and almost chuckled, enjoying the sight of his uncle in this unusual and uncomfortable role.

But if Rupert felt irritated at Miranda's grudging acceptance of the engagement ring, he did not evidence it. Turning away as if the conversation had ceased to interest him, he crossed the room to his sister and, taking a glass of wine from a nearby table, engaged her in desultory conversation.

"Really, Miranda, you were quite short with Uncle Rupert. He is not accustomed to having his consequence and his gifts so ignored," Peter reproved gaily.

"Do him good. He's an arrogant and unsympathetic man and deserves a set down. And I always feel he is sneering at me. It's not an attitude to promote harmony."

"And not an attitude which will convince the world that you are in love and wish to marry him."

"But, Peter, I always understood that mawkish displays of emotion were considered vulgar by the *ton*. I would not wish to cause embarrassment because of my lack of experience. Enough of this. I want to know all about Oxford. Were you able to make your peace with your tutor?" And the two fell to discussing with some animation common friends and incidents of the past.

Rupert, watching beneath his heavy-lidded eyes, wondered if Miranda cared more for Peter than she was willing to admit. He was convinced his nephew could be easily besotted by this unusual girl, not a prospect he viewed with equanimity. However, his first duty was to allay Charlotte's suspicions. If she had any idea of the real relationship between her brother and the house guest, she would be disgusted and remove her cooperation, grudging as it was.

"I must thank you, Charlotte, for your direction of Miranda's transformation. She looks most attractive," he approved.

"Really, Rupert, you talk of the girl as if she were some kind of puppet. Do I understand that you thought her less than appealing before her new gowns and coiffeur?"

"Not at all. A natural beauty, if a bit of a rustic, but I saw beneath the surface. How right I was to deliver her into your care. You have an unerring eye for fashion."

"And for intrigue, let me remind you. There is a mystery about this so-called engagement, I am sure. You do not behave like a man in love."

"Ah, Charlotte, you always accuse me of the most heinous crimes. Let me assure you I am deeply devoted to Miranda and think she will make a splendid wife," he returned suavely, noting that he must be more careful with his sister.

"She seems much more interested in Peter than in you," Charlotte mused worriedly.

"Not at all. They share certain interests, and no doubt she is a bit homesick and anxious to hear all the news of Oxford. Don't fret, Charlotte, Peter is in no danger from Miranda. I will see to that."

"Yes, any girl would be a fool to prefer him to you; and, whatever she is, I have decided she is not a fool." Charlotte's shrewdness often surprised Rupert, but he could not allow her to delve too deeply.

"Well, I will rescue her now and taker her into dinner, for here is Radleigh coming to announce it." And Rupert strolled leisurely across the room and neatly annexed Miranda, leaving Peter to escort his mother.

Chapter Seven

"I am much obliged to you, Charlotte, for arranging the voucher to Almack's for Miranda. Can't stand the place myself, but I realize it has a certain cachet," Rupert thanked his sister as they rode toward King Street.

"Emily Cowper was very accommodating. Naturally there could be no problem about the future Lady Hastings," Charlotte agreed rather smugly.

"Don't know why anyone would want to go to Almack's. Nasty refreshments—watery lemonade, over-sweet orgeat, bread and butter, stale cake. And the patronesses, starched-up dictators, the lot," Peter rumbled.

"Ah, dear boy, you must not cavil. It is the epitome of elitism. To be refused a voucher for Almack's is social suicide," Rupert chided sarcastically.

"You are quite paralyzing me with fear," Miranda said, not entirely in jest.

"Nonsense, you will be a great success," Charlotte assured briskly. Although the evening up to now had not been entirely comfortable she had great hopes of Almack's. She had never been able to lure her brother there before, and Peter had gone only occasionally, under great protest.

"Nothing but dullards," Peter continued to feel ill-used.

"The Duke of Wellington frequents the place more often

than not, and certainly you cannot call Lord Alvaney dull," Charlotte reproved.

"I had no idea you would transform yourself into such a pattern card of respectability, Uncle Rupert," Peter jibed wickedly enjoying his uncle's discomfort. But Rupert did not gratify him by replying to such infantile teasing. Almack's was one sanctum Chloe Castleton could not breach, and that was a relief. He would dance a few times with Miranda, if she knew how to waltz, and then retire to the card room where he would meet some cronies. A boring evening, but it must be endured to give some verisimilitude to this damned engagement. In no good humor, he saw they had approached King Street, where carriages had lined up to inch slowly forward toward the entrance of the Assembly.

"It is always such a crush," Charlotte observed as their own coachman waited patiently to disgorge his passengers.

"I am sorry, my lord, you are finding the evening so tedious," Miranda offered sweetly, giving her fiancé a speaking look.

Her appraisal appeared to restore Rupert's good humor.

"Not at all, Miranda. It's all in a good cause. But do not frown at me so. The august patronesses will think you are having second thoughts about our future felicity."

As there was to be no future for them, Miranda very properly ignored this barbed remark, but a smoldering look boded ill for Rupert when she had him alone.

At last they reached the entrance and were able to alight from the coach. Just as well, thought Peter, for he sensed an explosion. Miranda was not a girl to hide her displeasure, and he found it amusing that she should rip up his uncle whenever she had the chance. But she would have to act a bit more convincingly to persuade the *ton* she was in love with this formidable man. Peter frowned. He hated the necessity for all this posturing.

As they entered the hall, Rupert bent down and whispered

to Miranda, "You really must treat me with a little less animosity, my dear. We do not appear at all enamoured." He sighed as if regretting the lack in his companion.

"We are not," she snapped. "But don't worry. I will attempt to at least look as if I did not take you in abhorrence."

"But you do, alas," he mocked.

"Yes, I do, and I can only wonder why you would want it any other way. Perhaps I will discover an agreeable admirer tonight and that should absolve you of any responsibility." She had not liked his reference, when they had made their bargain, to the idea she was husband-hunting among the eligibles.

"But not until we have played out our roles," he objected, taking her cloak and handing it to the manservant standing in the hall. Then offering her his arm, he accompanied her into the hall behind Peter and his mother.

At first Miranda was surprised at the spartan decor of the huge, blue assembly room. She had expected a more elegant scene, but it was certainly crowded with ladies and gentlemen of the first stare whom she did recognize. As she looked around she was immediately aware that their entrance had caused a buzz of talk. She felt embarrassed at such avid conjecture, but before she could complain, a small, dark, vivacious lady of some thirty years bounced up to them, exuding excitement.

"Why, Rupert, you mysterious man, announcing your engagement in that shabby way and not telling any of your friends! And this must be the fortunate girl who has finally sealed your fate."

Rupert, surprisingly, smiled at her. "This is Sally, Lady Jersey, Miranda, known to her intimates as 'Silence' and no need to explain that. Sally, my fiancée, Miranda Houghton."

"From Oxford, I believe Emily Cowper told me. How divine to meet you! I must hear all the details of this whirlwind romance, but first we must see that you have partners. You will not want to dance with Rupert all evening, I know."

Miranda, rather dazed by this ebullient lady's reception, nodded her thanks and murmured a greeting. Rupert, however, had not done with the lady. "And Sally, I want your permission for Miranda to waltz." Turning to Miranda he explained, "You are not allowed such license without obtaining prior sanctions from the patronesses, severe guardians of the young."

"You do waltz, my dear?" Lady Jersey asked, as if such sophisticated behavior could not be expected from a rustic.

"Yes, of course. And may I have your permission, Lady Jersey?" Miranda asked prettily, thinking the whole matter a perfect hum. In Oxford she had often waltzed, although many matrons there still considered the dance a bit "fast."

"Certainly, and I will not insist it only be with Rupert. Do him good to have a little competition, and there are many gentlemen eager to make your acquaintance," Lady Jersey promised wickedly, giving Rupert a sidelong glance from her dark eyes. Before Rupert could demur, she had given a signal and several gentlemen appeared as if by magic, intent on securing the favor. Apparently a fiancé did not limit one's opportunities in these circles, Miranda observed. Immediately she was inundated with dance requests.

Rupert put his initials on the first waltz and the supper dance and stood by, watching cynically as her card was rapidly filled. Then, scattering the assembly with a few words, he drew Miranda onto the floor where the orchestra had begun the music.

"I can see you will be an enormous success," he promised as they twirled gracefully around the room, the object of many eyes.

"Obviously being engaged does not preclude the attentions of other men. How gratifying," she answered daringly, hoping to wound his *armour propre*.

"Not at all. You are not dealing with schoolboys. But do try to remember your duty to me, your promised husband," he replied smoothly.

"Oh, I could hardly forget that," she retorted with what she hoped was a languishing look.

"Much better," he approved. "Fortunately the assemblage can not see your furious eyes. I really must keep you in better order. I fear you have all the instincts of a flirt, my dear."

"But not with you."

"Of course not. You have already captured me, we agree, I think."

"You are the most maddening man. And I cannot brangle with you on the dance floor. I must mind my steps," she admitted with engaging candor, which drew a smile from her companion. In trust she was finding being held so closely in Rupert's arms a disturbing experience and only hoped he was not aware of the frisson she felt. She doubted it, he was far too experienced with women. They danced in silence until the waltz ended, and then Rupert escorted her to where Charlotte was sitting with the chaperons along the wall.

"Thank you, Miranda. You are a dainty armful. I will see you later when no doubt I will hear about your conquests."

Bowing courteously, he left. Miranda's next partner was Peter, which she found relaxing until he began upbraiding her for flirting. But since the intricacies of the dance separated them more often than it brought them together, she was spared most of his arguments. Evidently he had not reconciled himself to this false engagement and thought it was resembling too much of the real thing. But he could hardly pursue the theme on the dance floor with many listening ears and staring eyes.

Miranda, who had dreaded her debut at Almack's, was enjoying herself. Even Charlotte seemed relaxed, happy to be the center of eager listeners who wanted to know all the facts of this surprising alliance. Only to Emily Cowper did she really confide. Lady Cowper, an indulgent and kindly woman whose own long liaison with Lord Palmerston inclined her to view lovers with charity, looked benignly on Miranda.

"Really a charming girl, Charlotte. And I am sure you are pleased to see Rupert settled at last. I wonder what Mrs. Castleton is thinking," she added knowingly.

"Disappointed. Not that she ever had a chance to capture Rupert, at least legally," Charlotte retorted sharply. Pleased at her protégée's acceptance, she was apt to think now that perhaps Miranda might do.

"And how did they meet?" asked Lady Cowper.

"I believe my son Peter introduced them when Rupert visited him at Oxford." Charlotte would only go so far in her confidences, although Lady Cowper had an uncanny ability to root out secrets. Under her serene manner lay a shrewd knowledge of society and its facade.

"I understand her grandfather is an earl," she probed.

"Yes, but her mother's marriage to an Oxford professor did not meet with his approval so I hear, which is why I am sponsoring Miranda." Charlotte was prepared to go this far and no further, but she wanted to assure Lady Cowper that Miranda was completely respectable.

"I see, yes. I wonder could that be Moresdale. I had heard his daughter made an unwise marriage and he threw her out—or off, as the case may be. This daughter has a look of Anne, his wife. Her family, the Rutherfords, had just that color hair." Emily Cowper had her finger on every family tree in England, and Charlotte was not surprised that she would have delved into Miranda's antecedents.

"Moresdale always was an eccentric, never leaves his acres in Derby, you know. Probably wanted his daughter to wed some neighbor and she took exception to it. Can hardly blame her. Derby is so dismal. But this girl has done well for herself, catching Rupert. Never thought he would be so impulsive," she said, a question in her voice which Charlotte could not mistake.

"I believe he thought it was time to settle down, needs an heir, you know," she offered in mitigation.

"But a love match, I am sure," Lady Cowper replied kindly, looking across the ballroom where Miranda appeared to be entranced by the conversation of a young guardsman.

"Yes, of course." If Charlotte entertained any doubts of Rupert's passion, she was not fool enough to share those doubts with Emily Cowper; and the ladies abandoned the subject, turning instead to the latest *on dit* about Byron, now rumored separated from his wife, Augusta, and accused of insanity.

Miranda was indeed finding the young guardsman, the younger son of the Duke of Oldcastle, good company. And she was quite flattered by the attentions of her various partners, who mourned her engagement and spoke yearningly of her charms. She was wise enough to know that most of them would not be so effusive if she were not safely engaged to Lord Hastings and thus no threat to their freedom. But she was young and artless enough to enjoy this heady taste of life among the *ton*. So when Rupert came to claim his supper dance, she was in a most amiable mood, of which he was not slow to take advantage.

"I can see you have been having a merry time, Miranda, casting all these young blades into the boughs with your charms. Happy you find Almack's to your taste."

"Who wouldn't my lord, when everyone has been so kind? I am not accustomed to such attention," she confided frankly.

"What could the Oxford men have been thinking of? Well, just remember our bargain. You have plenty of time to make a selection before you throw me off," he mocked as they whirled around the floor.

"But you see, I must discover who is likely to offer the

71

most. It would be stupid of me to become attracted to a penniless nobody, wouldn't it?" she dared him.

"I wonder, Miranda, if you are as ambitious as I once thought," he mused, thinking that she would be hard put to find another man with his assets. Rupert Hastings was well aware of his worth and had eluded anxious matrons and their daughters vying for his attention for years. If she were really as blatant as she professed, surely she would make more of a push to engage his affections on a permanent basis. He frowned at the idea that she held him in such distaste she would not make the slightest effort to do just that. He didn't like that at all and wondered why.

"Don't look so ferocious, my lord. The company will think we are having a set-to."

"No, that would never do. Can't give the gossips any opportunity to think we are not the most cosy of love birds," he agreed. Then as the dance came to an end, "Come, we will now partake of the rather sparse refreshments. At least it will give you a chance to rest from your endeavors."

Although Miranda had heard Peter's warning as to the plain fare, she was not totally prepared for the diluted drinks and day-old cake. Still, she was pleased with the chance to rest a bit and contemplate the company. Rupert chatted lightly during the interval, pointing out figures of note. He could be an entertaining companion when he chose and she responded happily, completely engrossed, so that they were both surprised when a blond gentleman of pleasing manners interrupted their conversation.

"I believe this is our dance, Miss Houghton. Randolph Cary, in case you have forgotten." He smiled at her with an engaging candor, and she looked into his clear blue eyes and approved of what she saw.

"With your permission, sir?" Cary said tentatively to Rupert.

"Of course. You are an American, are you not, Mr. Cary?"

"Yes, just recently arrived from Virginia to serve at our ministry here," he explained. With his fresh open face and wholesome blond looks, he fascinated Miranda. He was different from the beaux who had attended her with flattery and practised manners.

"I have met your minister, Adams, several times. He is quite a forceful man. Not too fond of Englishmen," Rupert observed shaking the man's hand. "Rupert Hastings, and I am pleased to meet you, sir. Take good care of Miranda here. She is not used to all this gaiety."

"I can't believe such a Nonpareil has not been besieged, but you have my promise I will go gently, my lord," Cary agreed. Rupert watched them go toward the ballroom with a thoughtful frown. There was a quality in that young man he found unusual, but then he had little experience with colonials. Americans had as a rule little acceptance by the *ton,* but this Cary could never have been invited to Almack's without high-placed sponsors. He must make some inquiries.

Miranda was, in truth, finding Randolph Carter Cary a refreshing change from her earlier partners and the arrogant Rupert. He talked easily, explaining frankly that he found London society intriguing and formal after Virginia.

"Do you think you will enjoy your stay, Mr. Cary?" she asked. "Our countries were so lately enemies," she continued, referring to the war now some four years concluded which had not endeared England to her former colonies.

"Yes, but that is all in the past. Everyone has been most kind. I understand you are engaged to Lord Hastings. Quite an obstacle, the noble lord, but I hope he won't prevent us from becoming friends," Randolph Cary said with a pleading look to which Miranda was not entirely unsusceptible.

"Friends, certainly, Mr. Cary. And I want to hear about America. It sounds exciting and very adventurous."

"Perhaps I may call? Where are you staying?" he persisted. Wondering at his insistence, still Miranda could not be rude. She told him of her direction, and he seemed uncommonly grateful for the information. What a contrast to her other partners. So frank and honest and definitely attracted. She decided she liked Mr. Cary and said engagingly that she hoped he would call. They parted reluctantly as Peter came to claim a country dance.

"Who was that fellow?" he asked jealously as he handed her into the set.

"An American—attached to the ministry and quite nice," Miranda teased, earning another scowl. She smiled as if she had a secret, annoying Peter even more; and whenever the figure of the dance brought them together, he returned to the topic. He believed Miranda had no interest in his uncle, even disliked him; but other rivals were bound to appear, and this Cary might prove a serious threat to his own intentions. Peter had adopted a proprietary interest in Miranda and was not about to abandon it even if he were relieved to have come out of the botched elopement so happily. Miranda did nothing to disabuse him of her interest in the American; and at the end of the evening he, as well as Rupert, wondered just how taken she was with the charming American.

Chapter Eight

The week following her debut at Almack's passed in a delightful whirl for Miranda. Evidently she was approved by the *ton,* for a rush of invitations followed that evening. Randolph Carter Cary called several times and twice took her for a ride in the park. Miranda understood that it was perfectly respectable to accept such invitations as no one expected her to live in Rupert's pocket. But Peter took great exception to Mr. Cary's attentions and was quick to remind her that the attractive American was showing too much interest in the fiancée of another man.

What Rupert himself thought she had no idea, as his appearances in Mount Street were rare. However, tonight he was escorting her to Astley's Royal Amphitheatre to see *Mazeppa or the Wild Horses of Tartary.* The treat included Louisa Woolford, a luscious lady dancing on the back of a white horse, and other equestrienne displays for which the circus was famous. Lady Worthington considered the entertainment vulgar, but Rupert had insisted that Miranda must not miss it and would much prefer it to the Shakespearean drama at Drury Lane.

Little had altered in Miranda's relationship with Rupert. He had made no further effort to press upon her any of those caresses she found so disturbing, and she decided that the one

75

digression had been spurred by temper rather than any other emotion. Neither one of them had referred to the episode.

They never seemed to meet without brangling and she hoped tonight might prove easier, but she doubted it. He was a most maddening man, but she could not fault his honoring of their bargain. He paid without protest Mme. Berthe's outrageous dress bills and dutifully sent flowers as a sign of his spurious devotion. She still did not know what to make of him and wondered if he continued to see Chloe Castleton, the reason for this false engagement.

Well, she would enjoy her London stay and forget about Rupert's intentions. They did not concern her. If he gave little thought to her, she would not be so foolish as to worry about a man who appeared so indifferent. If he wanted to rid himself of Chloe Castleton, he was going about it in a rather casual fashion. And if he did not take this engagement seriously, why should she?

Miranda would have been astonished to hear that she was the subject of discussion between Rupert and his old friend and companion at arms Major Marcus Handbury as they sat over their wine that afternoon in White's. Almost a year had passed since Waterloo, and Major Handbury had finally returned from his military duties on the continent to take up the life of a half-pay officer in London. Fortunately he was possessed of a tidy family income, so he suffered none of the financial burdens other less fortunately placed officers were experiencing. A stocky, blond, blue-eyed man of phlegmatic temperament, little escaped his discerning eye. He served as a good foil for his more volatile friend and had often extricated Rupert from compromising escapades. Their friendship was long-standing and uncomplicated, and Rupert welcomed his arrival back in London. But for once Marcus was proving inquisitive, evidencing an inordinate interest in Rupert's engagement.

"Never thought you would take the plunge, old man. And

I must say you do not behave like a swain in love. I take it this engagement is a settled affair. I should like to meet the lady that has lured you into matrimony," he commented.

"Join us tonight. I am taking a party to Astley's, thought Miranda might enjoy it. She has never been to London before and finds the city intriguing," Rupert explained, his tone bored. Much as he respected and trusted Marcus, he was not about to confide in him about his arrangement with Miranda.

"Fine. I always enjoy Astley's. Some gorgeous legs to be seen. And I will meet this paragon."

"Hardly that. But she is an unusual girl. I met her in Oxford where my nephew is idly pursuing what passes for education. But I must warn you, she is no milk-and-water miss. You might find her a trifle astringent."

Marcus chuckled. "She will have to be to handle you. Somehow I cannot picture you as a tame benedict. Would it be out of order to ask about the fair Castleton? I understand that affair was in full spate. How has she taken this sudden *volte-face?* I suspect she meant to capture you permanently, Rupert."

"Chloe is for dallying not marrying, as I trust she now understands. Not a faithful type—which could be a disadvantage in a wife."

"Don't see why. You have cuckolded enough husbands. But it's typical. When it comes to your own wife, you expect fidelity."

"Yes, surprisingly, I do. Most unfair, I agree. But there it is," Rupert agreed languidly. Then, still casual, as if it were of little importance, he changed the subject. "You seem to know a great many colonials. Have you run across a young man, Randolph Cary, attached to the ministry? I have met Adams, of course, but few of his staff seem to frequent the circles I do."

"That's because you are an arrogant devil who thinks them

beneath you," Marcus teased, twirling his glass idly and then reaching for the bottle.

"Not at all, just rather gauche, most of them," Rupert replied, not at all offended.

"Well, I have met Cary, a likely lad. A Virginian—and they are not so straitlaced as those New England puritans. As a matter of fact, I saw him tooling a lovely auburn-haired creature in the park yesterday. He seemed most animated—on the verge of love—so I did not interrupt him, but I would like to have met the lady."

Rupert frowned. "I rather believe that was Miranda, my fiancée. She is seeing a lot of the fellow."

"Well, you had better put a stop to it. He is quite appealing to the ladies, I hear."

"He's joining the party tonight. Miranda asked and I did not want to make an issue of it, so I of course said yes."

"I can't wait for this evening," Marcus teased, thoroughly enjoying his friend's discomfort. Rupert seemed fairly caught. He had a record of treating his women carelessly. Unmoved by protestations of undying love, he claimed that excess of emotion wearied him. More often the pursued than the pursuer, his conquests had roused Marcus' envy. He had never understood Rupert's ability to attach any woman who roused his interest. Certainly the fellow was not overwhelmingly handsome; it was not the Byronic looks or romantic mannerisms that endeared him to those fortunate enough to catch his fancy. It would be rather amusing if he had at last met his match, and was the victim instead of the villain in this affair of the heart. Marcus shrewdly wondered if that were not the unknown Miranda's appeal. She had not attempted to attract him. Well, he would enjoy seeing how they went on together. Could be instructive to see Rupert get his comeuppance. Marcus genuinely cared for his friend and would not like to see him make a misalliance, nor be duped by a designing hussy, but he doubted that was the case. If Miranda could manage to make Rupert do the running, it would be a departure and genuinely salutary.

"I will be anticipating this evening, Rupert," he said with a wink before launching into reminiscences of adventures past.

One of the reasons Rupert found Marcus such a satisfactory companion was his ability to take life as he found it. Rarely was he put out of countenance, and he judged his fellows with a charity Rupert himself found impossible to emulate. If Marcus never reached the heights, he never fell to brooding. He was not a passionate type and Rupert respected him for his good sense and placid temperament.

If the party in the Hastings' box at Astley's that evening held undertones of disquiet, Miranda did not notice. She was thoroughly enthralled with the pleasure palace, a great rotunda surrounded by gilded boxes and lit by huge glittering chandeliers. To lend a semblance of balance to the company, Lady Worthington was escorted by a middle-aged man-about-town usually available for such duties. Peter reluctantly escorted a girl making her come-out, Maria Henderson, with whom Miranda had struck up a friendship and who fulfilled all Peter's mother's requirements. Randolph Cary and Marcus Handbury attended without companions, for the box only comfortably held eight.

No one would have noticed from Rupert's manner that he found Cary's attentions to his fiancée in any way exceptional, and that young man was wise enough not to give him cause to suspect he entertained any but the most lighthearted interest in Miranda. In that, he was cleverer than Peter, who scowled at the American and refused any overtures. Rupert, watching them both, conceded that his nephew could take a lesson in manners from the colonial whose courtesy could not be faulted. In the interval between acts, Marcus escorted

Miranda on a stroll around the amphitheatre while Rupert engaged Cary in conversation.

"Are you enjoying London, Mr. Cary?" he asked, ignoring Peter's attempts to join them and learn what Miranda saw in this undeniably handsome upstart.

"Yes, indeed. My duties at the ministry are not onerous, so I have plenty of time to take in the sights. Miss Houghton has been most generous in allowing me to share her own discoveries. I understand this is her first visit to London also," Cary explained with a respectful air that for some reason Rupert found annoying. "Of course, I realize that you would find such attractions as Westminster Abbey, the Tower, and Hyde Park mundane, but to us they are an adventure."

"Very kind of you to devote your leisure to educating my fiancée. But tell me, Mr. Cary, something of your life in Virginia. I find the colonies—or I should say, the United States of America—a mystery," Rupert commented suavely. He was not about to oblige the fellow by behaving in a gothic, jealous manner. Not that he would be justified, he reminded himself with a start. After all he and Miranda were not on those terms. If they were, he would not have allowed this young man the license he had already taken.

While Rupert was skillfully probing Randolph Cary's background and being adroitly, if politely, thwarted, Marcus Handbury was having an equally frustrating conversation with Miranda. On the surface she appeared compliant and friendly, displaying none of the false pretensions so many young girls employed. But he believed she was hiding something.

"I was astonished when I returned from the continent to learn of Rupert's engagement. He never appeared in the marrying mode," he remarked as they strolled the halls behind the amphitheatre.

"I always understood no man was in the marrying mode until he met the right girl," she riposted. She liked this plain burly officer and recognized that he was truly fond of Rupert. It would not do to antagonize him.

"True, you have me there, Miss Houghton. I suppose I am jealous of his happiness," he replied with appealing candor.

"I am sure you, too, will find a wife, if that is what you want. There are a great many lovely girls making their come-out, you know."

"I understand you are from Oxford. Are you finding London enjoyable?" he countered, avoiding his own availability. She was not the artless innocent he had at first supposed, he should have known better. Rupert would not be attracted to a ninny with little wit, and certainly she had obvious attributes any man would find desirable.

"Yes, indeed, and Lady Worthington has been most kind. She could not have liked having me foisted upon her, but Rupert felt I should have some time to adjust and taste the delights of the season before settling down." Her tone was light and her manner seemingly frank and open, but Marcus sensed a reserve. She would tell him just what she wanted to, and her reticence intrigued him. She did not behave like a girl greatly enamoured with Rupert, but then that gentleman had not conducted himself with any marked degree of passion, either. Of course he did not expect an experienced man-about-town like Rupert to act the besotted lover, but he had thought Miss Houghton would evidence some sign of satisfaction or warmth at acquiring such a husband.

Miranda had some questions of her own and did not believe in circling the subject warily. "Are you acquainted with Mrs. Castleton, Major?" she asked bluntly.

Marcus suppressed his amusement. Miranda Houghton was awake on every suit. She had heard the tales of Rupert's liaison with that lady and wanted confirmation.

"Yes, she has been on the town for some time, a very fetching woman," he admitted.

81

"I would like to meet her, but somehow our paths have not crossed. Does she frequent society?" she asked ingenuously.

"Certainly, though perhaps not by the hostesses you have met. But she is received in many of the best drawing rooms," he offered warily before realizing a bit of reassurance might be in order. "You have no need to fear Mrs. Castleton. Whatever her relationship with Rupert, I am sure it has come to a conclusion now that he has become engaged."

"Do you think so, Major? How kind of you to set my fears at rest," Miranda looked at him with artless charm, but he felt she might be secretly laughing at him and his interest deepened. Rupert had chosen an intriguing girl who would not tamely endure whatever that gentleman had in mind. This marriage, if it came off, should prove both challenging and unsettling. Marcus foresaw pitfalls ahead, and he wondered if Rupert had considered them.

"It is time we returned to the box, Major. I would not want to miss the next attraction. Fire-eaters must be brave souls," Miranda said, hiding her amusement. She knew the major in his bluff way had tried to discover the real story of her supposed romance and she had enjoyed their exchange; but she was not prepared to confide in anyone, not even this apparently honest and genuine man.

The evening proceeded, the program meeting the approval of all Rupert's guests. Even Lady Worthington relaxed enough to admit the entertainment was unusual. After supper at Grillon's, the party broke up—Randolph Cary, Marcus, and the gentleman who had acted as Lady Worthington's escort going their separate ways. Rupert and Peter accompanied the ladies back to Mount Street after dropping off Miss Henderson at her house in South Audley Street.

"Will you come in, Rupert?" Charlotte asked her brother.

"Yes, I think so. I want a few moments alone with Miranda, if you will grant your permission."

"Of course. You see so little of each other," Lady

Worthington noted dryly. She had been puzzled by Rupert's lax attendance on his fiancée and disturbed by Miranda's interest in the forthright American. Perhaps Rupert, too, was finding he could ignore Miranda only at the risk of losing her.

Miranda, not happy at the idea of a *tête á tête* with her fiancé, demurred. "I am really rather tired. Could we postpone any discussion till tomorrow?" she pleaded sweetly.

"This will only take a moment," Rupert insisted, not to be deterred. Miranda's reluctance only strengthened his resolve.

Throughout their exchange Peter had remained silent. Now he frowned, ready to protest, thinking Rupert would only rouse Miranda's anger. However, prudence prevailed, although he could not prevent a smirk when he considered the possibly stormy interview. Miranda was not accustomed to being reprimanded, and Peter suspected Rupert would interrogate her about her relationship with Cary.

They parted in the hall, having surrendered their outer garments to Radleigh. Lady Worthington ascertaining that refreshments were set out in the drawing room, departed upstairs with Peter. Rupert watched their disappearance and then dismissed Radleigh. Turning to Miranda, he ordered curtly, "In here."

Bridling at his tone, Miranda sailed into the drawing room, closely followed by her tormentor. Once inside, away from prying eyes, she turned and said sharply, "I don't appreciate being ordered about as if I were a mastiff."

"My apologies, but I doubt that any dog would behave so ungratefully." He strode to the fireplace. "If I begged you politely to sit down, would you comply, I wonder, or insist on standing just to prove your independence?"

Miranda sniffed, but settled into a chair as far from him as possible. "What did you want to talk about?"

"Surely it is not surprising that I should want to see you alone. We are engaged, if I remember correctly."

83

"I have not noticed that that bothered you much. You have not been exactly assiduous in your attentions."

"Were you disappointed? Well, that will change. If this engagement is to seem realistic, I must alter my conduct. I can't have you running about London with every colonial that strikes your fancy. Not at all the thing, my girl," he reproved, noticing with some amusement the angry flush rising to Miranda's cheeks and her efforts to remain calm.

Determined not to lose her temper and allow him any advantage, Miranda smiled disarmingly. "Mr. Cary does not encroach upon our betrothal, and I have found him nothing but open and sincere." She averted her eyes, affecting a rueful demeanor. "And how am I to find a suitable husband," she asked demurely, "if I don't encourage young men who admire me? That was part of our infamous bargain," she reminded him, returning her gaze steadfastly to his.

"I don't think Cary is a suitable young man," Rupert objected. "We know very little about him. He may be the most veritable bounder." He strained to keep Miranda from gaining an ascendency.

"I doubt that, but you have more experience with cads and bounders than I do. I must bow to your superior judgment."

"Don't act the shrew, Miranda. It's unbecoming." Conscious he was losing control, Rupert became stern. "I will not have you the object of gossip."

"What you mean, my lord, is that you will not countenance anyone suspecting I might prefer another to yourself. It is strange, I agree, but somehow I find Randolph Cary a more pleasant companion. He is polite and never goes beyond the boundaries of propriety."

"I should hope not. He will answer to me if he does, as will you. London loves scandal, and I will not have you providing the tabbies with any food for speculation."

"No, you do that yourself. What about your reputation and your own license? If we are engaged, you should act as if you at least found my company endurable." Too late Miranda realized she was behaving badly, criticizing him for not paying court to her when that was not part of the arrangement. Randolph Cary had soothed her ego; and the other young men who sued for her favors had flattered her, although she was wise enough to accept that it was just a game. But she would not have this hateful man reprimanding her conduct when his own was equally at fault.

Rupert, thoroughly maddened by her insouciant air and lack of respect for his advice, lost control of his own temper. Crossing to her chair, he jerked her into his arms and bent his head to bestow a punishing kiss on her shocked face. Furious at his breach of manners, she raised her hand to hit him, but he forestalled her.

"No, you don't, you vixen. What you need is a man to master you. And if it is attention you are wanting, I will be glad to oblige." Then he gathered her resisting form closer and his lips fastened on hers with brutal force. But somehow the kiss intended as a chastisement gentled under her yielding response to one of passionate warmth. She seemed unable to prevent the glowing tide of feeling that swept over her and insensibly her hands crept around his neck and her body softened against his hard strength. His lips became more insistent, coaxing her to open her mouth before his questing tongue. Lost to any emotion but the overpowering demands of the moment, they were rapidly discarding any remnants of sanity when a log broke on the fire, disrupting their desire.

Rupert, aware that he had transgressed, drew away first, forcing her hands from his neck and retreating to the fireplace. "What an avid little wanton you are, Miranda. I quite lost my head," he mocked, unwilling to admit that his own senses had been overwhelmed.

Angry and ashamed not only that he had noticed her response but that he had been the first to turn away, Miranda rushed into speech.

"You are a brute and a cad, sir. Mean-spirited, too. I promise you if your attacks on me continue, I will return to Oxford. Our bargain be damned."

Before he could make any rejoiner, she whirled from the room and up the stairs. He made no attempt to stop her.

He, too, was ashamed. He had been tempted to uncontrolled action by her refusal to admit to a dalliance with Cary. He had behaved monstrously, and now he must try to retrieve the situation. Composing himself, he accepted his coat from the impassive Radleigh, who had observed Miranda's hurried exit and had ideas of his own as to what had transpired. Not that the butler showed any curiosity.

"Good night, my lord. I suppose we shall be seeing you soon," he offered blandly, opening the door to Rupert, who departed with a scowl. Radleigh had certainly had the last word—and the right one. They would be seeing him soon.

Chapter Nine

Chloe Castleton had not forgotten nor forgiven the blow Rupert had delivered both to her pride and her pocketbook. She had honestly thought that her skills in the bedroom and her physical attractiveness would eventually lead to marriage, although he had never given any indication that he was inclined toward the altar. She had set her heart on becoming Lady Hastings and not merely because of the social *éclat* the title would bring her. Yet he had dismissed her as if she were some light skirt. Well, he would regret that, for a paltry ruby-and-diamond necklace was not enough to salve her wounds. She knew his decision was final. Rupert was not a man prone to change his mind, but he would pay for his casual rejection of her. How she would obtain her revenge she had not fully determined, but she had begun to formulate a plan.

Despite her inability to penetrate society at its highest levels, she kept in touch with the latest *on dits*. And she had learned that Rupert's fiancée was the object of other men's attentions, particularly those of a young American diplomat. The prospect of Rupert being publicly jilted in favor of a young colonial offered her vast satisfaction. She would pursue this Mr. Cary and see what use she could make of him.

Sitting in her pink boudoir, Chloe permitted herself a congratulatory smile. She would employ all her cunning to ensure that Rupert Hastings suffered for his treatment of her. She opened her desk and, taking out a sheet of scented pink paper, scrawled a note.

Rupert, believing he had successfully ousted Chloe from his life, had given her little thought. Now he was thoroughly engaged in bringing Miranda around to a more complaisant attitude and to that end he bent his considerable talent.

Radleigh had been quite correct in his supposition that Rupert would repair his neglect and spend more time visiting the Mount Street house. Having had an intimate knowledge of his lordship since Rupert was in leading strings, he realized that Lord Hastings would not entertain any defection by Miranda. Below stairs the opinion was that the young lady from Oxford was a rare one and just the match for Lady Worthington's brother.

"She won't put up with any nonsense," was Radleigh's solemn assurance to Mrs. Bellows, the cook and the only member of the staff in his confidence.

"I don't know, Mr. Radleigh," that rubicund woman, who looked a great deal like her own roly-poly puddings, disagreed. "His lordship has a way with the ladies—and a temper, too. He will not take any sauce from a chit like her."

"She has standards. I think she will put him through the hoop, and it will be good for him," was Radleigh's final pronouncement. Mrs. Bellows, yielding to a superior nature, bobbed her round greying head wisely. "Perhaps you are right. It's a treat the way she goes on, at any rate, even if she does make poor Master Peter jealous."

"Miss Houghton would never do for Master Peter. He's much too innocent to handle her. Too young, too, to be hanging out for a wife. We will see some ructions before we are through. Mark my words, Mrs. Bellows." Radleigh nodded with satisfaction. "Lord Hastings won't have it entirely his way this time."

Rupert, sadly, was coming around to Radleigh's view. He

judged that he would have to change his tactics. On the day following the Astley's entertainment, he presented himself at Mount Street, intent on facing Miranda and making his peace.

Requesting that Miranda drive out with him at the fashionable hour when the *ton* paraded in Hyde Park, he intended to apologize for his effrontery. Miranda received him warily.

"Really, Miranda, do not look upon me as if I were a monster. I apologize most humbly for my advances. Will that satisfy you?" He had meant to beg forgiveness but broke into an unrepentant grin.

"There is little humility in your manner, my lord," she reprimanded. "And I will not go on with this mock engagement if you keep treating me like one of your Cyprians. You think I am an adventuress with few morals and less sense, but I assure you that is a badly mistaken estimate of my nature." Belatedly intent on retrieving her character, she blushed at the recollection of her uninhibited response to his lovemaking.

"I assure you I hold no such low opinion of you," he protested earnestly. "I fear I was carried away last evening. You are most attractive, Miranda, and I succumbed to temptation. I promise I will not transgress again." He took her hand in proper redress but could not resist adding a brazen effrontery. "Unless, of course, you give me permission," he concluded, amused by her righteous indignation. He was, however, piqued by her refusal to find him in any way acceptable as a lover.

"Well, I don't trust you, but I suppose I was also at fault," she admitted honestly.

Rupert, although amazed and delighted by this confirmation that she had not been entirely loathe to accept his kisses, found her reaction extraordinary. Most young women in her position would have taken an attitude, simpered, or asserted that her virtue had been attacked. But he had known for some time that Miranda was of a different stamp than the vacuous debutantes he had met during a decade on the town.

"So, if I am forgiven, can we ride out? A breath of air will be good for you."

"I suppose being seen with you by society will quiet suspicions and be good for my consequence. All right," she agreed laughing. "But I must go to Hookum's. I promised Lady Worthington to return a parcel of books for her, and I want to get the new Jane Austen."

"Delighted to escort you." Thus they set off on their errand in charity with one another, beamed on by Radleigh who ushered them out with a fatherly air which vastly annoyed Rupert.

In Bond Street at the lending library, they accomplished Miranda's mission quickly, the cynosure of several eyes, for the engagement was still among the most fascinating of society's current *on dits*. But Miranda ignored the avid stares and concentrated on her reading list. Rupert, impressed by her bookish knowledge, lounged about negligently playing the part of a devoted suitor as she rifled through books.

Finally, she concluded her business and they turned to go. As they moved toward the entrance, the door opened and a middle-aged man bustled through, intent on his own concerns but not so preoccupied that he did not stop and take in their presence.

"Miranda. What a fortunate meeting. I was coming to call on you." He smiled benevolently, as if this chance encounter delighted him.

"How do you do, Professor Howland," Miranda replied weakly.

"And this gentleman must be Lord Hastings, who so rapidly replaced me in your affections," Howland jibed.

"Yes, this is Lord Hastings. Rupert, this gentleman is Horace Howland, a colleague and friend of my father's." Miranda grimaced as she turned to Rupert, and he was quick to comprehend not only who this plump and aging professor was but that his unexpected arrival had unsettled Miranda.

"Delighted, sir. I am sure Miranda is eager to hear news of her family and home," he replied evenly. But he took Miranda's arm in a possessive grip and aggressively met Horace's gaze to reinforce his claim.

"I don't think your parents mentioned your changed status when last I talked with them. Of course, I heard of it the moment I arrived in London," Howland continued. His tone was outwardly pleasant, but Miranda did not care for the innuendo in the least.

Fortunately, just then a solid matron of advanced years attempted to gain entrance to the library and the trio was forced to stand aside. Rupert, taking advantage of the interruption, announced that they must be on their way.

"No doubt you will call on Miranda at Mount Street. I am sure she will be happy to receive you, but you must excuse us now," he maintained and swept Miranda out the door and toward his waiting phaeton.

Continuing down Bond Street toward Piccadilly, he waited for an outburst from Miranda. She appeared both apprehensive and distrait but she kept her silence.

"So that is the erstwhile suitor you were escaping. Can't say I blame you. He looks a pompous old fool, but not one to dare any jape." Rupert felt inclined to fill the stillness with conversation. "Why haven't you informed your parents of our engagement, Miranda?" he asked. "Surely you could not have hoped to keep it a secret?"

"Well, not exactly," she evaded and then confessed, "I had only written that a kind friend had offered to give me a season. I thought it best not to discuss this bogus engagement." Shamefully she admitted that she had felt that if she did not tell her parents it would not be real. Yet she had known they would learn the truth eventually. "I do hope Professor Howland will not cause trouble. I don't trust his display of friendly esteem. He is inordinately proud of his reputation and standing, and I have dealt him a blow."

"Deserved, I am sure. What an old fool to think you would willingly enter into a marriage with him!" Rupert eyed her speculatively. "He won't give you any trouble," he promised to ease her concern. "And if he does, I will handle him."

"He appears to be taking his rejection well, and that makes me suspicious. I don't want to see him alone." Miranda voiced her fears, despite the glow of reassurance at Rupert's championship. He could have viewed the meeting with his typical cynicism; instead, he was being most sympathetic.

"I will write to your father and explain that I am at fault for not seeking his permission to address you," Rupert pronounced. "He cannot be but pleased that you have made such an advantageous alliance." He teased her, unaware that he had touched with inexplicable accuracy on Miranda's deepest fear. Unaccountably, he wanted to comfort her.

"Yes, and when I return to Oxford, having broken the engagement, he will make my life a misery," Miranda sighed, envisioning the shoals ahead.

"Ah, but by that time you will have contracted an equally brilliant match, so you say," Rupert riposted. His foolery was bad form, but he could not resist. He recognized that Miranda had indeed been driven to elude the obnoxious Howland, and he was not pleased that she considered him the lesser of two evils.

"Of course. I must remember that you fear for your status as a reigning rake," Miranda came back, angry and confused.

"Now, Miranda, you are within an ace of losing your temper. I am mean to mock you, and I apologize," he said penitently. "I understand your dilemma and the reason for your reluctance to view me as anything but an expedient, but I will not take advantage of you. I promise." He patted her awkwardly, then forced a reassuring chuckle to shake off the gloom that enshrouded them. "Let us continue our outing in better spirits. If Howland plagues you, leave him to me."

Miranda nodded, miserable that she held little hope of

emerging from this fiasco with any advantage, but she could expect no more from Rupert. And indeed, what could he do? Pretend that he cared for her and would rescue her? Hardly. That was not part of the bargain, but why did that make her feel so despondent?

Randolph Cary, opening Chloe Castleton's note in his rooms in Wimpole Street, was not entirely surprised. He had heard of the lady and had made it his business to learn more about her. He knew she had once been the mistress of Lord Hastings and suspected she had not taken her *congé* tolerantly, if indeed the relationship had ended. A meeting with the lady should prove fruitful, he decided, and replied that he would call on her that very afternoon.

Cary was not unaware that Rupert had been making inquiries about him concerning his past and his present post at the ministry. Cary had no fears that Rupert would discover anything disreputable. His record was blameless; and the minister, John Quincy Adams, although a New Englander and apt to be wary of Virginians, had signified his approval of his latest recruit. Adams, unlike Cary, had reservations about the English, but he encouraged his staff to make forays into London society. Cary found the minister reserved and a trifle prickly, but he managed, by the exercise of his considerable charm, to stay on the right side of Mr. Adams. Cary preferred to remain in London, and his plans for the future included Miranda Houghton. He surmised that Chloe Castleton also had intentions toward that young lady, although her motives might be uncongenial to him. He looked forward to meeting Mrs. Castleton with some caution.

Chloe Castleton knew how to entertain gentlemen, and she welcomed Randolph Cary with a show of gracious enthusiasm. Arrayed in a fetchingly gossamer, pink-lace gown, she received him in her overdone drawing room with a suggestive smile. Offering him a fine madeira, she waved him to a settee before the fireplace and settled herself by his side.

"I can't imagine why we haven't met before, Mr. Cary," she frowned, but her dulcet voice promised happy reparation.

"I haven't been in London long, but I agree it is most regrettable that we have not been introduced," Cary agreed. "It was most kind of you to correct this omission."

Chloe placed a hand on his arm. "I think we have friends in common."

"Oh," Cary replied, determined to let the lady make the running.

"Yes, I understand you are acquainted with Rupert Hastings, a dear friend of mine, and his charming fiancée, whom alas, I have not yet met. But from all I have heard she's a lovely girl," Chloe cooed. However, Cary noticed the hard look in her eyes that belied her soft words.

"Yes, indeed. Miss Houghton is an exceptional young woman, and both she and Lord Hastings have been most kind to include a stranger, an American no less, in their circle."

"I fear Rupert has been a bit precipitate in announcing his engagement. I will be honest with you. I had every expectation he would pay his addresses to me, but we had a most unfortunate quarrel—my fault, I am afraid—and he rushed off to engage himself to Miss Houghton. I am desolate." Chloe leaned close to Randolph, allowing him a view of her enticing breasts, well-displayed by her *décolletage*.

"I know nothing about that. He appears quite devoted to Miranda, although he is perhaps too experienced and sophisticated for such an innocent. You seem much more suited to his lordship," Cary offered, testing the waters.

"Yes, well, I think, just from what I have heard—and you know what a rumor mill London society is—that you have a certain fondness for the young lady. She is fortunate indeed to have attracted so personable a suitor."

Cary, certain now of the reasons behind Mrs. Castleton's

eagerness to meet him, was not loath to encourage her. "I am exceedingly fond of Miss Houghton, and regret we did not meet earlier."

"Yes, it is a shame that you came late on the scene, but perhaps that unhappy chance can be altered. If I may speak frankly . . ." Her voice trailed away, implying intimacy.

"Of course." Cary could barely hide his amusement. It was obvious that the lady saw him as an ally in her efforts to regain the affections of the mercurial Lord Hastings. He did not doubt for one moment that her relationship with that gentleman had been close. And he understood all too well why Rupert would have preferred the fresh charms of Miranda to this accomplished seductress. But he allowed no sign of his thoughts to betray him.

Adopting a sympathetic manner, he said, "If I can be of any service to you, I would be delighted; but I fear Lord Hastings is a formidable rival."

"Then you do admire Miss Houghton and would like her for yourself?" Chloe pressed.

"I would be honored if she would marry me, but I believe she is irrevocably promised to Lord Hastings," he concluded sorrowfully. What could the woman be suggesting?

"Well, perhaps it is not too late. You could help me and at the same time secure your own dearest hope," Chloe suggested.

"And how would I do that?" Cary asked ingenuously.

Chloe then proceeded to tell him.

While Chloe and Randolph were plotting how to upset Rupert and Miranda's engagement, Horace Howland also contemplated how he might seek his revenge and reclaim his reluctant fiancée. In his rooms in Bury Street he pondered over how this could best be achieved. He believed he had disarmed Miranda by behaving pleasantly in their come-by-chance meeting at Hookum's, but he was not deceived into thinking that Rupert Hastings viewed him so charitably. His first outburst of rage at Miranda's defection had abated, but not so his frustration, for he greatly desired to claim her as his bride. He had had little recourse when Adrian Houghton had paid the debt he owed him but to accept the loss of his nubile young consort. His *amour propre* would not allow him to consider that Miranda might find him unacceptable as a husband, and he could only concede that she had not been able to resist the lures cast out by a nobleman. However, he had hidden his chagrin when her father explained that Miranda had felt she could not sacrifice the opportunity for a London season to wed Horace Howland, no matter how acceptable that gentleman appeared as an alliance.

"Young girls are so unaware. She did not realize, Horace, that you would have made her a fine husband," Adrian had pacified.

Since no mention was made of another engagement, Horace decided that the Houghtons had not yet learned of their daughter's good fortune. Compared to Rupert Hastings, he was not an enviable choice. He did not deceive himself on that score. Somehow he must turn to his own advantage this news, which had come to him on his arrival in London. Could he persuade the Houghtons to forbid the engagement once they learned of it? He doubted that. But he was determined that Miranda would not escape him. He would look the fool in Oxford, and he did not relish the role of a jilted suitor abandoned for a more exciting prospect. He would remove Hastings and get Miranda back—of that he was determined.

Chapter Ten

Unmindful of the hatchling plots to break her engagement to Rupert Hastings, Miranda continued to enjoy her season. Although incensed by Rupert's opinion of her as an opportunist, she did nothing to disabuse him of his misguided notion, despite the fact that she had no intention of luring some eligible gentleman to the altar. She planned to return to Oxford uncommitted to any man, but she would continue to play the role Rupert had assigned to her. She quite liked Randolph Cary and found him a flattering antidote to her irritating fiancé. However, she did not see him as a husband and she doubted that she would ever feel more for the personable American than a warm friendliness. Still, it would not be wise to acknowledge that to Rupert; it would do him good to believe he had a rival. Unfortunately, Rupert did not respond to this threat in quite the manner she liked. Conceited man. No, she conceded honestly, just assured of his assets.

Now if only Peter could accept that both Cary and his uncle were not serious claimants for her hand, she would be comfortable. But Peter continued to glower and posture whenever either gentleman paid her their addresses. Miranda was fond of Peter and felt she owed him a great deal. She did not want to hurt him but saw no way to calm his suspicions. She wished he would rid himself of this stupid jealousy and form an attachment to Maria Henderson, a much more suitable object for his affections, as Miranda was certain his mother agreed. Miranda liked Maria, thought her a sensible girl, and was convinced Maria had a *tendresse* for Peter. Of course, they were both too young for marriage, despite Lady Worthington's encouragement. but she would do what she could to further that romance.

Horace Howland created yet another problem. Correctly suspecting that the professor would not be content to accept her engagement, she anticipated trouble from him, and hoped she would be well able to deal with it. Brooding in Lady Worthington's morning room, she came to the conclusion that the time had come to inform her parents of her so-called engagement. She could not tell them the true story; they might upbraid her when they discovered the ruse, but she needed their support now. Resolutely, she selected a sheet of writing paper and set out her new circumstances to her mother. She would leave it to Mrs. Houghton to explain to her father that she had become engaged to Lord Hastings without his permission. No doubt he would be furious, but Rupert could handle Adrian Houghton if it became necessary. She stressed the opportunities she was enjoying and hoped her parents would applaud her stroke of good fortune.

Throwing down the pen, she sealed the envelope. She had done the best she could under the circumstances, but she still felt restless and edgy. From the window she looked out upon the bright April day. She was unaccustomed to leisure and found life in Lady Worthington's household confining and burdensome, but she had no right to complain. She had wanted to escape Oxford and Professor Howland, and she should not cavil at the means which had provided that escape. Although her evenings were crowded with engagements, she often felt the daytime hours a trial for she had not established a comfortable relationship with Lady Worthington despite that lady's surface acceptance of her house guest. She had just about decided to return to her room and read, when Radleigh announced a visitor. Maria Henderson followed the butler into the morning room.

"Good afternoon, Miranda. I hope I am not interrupting you, but I was feeling bored and thought you might like to accompany me to the new Soho Bazaar for a bit of shopping," Maria said tentatively. Maria, who much admired Miranda, was not convinced that regard was returned. The daughter of a famous beauty and successful hostess, Maria had little confidence in her own attractions. A small girl with a certain gentle charm, she much envied Miranda's spirit. How, she wondered did she cope with the arrogant Lord Hastings? She did feel some fondness toward Peter Worthington but doubted that young man noticed her when Miranda was present. She did not blame him, for she suspected any man would prefer this vivacious girl to herself. Yet she badly needed a friend and a confidant and hoped Miranda might fill that role. So she had bravely decided to make the overture.

"Thank you, Maria. You are just the tonic I need. I, too, am feeling out of sorts, and I would enjoy some shopping, although I certainly do not require any fripperies," Miranda accepted kindly.

"Yes, you always look so smart," Maria agreed. "I—on the other hand—have no fashion sense. I hate these pale muslins and silks mother insists upon, but I do not have the courage to protest."

"Nonsense. You look charming, and I am sure your mother knows what she's about, but perhaps you might try a slightly bolder accent," Miranda suggested, smiling at her visitor. "Come, let us search out some shocking gloves or an *outré* parasol." This might be the occasion to press Peter's assets on the girl, she thought. At any rate, she might discover Maria's true feelings. Taking her new friend by the arm she shepherded her from the room, prepared to listen to whatever confidences Maria would divulge.

Maria had come in her family carriage and within a few minutes the two girls were riding down Piccadilly. Maria's abigail had accompanied her, so their conversation was perforce limited to mundane matters. The bazaar, on the northwest corner of the square, had been opened but a year and was considered more fashionable than its rival the staid Pantheon Bazaar in Oxford Street. The latest imports from France and a lavish selection of ladies and children's notions—parasols, ribbons, lace, gloves, jewelry, and millinery—were displayed by young prim females, who paid two to three shillings a day for the privilege of displaying the wares. The Henderson carriage joined a line in the square for this newest addition to London's shops which attracted a most distinguished clientele despite its raffish location.

Trailed by Maria's abigail, the two girls wandered among the booths. Maria, encouraged by Miranda, bought a stunning parasol in brilliant cerise, trimmed in lace, and a pair of matching gloves. Miranda could not resist a piece of fine lace to freshen a favorite muslin morning dress, so the expedition was deemed a huge success. Electing to take some refreshment before leaving, the two hesitated at the entrance of a small cafe, unsure if they should enter, when Miranda was approached by a stunning woman who boldly made herself known to them.

"Miss Houghton? I know you will think I am quite rag-mannered, approaching you this way, but I felt I must introduce myself. We have so much in common. I am Chloe Castleton," said the brunette.

Sensing the lady meant trouble, Miranda knew of no way to avoid acknowledging her. "Yes, Mrs. Castleton, I am Miranda Houghton, and this is my friend, Maria Henderson," Miranda admitted with some reserve.

"Were you about to take tea? Perhaps I may join you?" Chloe cajoled.

Courtesy brooked no refusal, and Miranda indicated that would be acceptable as Maria followed along, goggle-eyed at this brazen confrontation from a woman whose reputation was not what it should be. She knew her mother would never receive Mrs. Castleton, but she found the situation intriguing. Debutantes, who were shielded from the Chloe Castletons of their world, nevertheless knew quite a good deal about the behavior of such types on the fringes of society. Maria was well aware that this voluptuous woman had been Rupert Hastings' mistress, and she was indignant for Miranda and prepared to champion her in any contest with the creature.

Directed to a table by a waitress, the trio settled down in uneasy alliance and gave their order for tea and cakes. Chloe, looking extremely dashing in an emerald-green Hussar's frigged redingote and a matching shako with a plume, leaned toward Miranda in a confidential manner.

"I realize you must think me the most encroaching person, but I noticed you by the lace stall and resolved I must make your acquaintance. I know you have recently become engaged to my dear friend Rupert Hastings and that surely makes a bond for Rupert and I are so close. No doubt he would have effected an introduction before long, but I was impatient to meet you," she cooed, implying what Miranda had already known, that her relationship with Rupert was most intimate.

"Of course, I knew of you, Mrs. Castleton," Miranda said shortly, letting Chloe make what she would of her ambiguity.

"Well, naturally, I was among the very first that Rupert told of his good fortune. It must have been a whirlwind courtship, I vow," Chloe trilled, as though agog over the romance.

"Not exactly. I had known Lord Hastings for some time," Miranda lied, unwilling to give her adversary any information. Fortunately their refreshment arrived, deferring any further questions as Chloe poured the tea and pressed cakes upon the girls.

"And when is the wedding? I am sure you won't mind my asking. Rupert is so reticent about these things."

"I suppose he feels it is no one's business but our own," Miranda replied pointedly, hoping the woman would take the hint and cease her probing.

"Oh dear, you think I am such an inquisitive creature," Chloe worried, "but it is only that I am so interested in dear Rupert's future happiness." She leaned forward with a suggestion of intimate disclosure. "I never really thought he would settle down. He has the reputation of being averse to matrimony." She ceased her prattle with an abrupt show of dismay. "Now I shouldn't have disillusioned you. Naughty of me."

Miranda had no illusions about Mrs. Castleton and her intentions, she showed no sign of discomfort. The more-sheltered Maria could barely restrain a gasp at this effrontery. Determined to come to Miranda's aid, Maria ventured, "But surely all men avoid the thought of matrimony until they fall in love."

Chloe treated her to a nasty look, but then ignored her.

Miranda, touched by the timid Maria's attempt to put Chloe in her place, countered smoothly, "I am sure Rupert will let you know our news when it is appropriate, Mrs. Castleton. It is kind of you to take such an interest."

If Chloe accepted the rebuff, it did not deter her. "Well, you know, he is not a dependable sort. I would not like you to be hurt, my dear." She spoke as if Miranda's happiness were of the utmost importance to her, but again Miranda was not deceived.

"I do not think that is possible, Mrs. Castleton. You see Rupert and I understand each other very well."

Barbs traded, Chloe retreated and brought up her secondary defense. "And we share another acquaintance, I believe. That very nice American, Mr. Cary. Such a charming man, wouldn't you say?"

"Yes, Randolph Cary has proved a most pleasant addition to our circle," Miranda enthused. "Don't you agree, Maria?"

"Oh, yes," the girl concurred, albeit weakly. She wondered at the turn in the conversation and was impressed with Miranda's cool reception of Mrs. Castleton. She only wished she shared her friend's aplomb in this difficult situation.

"Since we are both strangers to London, Mr. Cary and I have been occupying ourselves by visiting all the historical sights. Very illuminating," Miranda said. "But perhaps you do not share our interest in such matters, Mrs. Castleton." She doubted very much that Mrs. Castleton's interest in Randolph Cary included discussing London's landmarks. Really, the woman was a sly creature, hoping to upset Miranda with innuendoes and infamous suggestions, all delivered in the most candied of tones. Well, she had had enough of it. If she had cared deeply for either Hastings or Cary, Mrs. Castleton's remarks might have wounded her, but fortunately only her pride, not her heart, was involved. How dare Rupert's ex-mistress accost her this way! She would allow her no more license.

"I really think, Maria, we must be going. We have dallied quite long enough over our shopping, and Lady Worthington will be expecting me. Are you ready to leave?" Miranda turned to her friend seeking her assent.

"Of course," Maria rose hastily, only too happy to put an end to the encounter. She could hardly wait to get Miranda alone and learn her views. Bidding a polite goodbye to Mrs. Castleton, who insisted on paying their bill, the two girls left without further discussion.

Chloe, left her thoughts, wondered if she had accomplished what she had meant to do. Really, the girl was a cold fish. What could Rupert find so appealing? The meeting had not proceeded along the lines she had planned, and she regretted now she had yielded to the impulse to place some suspicion in Miss Houghton's mind about the faithfulness of her fiancé. Perhaps she did not care and was interested only in acquiring status as Rupert's wife. Miranda did not behave like a young innocent besotted with the man. Well, at least she had given her rival something to think about. Chloe gave only a passing thought to what Rupert would say if Miranda told him about their meeting. Any discomfort she could cause that arrogant lord would be a victory.

In the carriage Maria could barely restrain herself. Ignoring her abigail, she said with some indignation to Miranda, "How could Mrs. Castleton be so rude, forcing herself on you? She must have known it would cause embarrassment."

"If so, she was disappointed. I found the whole affair unusual, but I was quite pleased to meet her, having heard so much about her. It's always wise to study one's opposition, you know," Miranda replied, not at all angered. She had found Mrs. Castleton transparent and rather foolish.

"You are so sensible, Miranda. I would be consumed with jealousy after meeting such a woman. She is beautiful and, I hear, has had a number of men eager for her favors."

"No doubt. But a trifle lush in her charms. And she craves respectability, which I fear she will not achieve. Really, she is pathetic," Miranda observed without emotion.

"Will you tell Lord Hastings?" Maria asked, apprehensive.

"Perhaps. It really was of no moment, and now let us abandon this fruitless discussion of a regrettable episode."

Maria, realizing Miranda would not be drawn further and unwilling to antagonize her, rushed into a discussion of their purchases and thanked Miranda for accompanying her. They planned to meet again soon and parted at the entrance to Mount Street both feeling that a bond had been established. Miranda regretted she had not quizzed Maria about Peter, but she would defer those questions until a more appropriate time.

As Miranda entered the house, she met Randolph Cary just turning away.

"Oh, well met, Miranda. I dropped in on the chance you might go with me to view the Elgin Marbles. So much controversy surrounds them I thought it was a good idea to take a look," he explained cheerfully. "But alas, I think it too late now. Perhaps another day."

Miranda, who wanted to ask Randolph a few questions, made a moue of disappointment. "I have just had tea, but do come in for a moment. I have had the oddest encounter at the Soho Bazaar and am feeling jumbled."

"Delighted," he replied, following her into the hall, where Radleigh hovered.

"Mr. Cary will be taking some refreshment, Radleigh, if that is convenient. Is Lady Worthington at home?" Miranda asked, surrendering her shawl and bonnet to the butler.

"No, Miss Houghton. She and Master Peter went around to the Egertons, but I will send in some wine to the drawing room immediately."

"The morning room will do, Radleigh. Thank you."

Miranda chatted inconsequentially with Cary until the madeira and biscuits had been delivered, telling him of a Roman breakfast she had attended with the Worthingtons some days before and making an amusing story of her attempt to eat sprawled on cushions. Randolph listened with appreciation; when she paused, however, he leaned forward and looked at her with a troubled frown.

"I did want to talk to you, Miranda, about a strange encounter myself, but I will let you go first."

"Well, it's just that I met Mrs. Castleton at the bazaar. She introduced herself and during our conversation mentioned that she was a friend of yours. It's really not my business, but I wondered about it, what you thought of her. I am insatiably curious," she added with a disarming grin.

"By gad, that is too much. The lady, if I may call her that, summoned me to her presence and we had a very peculiar chat in that atrocious pink drawing room of hers," Cary said, disturbed.

"How enthralling, do go on."

"Well, she asked what my intentions were toward you. It was most brazen, but then she is quite beyond the pale." He hesitated and then blundered on, embarrassed. "You must be aware of how I regard you, yet I would not cause you any distress by pressing unwanted attentions on you. I respect your engagement; and, of course, Lord Hastings is not a man to allow any license. He has been most generous in allowing me to escort you now and then. And I admit I regret exceedingly that we did not meet before you became engaged, not that I would have stood a chance with such a wonderful girl," he concluded wistfully.

Miranda, charmed by his modesty and frankness, smiled but was not willing to let him off with such a sketchy report. "Well, what did Mrs. Castleton want from you?"

"She believes that if Lord Hastings were not on the scene you might have looked favorably upon me. Of course, I denied any such suggestion, but the lady persevered. In all honesty, she is the most blatant intriguer I have ever met."

"But vastly attractive, I think," Miranda suggested.

"Not to me. However, what she proposed was shocking. She wanted me to arrange an abduction or some compromising situation which would result in your breaking your engagement and marrying me instead. Not that I encouraged her, you understand, and I could not deny that that is the dearest wish of my heart; but I would never do anything to cause you unhappiness. I let her know that she had gravely mistaken her man," he explained in some confusion, a blush rising to his cheek.

Miranda's reaction ran contrary to his expectations. Placing her hand on his, she smiled, "Dear Randolph, how nice you are. You need not have told me this scurvy tale, but I am

106

grateful for your warning. The woman obviously wants me out of the way, thinking she can capture Rupert by fair means or foul. Perhaps she may yet, but at least not with your contrivance."

"She is a dangerous enemy and not a woman who you should have anything to do with," Randolph insisted. "Will you tell Lord Hastings?"

"Oh, I don't think so. He would only laugh and make light of it. Let it be our secret, but I wonder if your refusal will stop her machinations. Still, I have been warned and will be most careful."

"You do care for Lord Hastings. I suppose there is no chance . . ." Randolph looked pleadingly at her, hoping for some suggestion that Miranda found the noble lord lacking in the devotion he himself so eagerly offered.

"Dear Randolph, you are kind. I hope we can continue to be friends, but I am firmly attached to Rupert and could not consider any other man. That would be a deplorable act." Miranda was moved by Randolph's profession of affection, but she was apt to discount it. Would he have been so vehement if there were any chance she would accept him? What a cynic she was becoming! Her experience with society had not altered her views that London beaux were a volatile lot, only concerned with fashion and manners, not with sincere emotion. Perhaps she was unfair to this engaging American. She was both pleased and surprised that he had been so forthright with her, but she could not abandon her bargain with Rupert. She was not even tempted, despite her boasts to him that she was on the watch for a suitable husband. She was almost as brazen an adventuress as the odious Mrs. Castleton, but she could hardly explain her dilemma to this charming friend.

"I felt I must tell you. I want you to trust me, and I hope our friendship will continue. I promise not to presume," he added with a rueful sigh.

"Thank you, Randolph. I would like that, and I would enjoy viewing the Elgin Marbles. We must set a date. And now I have to dress for dinner. Let us simply forget Mrs. Castleton and this conversation."

Randolph, accepting that further discussion would not be welcomed, made his adieux, promising to see her again soon. Left alone, Miranda made no move to rise and retire to her bedroom. She found the whole business of the conspiring Mrs. Castleton worrying. The woman must be mad to think she could recapture Rupert, if indeed she had lost him. Really, they deserved each other, and Miranda frowned wondering why that possibility bothered her so much. Randolph Cary was a decent and sincere young man, but she would never consider him as a husband. He might be far more devoted and kind than Rupert, but he lacked that gentleman's presence and arrogant charm. What a fool she was to even compare the two. Shaking off her confusion, she finally departed to prepare for the evening, close to admitting that her life was becoming too complicated for words.

Chapter Eleven

Several nights after Miranda's encounter with Chloe Castleton and Randolph Cary's odd disclosure of his interview with that lady, Miranda and Rupert went to an elegant dinner party at Kenwood House, the family seat of the Mansfields. The company was high-toned, including the Prime Minister, Lord Liverpool, the Palmerstons, and the Duke of Wellington. The mansion, set on the northern edge of Hampstead Heath, had been enlarged by the first Earl of Mansfield, a seventeenth-century Lord Chief Justice, after his home in Bloomsbury had been destroyed in the Gordon Riots some forty years ago. Kenwood had been the family country seat, saved from looting by the landlord of Spaniards Inn, who had served the rioters enough liquor to distract them. Robert Adam had designed the classic villa with shallow arches and columns, and the Mansfields had filled it with stunning French and Adam furniture.

"If you find the company oppressive at least you will enjoy the house. It's one of the finest in England and boasts some outstanding paintings," Rupert had promised Miranda, who had been awed by the guest list.

"It is very kind of you to include me in such an evening," Miranda thanked him primly. "I hope I do not disgrace you."

Rupert's lips quivered at the corners, but he merely replied,

"You seem too interested in exploring London's historical sights with Cary; it behooves me to also offer a special treat."

Miranda, annoyed by his condescension, did not rise to the bait although she was greatly tempted.

As it turned out, the party went off quite well. She found Lord Liverpool kindly and distinguished and was almost overcome by the attention of the Iron Duke, who congratulated Rupert on acquiring such an attractive and knowledgeable fiancée. She was by far the youngest woman present and was careful to behave with the utmost circumspection, aware that Lady Palmerston, her hostess, Lady Mansfield, and the other dowagers were watching her with an appraising eye. She had donned her most genteel costume, a gown of white shirred muslin with a patterned gauze weave, short puffed sleeves, and a demure *décolletage*. And since the evening was mild, a lacey white shawl was enough to protect her from errant breezes.

Rupert, assessing her with his connoiseur's eye, had informed her she looked just the thing, a dubious compliment she received with a grimace.

"I really don't care for the present fashion of white gowns, so impractical, but Lady Worthington insists they are of the first stare and the only proper dress for young maidens," she explained with a certain honest disgust.

"Charlotte has impeccable taste and you do us both an honor," he dissented, repressing his amusement. Miranda never ceased to enchant him with her opinions of style, fashion, politics, and social conditions. He often teased her on the danger of becoming a bluestocking.

"I see nothing untoward in being interested in concerns more pressing than the cut of a gown or the decoration of a bonnet," she had replied with some hauteur.

"Of course not. You are always a great credit to me, Miranda, as well as being an Incomparable."

Pleased as she had been with his compliment, she would

not acknowledge her pleasure beyond giving him a speaking look which intended to express reproof. However, this evening she was quite in charity with Rupert. She no longer worried that he might pounce upon her with an unwanted caress. She only wondered at her own reaction if he did.

Dinner had been most enjoyable, since she was partnered with Antony Egerton, the young Deputy Home Secretary, an amusing and kind companion whose wife, a stunning blonde, had drawn her husband's chief, Lord Sidmouth.

Looking along the table, decked with Georgian silver and a massive epergne filled with yellow and white roses, Miranda confided boldly, "The company is almost too rich for me, my lord. I had no idea Rupert was so intimate with members of the government."

"A very intelligent chap, your fiancé. Do not be deceived by his casual manner. He has an astute brain and could well fill a cabinet post if he were so inclined. Alas, he finds us all rather prosy, I fear, and misses the excitement of the battlefield. Wellington thinks very well of him, you know."

"He never talks about his role in the war," Miranda said wistfully. Somehow she was not surprised that Rupert was applauded by these peers.

"Well, he wouldn't, you know. Not good form," Lord Egerton explained cheerfully. "My wife calls the present government *the mouldy ones*. It's a popular view, I fear."

"She's very lovely," Miranda said gazing at Lady Egerton with admiration.

"Yes, and very obstinate. I am quite under her thumb," Tony Egerton confided with a grin.

"I must ask her her secret in handling mettlesome men. I am sure she would give me some good advice," Miranda riposted, not at all convinced that the lady in question dominated her husband. She was sure they had a happy marriage, a rarity in these refined circles.

"Ah, Rupert has my sympathy, but a spirited bride is more

111

of a challenge than a meek and carping one. Kitty Wellington, for example, tries the patience of the duke, and he is not a patient man."

Looking at the Duchess of Wellington, unbecomingly dressed in a puce satin creation and making heavy weather of Lord Liverpool on her right, Miranda could well believe it. She had heard that the duke preferred sprightly and stunning ladies to his own much-tried wife.

"We are wicked to gossip like this. You are luring me into indiscretions, Miss Houghton. I sense you're a dangerous woman," Tony Egerton teased.

Miranda rather regretted leaving her charming dinner partner when the ladies retired. The proper matrons did not seem as inviting. However, once esconced in the great library, a pillared room lined with leather-bound volumes, Miranda was approached by Lady Egerton who appeared as friendly as her husband.

"I must tender you my best wishes. Rupert has always been a favorite of mine, and I am pleased to see he has captured a girl worthy of him," she said with an engaging smile, settling down next to Miranda on a brocaded settee.

"And how do you know I am worthy of him, Lady Egerton?" Miranda responded, questioning the intent behind the remark.

"Because you managed to charm Tony, my husband. He must be grateful to have drawn such a lovely and witty partner for dinner. He might have been lumbered with Kitty Wellington," she whispered.

Miranda grinned and could not repress her satisfaction. "I am glad not to have disappointed, but I can see he has a very high standard, Lady Egerton."

"Oh, do call me Francey. I feel we could become firm friends. After you return from your honeymoon, you must let me give you a party, ease your way into domestic harmony."

Miranda gave a passing regret that she must deceive the lady. Domestic harmony with Rupert was not in the cards.

Before she could either agree or demur, the doors opened and the gentlemen appeared. Rupert came immediately to her side.

"I see you got on famously with Tony at dinner, Miranda. And I hope Francey is telling you what a fine fellow I am," he bantered, giving Lady Egerton an endearing smile.

"Not at all, Rupert. I am warning her to put you on a tight leash. You have a shocking reputation," Francey replied, not in the least discomfited.

"Ah, Francey, you distrust me, and now Miranda will have second thoughts about our future felicity."

"I do not see you as a tame benedict," Miranda said sharply, suddenly confused by their repartee.

Before Miranda could be betrayed into making an intemperate remark, Lady Mansfield announced they would be honored by a programme of song from the famed diva Madame Canelli. Typically, the Italian star, while not invited to dinner, had been asked to provide the entertainment. Opera singers, even the most acclaimed, were rarely received socially in the drawing rooms of London's *haut ton,* a distinction Miranda thought both snobbish and inexcusable, but she did not voice her opinion. They adjourned to the gilded music room for the entertainment.

Madame Canelli sang two Verdi arias and a light country air which charmed all the guests. After some conversation and light refreshment, the evening ended on a pleasant note, and Miranda believed she had brushed through the affair creditably.

After thanking her host and hostess, she and Rupert prepared to enter their coach for the ride back to London.

As they were stepping into the carriage, Lord Mansfield, standing at the entrance to bid his departing guests farewell, looked over Rupert's entourage.

"Surely you are not going across the heath without outriders, Hastings?" he asked worriedly.

"I have no intention of going an extra ten miles just because of the rumors that some pesky highwaymen are lurking on the heath. I won't be intimidated by the rogues," Rupert replied.

"Take care. You have Miss Houghton to think about," Lord Mansfield warned.

"I am prepared for all eventualities. My coachman is a formidable man, more than capable of dealing with any mishap," Rupert assured his host and then cut off any more forebodings by handing Miranda into the coach and excusing himself to speak to the coachman. Seeing that he was making little impression on Rupert, Lord Mansfield remained quiet as Rupert turned at the top of the coach steps to bid him goodbye.

"Thank you again for a very enjoyable evening. I know Miranda was delighted to be included and to view your splendid house." He nodded and entered the coach, the footman putting up the steps and closing the door.

Lord Mansfield shook his head at such rashness and stood watching as the Hastings carriage, with its distinctive crest, rolled down the drive. They were the last to leave, and Mansfield hurried to return to his guests who were staying the night.

Miranda wondered, not for the first time, as they proceeded down the drive why Rupert was allowed such license by his friends. Charm, wealth, and arrogance probably explained it, she conceded silently. Really, he tried her temper. Was he never put out of countenance?

It seemed not. Rupert leaned back against the squabs and contemplated Miranda with approval. "Upon my honor, it was quite astute of me to wrest such a gem from Oxford's shining towers. I was proud of you tonight, Miranda. And I think you enjoyed yourself."

"Yes, I did. Kenwood is a magnificent seat. But I might remind you, Rupert, you did not choose me. You contrived to make use of a situation which put me at your mercy," she said sharply.

"Why is it, my dear, whenever I try to pay you a compliment, you shrug it off and view me with disgust. Very offputting, I assure you, and disastrous to any attempt to make love to you."

"Ah, I suppose it's because I know how false your words are, and I am not interested in being the object of your practised address. But I do thank you for allowing me a glimpse of such august personages. Especially the duke. What a lovely man he is."

"Not everyone's assessment, but then he has always had an eye for a beautiful woman. And who could blame him, tied to that drab Kitty? Such a gauche duchess. Poor dear, she has never learned how to go on even after all these years."

"How you do gossip! I find London society much too prone to spitefulness," Miranda criticized.

"But you are not very charitable yourself, my dear. You treat me with the utmost scorn, and here I am eager to win your approval and inveigle myself into your good graces."

"Pooh, you could care less. It's just your conceit is damaged because I do not fawn and simper like most of your conquests." Miranda found sparring with Rupert stimulating and was convinced she could respond to any of his efforts to put her in the wrong. The coach was now entering the deepest depths of the heath, and she looked idly out the window, wondering if Lord Mansfield's warning had any validity.

For some reason she had every faith that Rupert could handle any mischance that happened, although it did indeed look dark and menacing beyond the comfort of the coach. As if in answer to her disquiet, the coachman whipped up the horses to greater speed, hoping to put the miles of this treacherous landscape behind them as quickly as possible. She looked at

Rupert, sprawled negligently beside her, and wondered if he felt any apprehension. Even if he did, he would never show it; nor would he bow to prudence and take a safer course back to London. Just then, she heard the hard clop of horses' hooves and a shout. The coachman jerked hard on his reins, and the coach shuddered to a stop. Muffled voices rang through the night air and Rupert, losing none of his cool careless demeanor, rolled down the window, letting in a gust of damp air. Miranda heard a gruff voice cry, "This is the one. That's the crest."

Then the door of the coach was flung open and a man, completely masked by a hooded cloak, peered inside.

"What have we here? A fine toff and his lady friend. Good pickings. Step down, me fine buck, and I will relieve you of your pocketbook," growled the intruder, lending emphasis to his threat by waving the gun he held in his hand.

"I think not, my friend." Before Miranda could do more than stifle a cry, a shot rang out and the highwayman fell back. Rupert coolly leaned forward and closed the door, then called from the window, "Drive on, John."

"You shot that man. He's wounded. You cannot just leave him there," Miranda protested, shocked.

"Would you like me to bring him into the coach so you could tend his wounds? I think not as he might bleed all over the squabs and they were just recovered last week," Rupert retorted tersely.

Just then another shot rang out, and the coach gathered speed. They were on their way. Miranda hardly knew what to say, and she looked in dismay at Rupert who was examining the pocket of his coat, which displayed a scorched and burnt hole.

"Where did you get that gun? Surely you did not carry it into Kenwood tonight?" she asked catching her breath.

"Naturally not. It would have destroyed the fit of my coat and my tailor would have been appalled. He will be most annoyed at this damage. I relieved John of one of his weapons before I stepped into the coach. I assume he used the other one to good effect and dispatched our intruder's companion."

Now that the danger was past, Miranda felt shaken and weak, not that she would admit to any faintness before Rupert. He would only laugh and despise her for such timidity. But just how did one react after a hold up by highwaymen? Then the remembrance of the villain's words distracted her from any cowardly reaction that might make her vulnerable before Rupert.

"He was looking for you. He recognized the crest on the coach. What did he mean by that?" she asked.

"Ah, Miranda, you never cease to delight me. Any other lady of my acquaintance would be screaming and having the vapors, throwing herself on my breast and calling for protection. But you are only interested in the motives of the highwayman. I commend you, my dear, for your good sense. Although I admit a little gentle shrinking against my manly bosom would not come amiss."

"Don't be ridiculous. If the man knew your coach, he was waiting for it and intended you some harm. If you had followed his commands and left the coach, who knows what would have happened? I don't think he had simple robbery in mind."

Rupert gave her a quick piercing glance and then lowered his lids, masking his feelings.

"Ah, Miranda, you are entirely too perceptive. That thought had also occurred to me. I wonder who among my, no doubt myriad, enemies, dislikes me so much that my removal seems advisable. There is your erstwhile suitor, Horace Howland, but somehow I cannot see him managing this affair."

"No," Miranda agreed doubtfully. "Horace would not know how to go about hiring ruffians to carry out his designs no matter how much he wanted to embarrass you or cause you harm. But you must have other people who might rejoice at your downfall."

"What an opinion you have of me, Miranda. But to answer your question, I can't recall any disgruntled folk who would go to those extremes."

"Who is your heir? Peter?"

"That is why I want to get married, my dear. If I meet an untimely end, there is no heir. I am the last of my line. Peter would inherit my estates as things stand now because I have no other relatives. The Hastings were not a prolific brood. Which brings me to a serious concern. Having seen you in some very fraught situations, I am impressed with the way you handle these vexing affairs; and it seems to me, Miranda, I would never find a bride with such beauty, intelligence, and capability in handling a crisis. They are incredible and rare assets in one so young."

Miranda, not entirely sure whether he was funning or not, tossed her head. "Don't try to gammon me, Rupert. You don't want a wife. You want to be free of designing women, which makes me think of your Mrs. Castleton, a cast-off mistress and a dangerous one at that, don't you think?"

Rupert roared with laughter, then drew Miranda close to him. "What can I do to persuade you I am not an evil ogre with an unsavory past and a reputation for treating women badly? You may be making a grave mistake, my dear, in turning down my proposal so abruptly. I might make a most agreeable husband. Think about it."

Before she could collect her disordered thoughts, he gathered her into a close embrace, pinioning her hands so she could not resist, and kissed her with lingering competence. Overcome, Miranda did not resist and wondered why she did not find his kisses repellent but, instead, warm and comforting. She wished fleetingly that she could stay in his arms forever. Rupert made no further incursions than this series of drugging kisses, and she felt her body softening and her heart racing in response. But before she could completely betray herself, he drew away, patting her comfortingly on her shoulder.

"You see, Miranda, you did not find that disgusting. In fact, with practice, I think you might even enjoy it. Do not be so hasty in dismissing me. We might yet be able to accomodate one another."

Miranda, not sure whether the kisses were a punishment or a promise, was bewildered by Rupert's ambiguous words. So intent was she on behaving with insouience under his keen regard, she almost forgot about the incident with the highwayman, which might have been Rupert's intention. On the other hand, he might have been sincere in his proposal. If so what was she to do now?

Chapter Twelve

Lady Worthington had retired when Miranda and Rupert finally reached Mount Street after their nocturnal adventure. Which was just as well since Rupert warned Miranda there would be little purpose in informing his sister of their encounter with the highwayman. Escorting her to the door, he apologized for exposing her to such a frightening experience and only raised his eyebrows when she insisted it had not been so much frightening as puzzling.

"Who would single out your coach for such an attack? I am not at all convinced that it was a mere raid on any convenient wealthy traveler," she said.

"Don't worry, Miranda. It will sort itself out. Unfortunately, I must leave town for a few days. I promised Marcus to join a party at his manor in Berkshire. It's an all-male affair so don't start imagining mischief. And try to stay out of trouble while I am away. You might give some thought, too, to my earlier suggestion of making our engagement a reality," he concluded and then, before she could question him further, kissed her lightly on the forehead and bade her goodnight.

Despite her expectation to toss and turn until dawn, she fell immediately into a deep sleep. But her rest was disturbed by strange dreams in which Rupert, Peter, Horace Howland, and Randolph Cary all figured in a confusion of claims and counterclaims. When she awoke in the morning she felt sluggish and unrefreshed. The problem of the highwayman receded to be replaced by Rupert's surprising offer to make their engagement a real one. What had prompted such an idea? Certainly he showed no signs of being in love with her. He treated her with a mixture of brotherly condescension and rakish attention which left her unsure of his feelings, although she was beginning to know her own. She must not allow herself to fall in love with Rupert for she feared it would only bring her disappointment and unhappiness. He could offer her a great deal, but not what she craved: an abiding and faithful love and, even more, respect. The attack by the highwayman must have impelled his offer. Perhaps it brought home to him that his estates, title, and wealth had no heir of his name. And she knew well-born gentlemen set great store by perpetuating their families. She had no intention of serving as a convenient breeder for future Hastings scions, and she would let Rupert know that she found his careless proposal insulting.

The day which had begun so doubtfully did not improve. Her favorite blue-muslin morning dress tore when her abigail helped her into it, and she looked into the mirror to discover a wan-faced, heavy-eyed girl, far from her best. Deciding that she would have a quiet day, she took a book into the garden after chatting politely with her hostess. Even that innocuous conversation brought problems. Lady Worthington handed her a letter from her father which had come late yesterday.

"Do you suppose your parents want you home, Miranda?" Charlotte asked with what Miranda sensed was a hopeful note. Miranda knew that despite her facade of acceptance and general courtesy, her hostess longed to see her depart but was too in awe of her brother to make such a suggestion. It was not pleasant to be a guest under sufferance, but Miranda stifled her inclination to agree that it would be best if she left. Her affairs were too precarious to escape. Of a certainty if she did leave, Rupert would travel to Oxford post-haste and drag her back, not for any reason but that he did not allow anyone to challenge his decisions. He would dispense with her when he felt she had served her purpose. Then she remembered his offer to put their relationship on a more permanent basis. She knew how Charlotte would regard that. Sighing with frustration, she took her letter into the garden. As she expected, her father's letter was a combination of satisfaction on her good fortune and annoyance that he had not been consulted, as well as a diatribe on her selfishness and Rupert's arrogance. He ended on a rather threatening note: "I am, after all, your father and responsible for your welfare. You saw fit to disobey me over the Howland business, which happened to resolve itself happily, but that does not allow you to decide your future without any advice and guidance from me. I might remind you that I have the final say on whom you will marry, and I hope you will remember your duty to your mother and me and act accordingly."

Really her father was almost as arrogant as Rupert, thinking she had no right to manage her own life. She knew that her father's interview with Horace must have been painful as well as embarrassing. And much as he might be impressed with Rupert's obvious assets, the fact that this current engagement had been effected without his knowledge or consent had touched his pride and self-importance. Typically, he made no mention of his debt being settled by Miranda's efforts, nor did he ask from where she had acquired the funds. Well, he would have to compose himself in patience. The dilemma she now faced would not have happened if he had not behaved in such a cavalier fashion.

Tossing aside the letter, Miranda turned to her book and was able to read a few pages before there was another and even more unwelcome interruption. Radleigh appeared at her side announcing that she had a caller whom he had placed in the drawing room.

"A Professor Howland, miss, tenders his compliments and craves a moment with you."

"Oh, Radleigh, could you not have denied him? I really am not up to callers today," Miranda complained with a grimace.

"I am so sorry, miss. Lady Worthington thought you might like to see a friend from Oxford. She is entertaining him now and requests you join them."

Seeing there was no help for it, Miranda acceded. After all, neither Radleigh nor Lady Worthington knew how much she dreaded meeting Horace.

Bracing herself for what she suspected would be an unpleasant interview, she walked listlessly into the house, taking her time in an attempt to sort out how she would handle her former fiancé. Veritably, she seemed to have gathered too many unwanted suitors lately. She recalled her dream and gave a small shrug. Why was the only fate offered to a respectable girl marriage to some man? She wished she had the courage to tell them all to go to the devil and escape to Wales like the notorious Ladies of Llangollen. In her innocence, Miranda did not understand the relationship between these two remarkable ladies, but their boldness and independence appeared admirable at the moment.

"Good morning, Horace," she said demurely upon entering the drawing room, rather amused at Lady Worthington's vinegary aspect. Horace could be heavy going, and obviously her hostess felt much tried upon having to entertain this prosy professor. She rose with some relief at Miranda's entrance.

"Since Professor Howland is an old friend of your parents, Miranda, I believe propriety would not be offended if I left you to entertain him. I have some pressing letters to write," she explained, edging toward the door.

Miranda, barely suppressing a smile at this threadbare excuse, signified that she understood.

"I am sure Professor Howland has just come to pay his respects and give me some news of my parents and Oxford. I did receive a letter from Father today, but he did not mention that you were remaining in London long, Horace."

"I decided very suddenly to take a small break now that we are in the long vacation," he replied sullenly. Horace did not like having his decisions questioned, but politeness demanded he acknowledge Lady Worthington's graciousness. "Thank you for receiving me, Lady Worthington. It has been a pleasure to meet you," he said punctiliously.

"Goodbye, Professor Howland." Charlotte nodded and was through the door before Miranda could delay her.

Taking a seat on a spindly French chair, Miranda sat stiffly upright and regarded Horace with some disfavor.

"What do you want, Horace?" she asked boldly, determined to put him on the defensive.

"Why to see you, Miranda, and demand some explanation of your flight. Your father was vague about your *volte-face*, and I believe I deserved better of you. I had made you a very respectable offer, which I thought you were happy to receive. Yet, without a word to me, you suddenly decamped only to turn up in London supposedly engaged to the utmost libertine."

Amused at Horace's scorn for Rupert, Miranda was also annoyed at his characterization and could not let it go by unremarked.

"Really, Horace, must you talk such cant? Lord Hastings is an exceptional *parti*—titled, handsome, well-endowed; and he has treated me with every courtesy. I am very fortunate."

"Of course I understand a mere Oxford pedant has little to offer in comparison to a title, but you treated me very shabbily, Miranda," he moaned, determined to put her in the wrong.

Although she realized the justice of his complaint, Miranda found the discussion distasteful.

"Oh, for Heaven's sake, Horace, let's be honest. You know I would not have accepted you if my father had not incurred that monstrous debt. You blackmailed us both into accepting your offer. The disparity in our ages would not have mattered if I held you in affection, but we have nothing in common and I would never have come to care for you as you might have hoped. You simply cannot believe I would prefer you to a young virile nobleman who cares for me." What she did not also say, but felt strongly, was that Horace was a self-complacent man with lascivious intentions whom she found utterly repulsive.

"The debt had nothing to do with it. You wound me with your intemperate remarks. I had admired you for some time and had every intention of making you my wife when you had reached the proper age," he protested, thoroughly upset and unwilling to admit Miranda had any basis for her attack on his probity.

"Well, that's all past now and you must accept I thought marriage with you would be distasteful in the extreme. Come now, Horace, let us abandon this fruitless discussion and part as friends," Miranda said cheerfully although she had little hope that Horace, so pompous, so wounded in his pride and disappointed in his efforts to get her into his bed, would accept her dismissal of him.

"I will never forgive you, Miranda; and do not think you can brush easily through this shameful affair," the professor warned. "I was eager to accept your apologies and reinstate you in your rightful place, but I see you have overblown ideas as to your station. I suppose this licentious London society has spoiled you beyond recall," he added viciously.

"Probably," Miranda agreed, not one whit disturbed by his words.

Radleigh, understanding that he had placed Miranda in an uncomfortable position, was eager to make amends and took that moment to interrupt them.

"Mr. Cary, miss," he announced, and on his heels Randolph walked into the drawing room.

"Good morning, Miranda," he said, then—seeing her visitor—exclaimed, "Radleigh did not tell me you had another caller. I hope my arrival is not inopportune."

"Not at all, Randolph. Professor Howland was just leaving. Horace, this is Randolph Carter Cary from the American ministry. Randolph, this is Professor Horace Howland, a friend of my parents from Oxford," Miranda explained with relief. Now she could be rid of Horace, who was becoming most tiresome. However, the professor did not immediately respond to her unmistakable desire for his absence.

"Your servant, sir," Howland said stiffly. Then, thinking perhaps more was required, he tried to assume a jovial air. "I hope this does not mean Miranda is thinking of emigrating to the colonies."

Randolph did not easily take offense, but he found this archaic fool annoying. "We would be delighted to welcome Miss Houghton to the United States of America." He deeply resented this insular Englishman's calling his country the colonies.

If Horace stood rebuked, he did not accept it; but neither did he make any move to leave. Finally, after an embarrassing and uncomfortable silence, Miranda rushed to persuade him.

"Mr. Cary and I have a prior engagement. I am sure you will excuse us, Horace."

Courtesy demanded that the professor take his *congé*, and, not liking to be shown up before this young American, he reluctantly decided he must obey his hostess.

"You have not seen the last of me, Miranda. We still have a great deal to discuss," he warned. Ignoring Cary, he bowed slightly to Miranda to quit their presence.

At his departure Miranda gave a huge sigh, then—realizing that Cary must think her attitude strange—hastened to explain. "Horace Howland is a particularly boring man, and I am most grateful for your interruption. I hope you did not think me brazen to claim we had a prior engagement, Randolph."

"Not at all. I could see you wanted to get rid of the fellow. And I have come to see if this was an opportune time to see the Elgin Marbles." He looked uncertain, as if he thought she might refuse and would require some persuasion.

"I would like it above all things. Just let me get a bonnet and shawl and tell Radleigh of my direction," Miranda agreed, happy to escape from Mount Street and her problems.

In Randolph's phaeton on the way to the museum she chatted gaily, determined to banish all thoughts of the disagreeable encounter with Horace. Cary, seeing she did not want to discuss the gentleman, asked no questions about him.

"And how is Lord Hastings? In fine fettle, I hope?" he asked as they rode along.

"Yes. I saw him last night. He escorted me to a very elegant dinner at Kenwood House." Miranda was within an ace of confiding to Randolph about their attack by the highwayman, but a sixth sense told her to keep silent. Instead, she rushed on. "He has gone to Berkshire for a few days with Marcus Handbury. You remember Marcus, of course."

"Certainly, a most companionable fellow. He and your fiancé are old friends?" he asked.

"Yes, indeed, and Rupert assures me this is a shooting party—no women invited. Not that I worry on that score," she confided artlessly.

"You would have no need, I am sure," Cary answered automatically. He seemed to find the news of Rupert's departure distracting and as they pulled into Great Russell Street appeared deep in thought. However, Miranda, with her own concerns, did not notice. Then she shook off her worries and talked brightly about the coming exhibition, but Randolph did not respond with his usual flattering attention.

When they entered the museum, she made a determined effort to behave as if the Elgin Marbles were of vast interest to her. In fact, she rather disapproved of the nobleman's wresting these artifacts from Greece. Surely it was a type of vandalism, robbing a country of its treasures. She whispered this opinion to Randolph as they paraded sedately before the truncated statues.

"I suppose he thought they would be cared for here and that the museum was a safer repository. A great deal of damage has been done through neglect already," he pointed out to her.

"Probably. But I hear they cost him dearly and that he had to sell them to the government," Miranda offered.

"Collectors are passionate men, ready to dare all for their acquisitions. But come, if you have seen enough, let me take you to luncheon," Cary invited.

"You amaze me, Randolph, with all the free time you have from your ministerial duties; but, yes, I would enjoy that."

"Part of my duties are to ingratiate myself with the local populace, and I prefer that to copying mouldy reports which never seem to inspire action on the part of either of our governments," he admitted ruefully.

As Randolph set out to entertain his companion over a splendid luncheon at the Clarendon, Miranda had to agree that his duties lay along pleasant lines. They decided that the Elgin Marbles were vastly overrated and thought the pictures at Somerset House much better value. No further mention was made of either Horace Howland or of Rupert until they arrived at Mount Street.

"Thank you for your company, Miranda. As usual it was a delight, and you are kind to take pity on this lonely colonial," Randolph said lightly, then hesitated as if unsure whether he should persevere.

"Perhaps if Lord Hastings will be gone some time, you would allow me to escort you to the theatre this week. There is quite a popular play starring Jessica O'Neill at the Haymarket. How long will he be gone?" he asked carefully.

"About a week, I assume. I will have to let you know about the theatre, Randolph, because I must cooperate in any plans Lady Worthington has made," Miranda explained.

"I quite understand, but I will see about a box and hope you can join me with a small party. I have many kind invitations to repay. *Á bientôt,*" he said charmingly, doffing his hat and looking at her warmly as they bid goodbye on the doorstep.

Miranda was not best pleased upon entering the house to see Peter in the hall. She had been trying to avoid him lately since his reproachful looks and dejected airs sorely tried her temper. She was grateful to Peter, but she did not feel that gratitude could be translated into more than a tepid affection and he would not be content with friendship.

"Good afternoon, Peter," she greeted him with a smile, determined not to be thrown out of countenance by his sulks. But Peter appeared to have abandoned his pose of jealousy and sullenness.

"Ah, Miranda. Haven't seen much of you lately. I came home for luncheon hoping we could have a chat," he answered. He trailed after her into the morning room, which the Worthingtons preferred to the formal drawing room when they were alone.

Seeing that his mood was cheerful, Miranda welcomed him. "And what have you been doing, Peter—some of that reading required in the long vacation?" she teased, knowing he rarely opened a book unless coerced.

"Actually, I have been driving Maria Henderson to Hatcherd's. She came hoping to find you and had to settle for me instead," he informed Miranda smugly. "You know she's not such a bad girl. She seems to have some understanding of what a chap must endure in this ghastly season."

"Yes, I find Maria's shy ways deceptive. She has a great deal of sympathy and tolerance for a girl who has led such a sheltered life. I like her a great deal," Miranda responded happily. If Peter could transfer his mercurial affections to Maria, both his mother and Miranda would be greatly relieved.

"Of course, she's no beauty, but she is sensible," Peter offered, as if this discovery were peculiarly his own.

"I think she is lovely, under that quiet demeanor; but having the mother she does, she often feels cast in the shade. You can bring her out, Peter, as she admires you exceedingly," Miranda confided, rather amused at Peter's assessment of Maria's character and looks. In point of fact, men were conceited, and it needed only the smallest appeal to their vanity for them to become completely captivated. But Peter was young and had a great deal yet to learn. Suddenly Miranda felt years his senior and wondered how she could ever have considered using this boy to solve her problem with Horace.

As if he read her thoughts, Peter broadened the subject. "Radleigh tells me that beastly Howland called on you this morning. Wish I had been there, since Rupert is away. You need protection from him, Miranda." Peter spoke manfully, convinced he could have handled Horace with dispatch.

Touched by his concern, Miranda thanked him, "You are a dear, Peter, always so willing to help me out of my dilemmas. I don't think I have told you how much I appreciate all you have done in effecting my rescue from Horace, soothing my parents, and welcoming me to your home."

Reddening, Peter looked embarrassed and at a loss for words. "Well, I wish I hadn't introduced you to Rupert, but somehow you seem able to cope with him. I admire you for the way you stand up to him. I never can," he concluded wistfully.

"Our situations are a bit different," Miranda offered wryly.

"Yes, and I hope you come out of this imbroglio without any damage, Miranda. I would not want you to suffer any unhappiness, you know."

"I expect I will muddle through. After all, I will not be married to Horace, which is the main thing. You managed to safeguard me from that fate, and I will be forever in your debt. Now we are friends again and you will not worry about Rupert, I hope," she said tentatively, hoping for the best.

"You can count on me always, Miranda. All may work out to your advantage yet, and you may even end up as Lady Hastings," he suggested doubtfully. He was not persuaded that was a resolution he liked; neither, for that matter, was Miranda. But no more was said on the topic, and they talked easily about Maria and a host of other uncontroversial affairs completely at ease with one another.

Chapter Thirteen

Miranda was loathe to admit it, but she missed Rupert. Although she told herself he represented all that she disliked in a man—cynicism, arrogance, and a rakish charm that appeared to attract women no matter how he treated them—there was no denying he brought with him a certain excitement. She felt, despite all his faults, he could be relied upon to handle fraught situations and that he could be trusted to stand by his word. She had been secretly impressed by his masterful handling of the highwayman, although his callous solution had shocked her. Still, if he had not taken action, who knew what might have happened? No doubt Rupert had enemies of whom he was unaware, and a man in his position with his disregard for danger was not entirely invulnerable. A disgruntled husband, perhaps, or some thug Chloe Castleton had hired. Both possibilities Rupert would laugh off as nonsensical, but someone wanted to injure him, of that she was convinced.

Rupert had a reputation for striding through life pleasing himself and paying little heed to envious critics. She remembered his saying that he had no relatives beside Charlotte and Peter and that he had lost his parents while still young. Perhaps this lack of domestic affection was responsible for his ironic attitude, a protective facade hiding his true emotions.

Miranda pondered this idea and then dismissed it, chiding herself for being so naive. Rupert would have been disgusted at that explanation of his foibles and, she suspected, would scorn her as a hopeless romantic for such a charitable view of his excesses. He would be right, too, and she must guard against casting him in a too-favorable light or she might find herself in deep waters, indeed. She must think of him as he had been in that inn when she first met him—haughty and sarcastic, demanding and self-assured, as if no one would question his right to arrange his life along the lines he preferred whatever the cost to others. That was Rupert, and she would be a fool to cast any halo over his actions or to be beguiled by his caresses or his careless insistence that they might marry. He would be an uncomfortable husband and she was not the material of a complaisant wife. Rupert might be an exciting companion, but as a life partner he had more faults than assets if one discounted his title and his wealth. And Miranda, although she was enjoying the luxuries of this London season, had no thought of marrying merely for material gain. However, she found it difficult to dismiss Rupert's suggestion—or to dismiss Rupert, for that matter. She might have been gratified to learn that he was experiencing some of the same confusion that dogged her.

Although the season was unsuitable for serious hunting, Marcus Handbury had prevailed upon a group of friends, all veterans of Wellington's Peninsular campaigns, to join him at his modest manor house in Berkshire for a few days. With the exception of Rupert, the guests were bluff, hard-riding, hard-shooting men who avoided London's fashionable salons and spent most of their time on their own estates. Although they did not share Rupert's taste for London life, they respected him for his wartime exploits and his keen eye and skilled hand with a gun. He was as much at home on the grouse or pheasant moor as he was in Countess Leiven's drawing room.

Usually he enjoyed a respite from London's sophisticated

society, and he was genuinely fond of Marcus, an uncomplicated, unpretentious, and loyal friend whose company he found relaxing. But this party of companionable males, from whom he had expected an easy, informal fellowship, for some reason failed in its purpose. Instead he felt both edgy and distrait, although the company would never have guessed it. He was loathe to admit it to himself, but he missed Miranda and worried about what she might be doing in London.

That cub Cary would lose no time in taking advantage of Rupert's absence, he suspected, and he wondered just what Horace Howland was plotting. His one brief meeting with the Oxford professor had not reassured him. Recognizing Horace as a vain, easily affronted man with an inordinate belief in his own superiority, Rupert perceived that the professor was not one to take dismissal kindly.

Miranda boasted that she could handle both Horace and Cary, but Rupert was not convinced. And then there was Peter, always available and still enamoured of Miranda despite her efforts to depress his attentions. But this trio of suitors did not pose nearly the same threat as Miranda's own independent and honest spirit in obstructing Rupert's efforts to change her opinion of him. Why it was important that this one, unexceptional girl should regard him with favor he could not fathom. Was he so conceited, possessed such overwhelming pride, that he could not contemplate a female rejecting him?

No, he admitted at last, it was because he had come to care for her. To love her, he sighed ruefully, and he did not overestimate his chances with her. Their relationship had begun badly, and events had not tempered the initial antagonism. And he had done little to convince her he was not the haughty, all-knowing, and sarcastic brute she had first met. He had not handled the suggestion that she consider making the false engagement a reality with either sincerity or passion. She neither trusted him nor liked him very much, he decided.

How to change her mind and persuade her that they were meant for each other was the problem. He jeered at his dilemma, unaccustomed to doubting his footing with women. He had never before cared whether they found him acceptable or not. On reflection he determined he had made a grave mistake in confiding his problem with the experienced Chloe to Miranda. The girl now thought him a haughty uncaring brute with little feelings beyond satisfying his own desires, and she had every reason to think so. He must alter that impression or she would reject him firmly.

For once in his life, Rupert approached a new relationship with a woman humbly, wondering what he could do to make Miranda care for him. The future of their romance did not hold much promise, and he had an uneasy feeling that danger threatened from an unknown quarter. Despite having told Miranda otherwise, he had puzzled over the attack by the highwayman. Discreet inquiries had revealed that two injured men had ridden up to the Wounded Stag at the edge of the heath, a notorious hangout for robbers, but he could glean no information about them. To insure their silence, whoever had paid them must have been unusually generous, because Rupert's own minions had been able to get no further information, despite their offers of hard coin. Either they had been paid lavishly or they feared their employer too much to talk. It was a mystery which nagged at Rupert—not from worry about his personal safety, but because he disliked not knowing what his faceless enemy intended.

Marcus, who was more perceptive than Rupert realized, was quite aware that his friend had a problem, but he respected his silence. Rupert appeared in his usual spirits, entering into the drinking bouts, the ribald tales of wartime service, and the all-day hard-riding to the hounds that made up their routine.

On the next to the last day of the party, Rupert and Marcus decided to forego the usual hunting and ride to a neighboring farm to inspect some horses. Marcus wanted to extend his stables, which had suffered during his long absence, and Rupert was always on the lookout for a good matched pair. He thought he might find a likely young mare for Miranda, although he did not know whether or not she enjoyed riding. It might prove a bond between them, he conjectured, and they certainly needed one.

The stud farm, run by a harsh-faced, bandy-legged trainer, Tom Richards, for his noble owner, proved to be a lavish establishment with more than fifty horses in the stables.

A groom brought out a lively pair of matched chestnut yearlings, and Richards, running a loving hand over the horses' forelocks, pointed out the attributes of his charges.

"His lordship is thinking of running these two at Newmarket next fall, so they command a high price, five hundred guineas a piece, sirs," he confided slyly with the horse coper's shrewd assessment that these buyers were high-sticklers who could afford a bit over the usual.

"Come now, Richards, do you take us for sapskulls?" Rupert grinned. "I know the Earl of March, and I know horses. They are prime cattle, I agree, but March will not run them at Newmarket. They might do for my stables. I'll give you seven-fifty for the pair."

After some hard chaffering, Richards allowed as though he might sacrifice his horses. "But what the Earl will say, I can't fathom," he worried. "He'll give me what for, I guess."

"Nonsense. He will applaud your good sense. I will have a man here next week to collect the pair. See you take good care of them in the meanwhile."

Marcus decided on a gray hunter and two promising foals. Hacking home from the stud farm, they discussed their bargains with satisfaction and conceded the day well spent. About ten miles from Marcus' manor, they entered a deep copse of pine trees which shut out the sun of the bright early May afternoon. Both horses shied nervously, pulling on their bits as they cantered, eager to put the depressing woods behind them.

"Rather a gloomy spot, this, but it cuts off five miles and I am yearning for my bath and a whiskey," Marcus explained to Rupert.

"Apollo, here, doesn't like it. Steady old fellow," Rupert said to his stallion, a high-strung horse who took exception to the dank woods. "I see the end just beyond here another fifty yards or so." He gave a light flick to his wrist, and Apollo bounded forward eagerly, putting some distance between Rupert and Marcus.

Suddenly a shot rang out, catching Rupert in the arm. It might have hit a more vital spot, but, as the bullet sped toward him, Apollo snorted nervously and reared high, causing Rupert to lean forward and pull on the reins. He both heard and felt the impact of the bullet, and his first reaction was to halt his horse and investigate, despite the wound.

Marcus, riding up behind him, yelled, "Ride on, Rupert, for God's sake. Some fool is shooting blindly. Let's get out of here to where we can see our way." He spurred his own horse, causing Apollo, who disliked being passed, to gallop forward. Once beyond the thinning woods and into the gorse, the two men pulled up and dismounted.

Rupert grimaced, looking at his sleeve, from which blood was spreading ominously. "Damn, another coat ruined. Weston will be furious," he joked, but Marcus noticed his pallor. Knowing that Rupert would discredit the pain and pretend not to feel it, he insisted in a concerned voice, "Here, old man. Wait a spell. We had better bind that up and have a nip of brandy." He pulled a silver flask from his coat and offered it to Rupert, who took a deep draught. He appeared more surprised than hurt, but Marcus, who had experience with gunshot wounds, was not deceived. Taking a clean handkerchief from his pocket, he dressed Rupert's arm, tying a stiff knot at the end.

"There, that should hold till we get you to a doctor. I fear the bullet might be buried in your muscles."

"No, I think it passed through, a clean wound, but who in the world was loitering in that wood taking potshots at passersby? You have some rum coves in your part of the world, Marcus," Rupert joked, mounting Apollo with difficulty as Marcus held the reins.

"Can't understand it, Rupert. Has to be some careless farmer or poacher. We don't have highwaymen around here."

Rupert grimaced, remembering his last encounter with a highwayman. A coincidence, this latest fray? Too convenient. Someone meant to harm him, but who and why? Marcus scrutinizing him, scented a mystery and fixed on Rupert's remark about another ruined coat. Was this the second time his friend had been attacked? Had Rupert an enemy? Several questions occurred to Marcus, and realizing his friend had not told him of a recent adventure he was determined to have it out of him, in order that they might formulate a defense. Marcus was not about to be fobbed off with some specious narrative. Rupert was too cool by half, but this was serious business and must be investigated. First, however, he must get Rupert safely back to the manor. The questions could wait.

On Marcus' insistence, a doctor examined and properly bandaged Rupert's wound, confirming that the bullet had indeed passed through the arm.

"I suffered much worse on the battlefield," Rupert assured his friends before they sat down to dinner. Little more was said about the incident, the men deciding that a poacher had loosed the bullet and then decamped, fearing discovery.

"Our magistrate, Sir Humphrey Wells, is hard on poachers. He metes out stiff sentences," Marcus explained treating the matter lightly because he knew that Rupert would brook no questions before the company, but he was not satisfied. He doubted that Rupert had suffered from a stray poacher's shot

138

and intended to discover the real culprit. Later, after an early evening, Marcus challenged Rupert as the latter was preparing for bed.

"Rupert, I don't want to pry, but I am not convinced that bullet came from a poacher or a hunter's gun. You made some reference to spoiling a coat before. Have there been other attacks?" he asked, determined to get to the bottom of this strange affair.

Rupert grinned at his friend. "You really are the most complete hand, Marcus. There's no avoiding that dogged persistence of yours. I admit there was an earlier attack, by a pair of highwaymen as Miranda and I were returning across the heath from a dinner at Kenwood House. I sincerely thought at the time there was little in it, but now I am not as certain," he drawled. He sprawled before the fireplace, looking troubled but elegant in his paisley dressing gown.

"Do you know of any enemies who would take such a furtive reprehensible action?" Marcus asked, despising foes who would not meet one in a face-to-face confrontation.

"Miranda shares your poor opinion of me and is convinced some disgruntled husband hired assassins to wreak vengenence." Rupert laughed, but Marcus did not.

"Well, your reputation could lead to such ideas, I suppose; but I have not heard of any such a man and you are the subject of a great deal of gossip." Marcus shook his head in disgust. "I hoped your engagement signaled an end to such involvements."

"You mustn't listen to gossip, Marcus. I am not the devilish fellow you suspect. I have truly become a model of respectability since I met Miranda. But, like you, she doubts my change of heart."

"What happened exactly?" Marcus returned to the matter of the assault.

Rupert, seeing there was no way Marcus would be deterred, gave him a brief account of the encounter and its aftermath. "The thing that puzzles me is that my men could find nothing to discount the theory that we were just the targets of roaming robbers. Hampstead Heath has often been the scene of such incidents, as you well know."

"I don't like it," Marcus fretted. "You must be more vigilant. You were fortunate to escape two attempts to harm you. A third time they might be lucky," he warned. "I know you think you can take care of yourself, but there is foul hand at work here. These two efforts to kill you concern me."

"You are a good ally, Marcus, and a trustworthy one; but you must let me handle this. I promise to keep you informed," Rupert said, touched by his friend's words.

"I hope so. I rather pity the miscreant when you unmask him, Rupert. You make a formidable adversary."

Rupert frowned grimly but refused further discussion. Marcus left, after asking Rupert if he needed some laudanum in order to sleep. He had not been surprised when the veteran of the battlefield turned down the offer with scorn.

As Rupert climbed into bed and doused his candle, he wondered if Marcus were right and that some enemy had followed him to Berkshire with murder in mind. Outwardly he had dismissed Marcus' suspicions casually, but he did not intend to let the matter drop. Perhaps Marcus was right in his concern. Someone, for whatever reason, wanted him dead. But who would benefit from his demise? Peter, of course, but Rupert could not imagine his nephew, jealous as he might be, going to such lengths. There was the disgruntled Horace Howland, whose *amour-propre* he had offended by his engagement to Miranda. But Rupert doubted the Oxford professor had the courage to mount an attack himself and certainly lacked the resources to hire a band of rogues to do the job for him. Could Chloe be so misguided as to attempt this kind of revenge? She was a vindictive woman but surely would not go to these lengths, and what would it avail her? He would never resume his liaison with her, and she must know that.

That left the affable Randolph Cary, who obviously admired Miranda. Would he try to improve his chances by ridding himself of Rupert? Americans had a reputation for violence and for all this affability Cary was an enigma. It was a possibility and one Lord Hastings would investigate.

Having come to a decision, Rupert prepared himself for an uncomfortable night, his arm throbbing and his disordered thoughts insuring that sleep would prove elusive. He would return to London tomorrow, cutting short his stay. He wanted to see Miranda, for he had a lowering feeling that his absence had not improved his position with her. Hard-hearted female. Why could he not have found an amenable girl, one who was thrilled at his proposal and admired him extravagantly? Well, he was hoist with his own petard. After years of treating obliging females disdainfully, he was now on the receiving end of an indifferent, independent spirit who was not impressed with his assets. He must take a different tack with her now that he was in earnest about making her his wife. Tossing restlessly, he, for once, was not sure he would succeed.

Chapter Fourteen

When Rupert turned up in Mount Street the following day, his wounded arm in a sling and determination in his manner, Miranda received him with a wry exclamation.

"What in the world has happened to you? Surely your friends did not shoot you," she teased, instinctively avoiding a mawkish show of concern.

"I might have known you would have an unusual reaction to a battlescarred hero," Rupert responded with dry irony. "Actually some miscreant shot at me in Marcus' woods. Marcus dismissed the possibility of a poacher or careless hunter, but he would not allow me to investigate, insistent that I would bleed to death if the scratch were not immediately tended. I regret exceedingly I acceded to his protests," Rupert lamented. But he might have expected Miranda would not accept such an easy explication.

Her sarcasm vanished immediately, and she furrowed her brow, disquieted. "I don't like this, Rupert. It's too convenient to pass another attack off as a coincidence. I am now more certain than ever that the highwayman meant to harm you personally. You were not a chance traveler he intended to rob. Who could have taken you in such dislike that they would want to kill you?" she questioned.

"That you think such a person exists does not speak well

for your opinion of me. And here I was hoping for gentle feminine solace. I should have known better." Rupert sighed soulfully, but Miranda could hear the laughter that lurked behind his apparent disappointment.

"Don't be foolish. And sit down," she scolded. "It can't be good for you to be pacing up and down in such a heedless fashion. We must discuss this further and try to come to a logical conclusion." She eyed him sternly and then asked bluntly, "Have you made a will?"

"Of course I have made a will. But I am about to change it, if you agree to my proposal of marriage," he said, completely oversetting her with the reminder that he wanted to legitimize their engagement.

A fleeting expression Rupert could not define flickered over Miranda's face. But this was not the time to discuss their future; something else was on her mind.

"I wasn't certain whether to tell you this or not. For heavens sake, Rupert, sit down and stop looming over me, or I cannot go on. This is serious and may be part of what I see as a conspiracy against you—or me."

At last aware that Miranda was genuinely disturbed, Rupert sat beside her on the settee and took her hand. "Whatever is the matter I am sure we can settle it," he soothed. "I don't like to see you so upset, Miranda."

"Well, it is upsetting. Someone has been writing anonymous letters about me, casting slurs on my character. All the patronesses at Almack's have received these nasty screeds saying they should not be receiving such a deep-eyed adventuress and impugning my morals and decrying my attempts to deceive respectable society. Supposedly I am a threat to all decent people." Putting the accusations into words brought a blush of shame to Miranda's troubled features.

"You have to be making game of me. How do you know this?"

"Lady Worthington received a letter herself, condemning

her for sheltering me; and Lady Cowper called to tell her about a similar letter. They both discounted it and said it was probably the work of some jealous former *chère amie* of yours, possibly Chloe Castleton. It's all most worrying and so unfair, for there is no way I can challenge these statements. Lady Worthington says I must ignore them, hold my head high, and pretend it is all a hum. But this morning Countess Leiven crossed the road rather than meet me in Bond Street." Miranda had rushed into speech, her normal *sang froid* gone in the face of these backhanded attacks.

"You can be sure if it is Chloe Castleton, I will settle the matter forthwith, but I wonder.... It sounds more like your disgruntled ex-fiancé, Professor Howland to me," Rupert mused.

"Because the luscious Mrs. Castleton is incapable of such chicanery. Ha!" Miranda replied snidely, conscious that her vehemence revealed her jealousy.

"Don't be a little goose. I care nothing for the damn woman. And here we are within an ace of brangling again over such a nonsensical idea when we should be gathering some firm evidence about the culprit. I won't have your reputation damaged by these scurrilous tales." Rupert, looking at Miranda, felt an unusual emotion. It was the desire to protect and defend her against all critics, which just showed, he conceded, how deep he had fallen for this rare girl. He hated seeing her humbled and afraid, which was so foreign to her normal manner. He must settle her fears and reassure her.

"But what can we do to stop it?" Miranda asked. Now that she had confessed all to Rupert, somehow the whole miserable affair seemed less important. Obviously he was neither disgusted with her nor did he blame her in any way, and he had certainly had cause. Hadn't she played the role of adventuress in that Cheltenham inn, and hadn't he at first view seen her in that light? She was reluctant to remind him of this, but honesty prevailed.

"When we first met, you would have endorsed what these letters accuse me of. Why have you changed your mind?" she asked simply.

"Because I have come to know you and learn your real worth. I want to marry you, and I know you are not a scarlet woman with a dubious past intent on luring me into a misalliance. Now, how is that for a declaration of faith?"

"Quite satisfying. And I suppose this nasty letter writer is all of a piece with the attacks on you. We must try to discover who hates you—and, by extension, me—enough to go to such ends."

Seeing the color come back into her pale cheeks, Rupert was reassured. Anger rather than embarrassment would serve her better in this trouble. But now was not the best time to urge the marriage on her. She felt too insecure and unhappy to make any decision, much less one which would affect both their lives. However, he had not abandoned his desire to wed her and he was determined to eventually persuade her that her happiness lay with him. Regretfully abandoning any attempt to make love to her, he spoke briskly.

"Well, the first thing is for me to quiz Charlotte and make her show me the letter. Then I will know how to proceed." He had a fleeting idea that Randolph Cary might be involved in this villainous plot to discredit Miranda, but he decided it behooved him to keep silent about that suspicion.

Comforted by his masterful management of affairs, Miranda's spirits lightened. Somehow she had not expected his wholehearted championship. She had steeled herself for sarcastic or wounding remarks, for she had never been convinced he viewed her with charity despite his insouciant suggestion they make their engagement a true betrothal. How hateful of her to react so, when he was behaving so well. Arrogant and high-handed he might be, but, she decided despite all evidence to the contrary, he trusted her and believed in her.

"Good. Your spirits appear to be reviving. I never took you for a faint-hearted miss, Miranda. This situation demands both guile and determination, and you are not lacking in either quality. Now come, we will bring Charlotte in here to augment our council."

Rupert kissed her gently on the forehead, filling her with warmth and security. Then he rang the bell for Radleigh and sent him to fetch his sister.

"Now let me handle Charlotte, Miranda. I understand she might have behaved badly, but you must excuse her. Basically she is a kind-hearted, if rather foolish, woman," Rupert explained.

"She doesn't like me, and who can blame her? These letters have confirmed her worst fears," Miranda said sadly.

"Well, she will just have to abandon them. I will sort her out," he promised in firm tones.

Lady Worthington, bustling into the room, looked askance at Rupert's arm in its sling. "What scrape have you got yourself into now, Rupert? A duel or something even worse, I vow," she asked waspishly.

"Your wits are wandering, Charlotte. Just a hunting mishap. Miranda has told me about the letters, and I want to settle this unsavory business once and for all. Surely you realize that I have an enemy who is striking at me through my fiancée," he said decisively. If Charlotte wanted to disagree, one look at her brother's hard and stubborn face changed her mind. She could never gainsay him when he took that lordly attitude.

"Well, really, Rupert, anyone would think I had written them myself the way you go on. Naturally I was disturbed by these allegations against Miranda, but I never thought that they were intended to involve you." She tried to excuse her lack of charity by this specious reasoning, but Rupert was not impressed.

"You put too much stock in the *on dits* of the *ton*, Charlotte. There is no question of Miranda's probity, and I will not have you making her uncomfortable with unwarranted allegations. Someone is out to make trouble in a most cowardly way. Now, let me see this letter," he demanded, his expression promising retribution if she did not obey.

"I have it right here. I dare not let it lie about in case any servant should see it."

She reached into the reticule by her side and pulled out the offending missive. The letter, on expensive paper, had not been sent through the post. Its message was brief and nasty.

"Dear Lady Worthington,

You have been victimized by an adventuress. Your house guest, and your brother's fiancée, is little better than a whore. With her beguiling ways and lying tongue she has greatly deceived you. She intends to claim respectability under the cloak of your sponsorship. You must turn her out or win the disgust of all decent members of society.

A well-wisher

"Not much of a well-wisher, I think," Rupert said angrily. "But a fairly educated one, which leads me to believe your disappointed professor may be the author."

"Not that reputable Horace Howland! Why he is a friend of Miranda's parents. He would not stoop to such disgusting hints," Charlotte objected.

"Not hints, but barefaced attacks, and he will answer to me if he is indeed the author," Rupert promised, grim-faced.

"Well, I can't understand why he would behave so. What has he to gain?" Charlotte argued, unwilling to abandon her good opinion of that boring but proper man.

Miranda laughed. "I doubt that Horace would have either the inclination or imagination to write such shocking stuff. He might feel maliciously toward me, but taking any action would not be his style. I rather fear you must look else-where," she hinted, not wanting to accuse Chloe Castleton again, especially before Charlotte.

Rupert raised a wry eyebrow. He knew exactly where her thoughts were centered. "Well, I will pay the professor a visit. He will not be able to resist confiding in me if he is indeed the author."

Charlotte, eyeing the couple nervously, wailed, "But how can we refute this canard?"

Miranda, not at all convinced that Charlotte did not believe the accusations, remained silent; but Rupert, who understood his sister's horror of scandal, said decisively, "You must ignore the whole matter. Surely your own standing is above reproach. And if that group of high-in-the-instep patronesses at Almack's make barbed remarks, you must laugh the letters off as being no more than the diatribe of a disappointed suitor. I will handle the rest."

Lady Worthington, who would have liked to have pursued the accusations, had enough respect for her brother's temper not to persist, but she was not completely reassured. Men were so easily gulled by a pretty face, and certainly Miranda was attractive enough to turn the head of any man.

"It's just as well you did not accept that Mr. Cary's invitation to the theatre, Miranda. I told you it would not do, with Rupert out of town. You would only have given the gossips more ammunition," Lady Worthington commented smugly. The girl had no idea of how to go on, nor of the impact such rumors would have on her reputation. If she did, she certainly was not behaving in a fashion necessary to dispell gossip. Charlotte wanted to ask Miranda to what the anonymous writer referred, but she was afraid of her brother's scorn to venture any questions.

"So Cary is still after you?" Rupert queried, turning to Miranda with a frown. That damn cub kept turning up, and

148

Rupert wanted him out of their life. But he knew any such suggestion would be met with resistance.

"Randolph is a good friend. He would be appalled to learn of these letters." Miranda dismissed Rupert's aspersions as ridiculous.

"I wonder," Charlotte muttered, but realized that Rupert would not take her suspicions kindly. She was not really worried about her own respectability, but she disliked being associated with this nasty situation. Any deviation from propriety worried Charlotte, and she remembered that Peter might be affected by his proximity to Miranda, if indeed she were a wanton hussy.

"Charlotte, I want no more fussing from you. I depend on you to champion Miranda and see to it that no harm is done by these unfounded rumors. You have influence, and I demand that you use it." Rupert made no attempt to soothe his sister, disgusted by her lukewarm reception. That she could believe Miranda capable of promiscuity irritated him. He refused to give any credence to the subterfuge, ignoring his own initial meeting with Miranda. Whatever doubts he may once have had about her had evaporated now that he had come to know her.

Miranda, well-aware of Lady Worthington's tepid endorsement of her, was not convinced that his sister's opinion did not hold weight with Lord Hastings, no matter how acute his avowal of faith in her. She wished they were alone to delve into the matter further, but she could hardly ask her hostess to leave.

Rupert, however, had no such compunction. "I intend to put a stop to this malevolent duplicity, and I expect you, Charlotte, to cooperate. Now, leave Miranda and me alone. We have several more important matters to discuss."

"There is no reason to be rude, Rupert. But I suppose I should not expect civility from you. Very well, I will go," she conceded and flounced from the room.

"Now you have made her angry, and you really can't blame her, you know. She has looked on me with suspicion from the day I arrived and probably agrees with every word of the letter," Miranda argued cheerfully. Rupert's passionate refusal to believe ill of her had raised her spirits immensely.

"You know, Miranda, you must disabuse yourself of this picture of me as the veriest nodcock. Of course, I discount this nastiness, as you must. We have more important concerns, chief among them being when we will be married," he announced coolly.

"Upon my honor, Rupert," Miranda gasped, still unsure of his intentions.

"You think I am a hardened reprobate after every woman in town, and the only way I can prove to you how I have reformed is to marry you. What about it?"

"As a persuasive reason for marriage, I can't see the scotching of scandal as a good motive. I thought you were joking. And since you have apparently rid yourself of Mrs. Castleton, the reason for our spurious engagement, you now have no need to continue it. You are not serious about wanting to marry me. It's only that your arrogance will not let you admit that there is a woman who could refuse you."

"Pride and vainglory are not a good reason to marry, but I will not press you now when you are so upset. But please don't refuse me out of hand. I believe we would go on together famously."

"And you need an heir," Miranda reminded him, disappointed that he did not profess a deeper emotion.

"Quite right, I need an heir," he echoed, disconcerted that she believed him such a cynic as to propose marriage without affection. He had handled the whole affair badly, but perhaps she was right and his pride prevented him from any mawkish pleading about his feelings for her. He must try to rectify his mistake, but first he must apprehend this letter writer and mete out an appropriate punishment.

150

If Horace Howland were the writer of the anonymous letters, he had shot his bolt and fled back to Oxford. On applying to the professor's lodging, Rupert was informed that he had decamped that morning. Obviously, if he were the author, he had planned his strategy cannily. Aware that Rupert was out of town, he would have had a safe interval in which to work his wicked ploy. Rupert, frustrated to be balked of his victim, considered traveling to Oxford to confront the man but decided that Howland would be all the better for a judicious delay. If the man thought he was safe from Rupert's accusation, he would relax. Then Rupert would pounce. Another factor weighed in his decision not to ride post haste to Oxford. He wanted to protect Miranda from the current gossip, and the best way to do that was to show the *ton* how much he discounted it.

Repairing to White's, he moodily threw himself in a chair and evaluated his tactics. Several of the regular members lounging in the drawing room of the club eyed him curiously. They would have liked to have questioned him about the slurs on Miranda's reputation but feared his sarcastic tongue and his expertise with pistol and rapier. It would be foolhardy to challenge such a Nonpareil. His mood did not seem auspicious, but Lord Alvaney, that arbiter of manners, was bolder than his fellows. He crossed the room and interrupted Rupert's musings.

Alvaney, reputed to be the wittiest man in England, had other shining attributes. He had entered the Coldstream Guards after an excellent education and served with distinction in the Peninsula. During those campaigns he had come to know Rupert well. Since resigning his commission, he had spent his talents in the House of Lords, where his gift for repartee stirred up the noble company. Although corpulent, he was a hard rider to the hounds. "A good plucked one" was the opinion of all who knew him. This recklessness on the hunting field transferred to the social scene, and Alvaney might dare where other less intrepid souls would hesitate. Rupert quite liked him, and when the dark-haired, florid-faced Alvaney settled beside him and took out his ever-present pinch of snuff, Rupert grinned at him, prepared to undergo a catechism.

"Been out of town, Hastings?" Alvaney queried, his small, dark eyes sparkling.

"Yes. Handbury had a small hunting party at his place in Berkshire," Rupert replied, wondering in amusement how Alvaney would broach the topic which accounted for his presence.

"Too bad. Your absence is to be deplored. There are a spate of rumors about your fiancée. Nothing to it, of course," Alvaney commented, but his tone was questioning.

Rupert smiled grimly. "Yes, I am sure Miranda's reputation has been the object of much discussion in every drawing room and club in London. The unfortunate result of anonymous letters to Almack's patrons and others." Rupert saw no sense in denying what the gossip mongers were spreading about gleefully.

"Not enough to do, that's the trouble with most of those old tabbies," Alvaney offered.

"How offended they would be to hear you describe them so. Unfortunately, they wield a great deal of social power."

"But not as much as I do," Alvaney countered.

"Quite true. If you have my assurance that the letter's accusations are completely unfounded, I hope you will do your best to quash them."

Alvaney, who along with his wit and intelligence possessed a notable charity, *was* willing, but not before he knew more about the matter. "Who do you think is the author of these screeds?"

"A disappointed suitor," Rupert answered promptly, not prepared to go further.

"Or a disappointed mistress," Alvaney suggested with a sly grin, thinking of Chloe Castleton.

"Perhaps. Whoever has taken such a cowardly revenge will pay for it," Rupert attested with conviction.

Alvaney sneezed, the snuff accomplishing its purpose, and waited a moment. "I would be careful, old man. Could some enemy be striking at you through your fiancée?"

Struck by Alvaney's acuity, Rupert did not argue. Instead he bent forward and directed a piercing gaze at his interlocutor.

"I think you are right. Someone shot at me while I was in the country, and I don't think it was a mere mishap. It's difficult to accept that anyone feels such hatred toward me, but I suppose it's possible."

Alvaney looked appalled at such a breach of social etiquette. Anonymous letters were one thing, attempted murder was far more serious. "What will you do?"

"Discover the perpetrator and deal with him. Or her," Rupert said shortly, his manner leaving no doubt that the miscreant would be attended to most decisively.

"Quite right. We can't have fellows shooting our distinguished peers or impugning their brides-to-be."

If Alvaney wondered what Rupert had done to inspire such enmity, he did not to ask; but he clearly deemed the besmirching of Rupert's fiancée beyond the pale. "I will do what I can to discount this rumor, but if I were you I would not leave town again in a hurry, both for your safety and to let society know you scorn this gossip," Alvaney proposed shrewdly.

"Thank you, Alvaney. At times like this, it is rewarding to know your friends will stand by you."

"Naturally." Alvaney dismissed Rupert's gratitude, but in pondering the affair had another suggestion to make. "Will you be escorting Miss Houghton to the Rutland Ball tomorrow evening?"

This was not quite the *non sequitur* that it appeared. Rupert sensed that Alvaney thought a public appearance of the couple would be a discreet sign that Rupert entertained no idea of abandoning Miranda.

"Probably. No doubt we will see you there," Rupert agreed, seeing the wisdom of the peer's counsel.

"And perhaps Miss Houghton will spare me a dance," Alvaney tendered, aware of the *cachet* this would bestow on her.

"I am sure she will. You are a Trojan, Alvaney. I am in your debt."

"Not at all, my good fellow. Glad to offer my services. She is a lovely girl and you are fortunate. When is the marriage to take place?" he asked.

"Soon," Rupert announced baldly, and they left it at that. But Rupert was in little doubt that the affair of the anonymous letters was serious, although Alvaney would do his best to lay the rumors to rest.

Chapter Fifteen

Dressing for the Rutland Ball the following evening, Miranda realized that the excitement of the London season, which she had hailed with such delight, was beginning to pall. Not even the delicate, cream-needle, French-lace gown Charlotte had chosen for her raised her spirits. The two mysterious ambushes upon Rupert had left her with an uneasy premonition that a third attempt might prove successful. She realized, unhappily, that Rupert had become a vital influence in her life. From the beginning his presence had produced chaotic emotions—first of hatred, then of scorn—that had been followed by grudging respect and now, perhaps, a much warmer feeling. She did not want to fall in love with the noble lord; and she doubted, despite his proposal, he held any such fondness for her. She intrigued him, maddened him, challenged him; but those were not suitable sentiments for marriage. Unfortunately, by comparison other men grew dim and inadequate.

Beside Rupert, Peter appeared sweet but shallow, and Randolph Cary, although charming and kind as well as handsome, did not inspire more than a halfhearted affection. The American wanted to marry her, so it seemed, although his offer lacked ardor. But she could not envisage a union with a man who would take her across the ocean to places and people who would be strange to her. Neither could she imagine accepting Rupert's blasé proposal based as it must be on expediency and the need for an heir. Perhaps she was foolish to think of refusing a man whom most girls would consider a nonpareil, but stubbornly she clung to her romantic and nonsensical dreams.

Of course she could always abandon Rupert, Peter, Randolph, and the season and go home, where her parents would ring a peal over her and life would be exceedingly uncomfortable for some time. Added to that was the ubiquitous Horace Howland, who would renew his suit, causing more problems. She might not have much choice if the London society which had been accepting her turned its back because of those scurrilous letters. She glared into the mirror on her dressing table, causing Martha, her abigail, to apologize.

"I'm sorry, Miss Miranda, if I pulled your hair. It's so heavy, sometimes it is difficult to dress it easily," Martha explained, feeling put upon. Normally Miss Miranda was the most cheerful and uncomplaining of mistresses, but Martha sensed her disquiet and believed she was at fault.

"Not at all, Martha. I have the megrims, a bad mood, not your fault at all," Miranda soothed her maid.

If Martha wondered why Miranda, who seemed to have all that any girl could desire, should be in such a state, she kept her questions to herself.

"There now, you look lovely," she concluded, laying down the brush and comb and surveying Miranda with satisfaction. She thought Miranda a beautiful girl and most fortunate to be engaged to a nobleman toasted by all of society. She could not understand anyone in such a situation not being in high alt.

"Thank you, Martha. As usual you have decked me out to a treat. I know I could never manage all this elegance on my own," Miranda praised her abigail. After all, it was not the poor girl's fault she was so distrait.

She dismissed her with a few more kind words and, after the maid left, continued to stare into the mirror as if searching for some answer to her dilemma. She had begun this adventure on a dare, angered by Rupert's arrogance and wanting to relieve her father of his debt. She had intended to enjoy the season and London's pleasures, heedless of the future, believing that time would take care of any difficulties engendered by her bargain with Rupert. Now she was befuddled, angry, and the target of unjust notoriety. That had not been part of her impetuous agreement to pose as Rupert's fiancée. And tonight she would have to face the scandal-loving *ton*, encounter barbed remarks and perhaps even ostracism, if those accusations were believed. Rupert would protect her, but would his championship be enough to lay aside all suspicion? She hated the idea of being the cynosure of contemptuous eyes and sly innuendoes. Still, she could not avoid the ball and give credence to the very gossip she wanted to deny.

Oh well, it was best she get on with it. There was no point in sulking here in the privacy of her room. Rupert would view such a spineless attitude with contempt, and he would be right. Not her style at all. Standing up and taking one last look at her appearance, which belied any worry, she clasped her pearls around her neck and departed, like a victim going to the scaffold. That picture amused her, and she was able to descend the stair case with aplomb.

Rupert was waiting for her, his gaze full of admiration. He had some idea of her turmoil and applauded her courage.

"Good evening, my lord," she greeted calmly, giving no evidence of the tenor of her thoughts. However, Rupert was not deceived. He knew this ball might prove an ordeal for her, yet he could not appear to doubt her ability to face up to the challenge. She would scorn such a fainthearted demeanor, and he was determined to behave as if nothing were unusual.

"I know my compliments are not well received, but may I venture to say you look charming," he offered.

"I am always happy to hear you approve," Miranda answered primly.

"Then shall we leave?"

The Rutland mansion in Grosvenor Square was alight as carriages wended their way to the entrance, an imposing affair of Doric pillars and marble steps. The arrival of Rupert and Miranda was the occasion for some sidelong glances and whispers but no overt exclusion. Lord and Lady Cowper were just ahead of them as they mounted the stairs toward the receiving line, and Miranda braced herself for that doyennès snub. Instead she was pleasantly surprised.

"Quite a crush, isn't it, Rupert? And how charming you look, Miss Houghton," Lady Cowper smiled benignly. Her husband, although handsome and wealthy, was a cipher who nodded absentmindedly. Despite her brilliant marriage and social position of impeccable standing, Lady Cowper herself, like many well-bred matrons, had been involved in some notable liasons, and her current lover was Lord Palmerston. In her early thirties, she was merry, slender, and could be—like all the Melbournes—completely unpredictable. Perhaps that was the reason she did not condemn Miranda, although she had been accused of sharp-tongued remarks and enjoyed a good gossip. Her brother Frederick called her a rattlepate, but generally she was good natured and a true sophisticate. Her approval did a great deal to alleviate Miranda's apprehensions.

"Thank you, Lady Cowper. Your gown is a triumph," Miranda offered bravely, staring the lady hard in the eye as if daring her to make some untoward remark. But Emily Cowper only smiled and turned away to greet their hosts. Miranda, just behind them, braced herself for the duke and duchess' icy stare and was grateful for Rupert's comforting squeeze of her arm as they faced the couple.

"Ah, Hastings, glad you could come," the duke said easily.

"I don't believe you have met my fiancée, Miss Houghton," Rupert replied.

"Your servant, Miss Houghton. May I present Miss Houghton, Elizabeth," he said correctly, passing Rupert and Miranda on to his wife, who nodded pleasantly. Miranda wondered if she knew half the guests, she looked so bemused, but then they had made their courtesies and strolled on into the ballroom.

If Mrs. Drummond Burrell, a very grande dame, looked them over with some contempt, the majority of the company, all of whom watched their arrival with keen attention, appeared neutral. Malicious as some of the ladies might be, most of them were too impressed by Rupert's wealth and acknowledged top-of-the trees reputation to press any direct slanders upon his fiancée. If Lord Hastings did not believe the rumors—and obviously he did not—then they would walk warily. Almost immediately Randolph Cary and an entourage of young men appeared at their side, begging Miranda for a dance. Taking a deep breath, she acceded graciously. Among the applicants was Lord Alvaney, for whom Rupert insisted she spare a waltz.

Her program comfortably full, Miranda was whirled onto the floor by Rupert, who studied her braced shoulders and smoldering eyes with approval.

"That's the spirit. Do not let the tabbies see that you are discomforted in any way. You will see; we will brush through this affair without trouble," he assured her.

"If we do, it is entirely due to your standing in society, my lord. You look quite formidable and prepared to take on any challengers."

"I am," he said shortly. "Ignore any slights and refuse to discuss the letters as beneath contempt. A haughty uncomprehending air is the ticket."

And so it proved to be not such a terrifying evening as she had expected. She was much cheered by Maria Henderson's championship, as that young lady, defying her mama, greeted Miranda affectionately and whispered, "I think you are so brave, Miranda. Not that there is any truth in the rumors. You will see; it will prove to be a tempest in a teapot."

Just before supper Miranda encountered the only really disagreeable confrontation of the evening. Repairing to the ladies' retiring room, she asked the maid on duty there to sew on a button which had become dislodged during an energetic german. Satisfied that she had gracefully handled her first public appearance since she had learned of the letters, she turned away, walking down the corridor toward the stairs to meet Rupert for supper. As she passed one of the alcoves where some couples were sitting out, she was hailed by Chloe Castleon, who had been lying in wait for her.

"Hiding from the vicious tongues, Miss Houghton," Chloe asked with a malevolent leer.

"I have no idea what you mean, Mrs. Castleton. But I am a bit surprised to see you here," she countered, implying that the Rutlands had not been as careful as they might be about their guest list.

"My reputation is not at issue," Chloe came back weakly.

"I am mistaken, then. You must excuse me; Rupert is waiting for me," Miranda answered blithely and sailed away, leaving her antagonist baffled and furious. But the encounter had left her shaken, and Rupert noticed her unease immediately.

"What has happened, Miranda?"

"Mrs. Castleton has happened. She approached me in the corridor and was most unpleasant."

"She can be," Rupert admitted, then hesitated. He was not sure how to proceed.

"I am sure she was the author of the letters, Rupert."

"If so, she must be deeply disappointed they did not achieve her aim. I think I will talk to the lady later."

"Is this the place and time to challenge her?"

"Indubitably. I believe the egregious Chloe had best absent herself from London for awhile. She has become a nuisance."

"And you will remove her?" Miranda smiled weakly, amazed that Rupert could talk so nonchalantly of banishing his former mistress.

"She is quite expendable. I wonder how she secured her invitation to this ball. Very negligent of the Rutlands. Now don't worry, Miranda. She is a spent bullet."

"I only hope so and that she is not the instigator of those assaults upon you. She seems intent on revenge."

"She may have written the letters, but she is incapable of planning a murder. Her toehold in society is tenuous and I have the means to force her into exile."

"You are a ruthless devil, Rupert. I trust you'll never turn your wrath on me," Miranda said bleakly.

"Inconceivable, my dear. Now put on your most delightful mask and let us enjoy supper. Forget Chloe Castleton. She is of no importance," he reassured her, but Miranda suspected from his formidable manner that he would deal with Chloe's mischief-making handily, disregarding his past feelings for the woman. If she had written the letters, she had made a grave miscalculation, one for which Miranda prayed she would pay grievously.

Obeying Rupert's command, Miranda summoned her resources and accompanied him to the supper room in better spirits, although not entirely comforted by his obvious intention to deal with Chloe Castleton in a manner that would silence her slander.

Later, dancing with Lord Alvaney, she noticed Rupert guiding Chloe Castleton from the room. She questioned his wisdom in escorting a woman the *ton* knew had once been his mistress. Would that quell the rumors or intensify them? But she let none of her disquiet show and chatted brightly of her enjoyment of London with this pleasant man, whom she realized was showing the company that she had won his allegiance. Miranda had been tutored by Lady Worthington in the importance of that elite group of men who sat in White's bow window and made judgments on society's foibles. His good opinion was paramount, and she suspected that Rupert had pressed him to invite her to dance.

"Have you visited Rupert's place in Wiltshire yet, Miss Houghton?" he asked as they twirled about the floor. Like many corpulent men, he was light on his feet and his graceful manners testified to his experience at dealing with difficult situations.

"No, Lord Alvaney, but Rupert mentioned we would be going soon. I am quite anxious to see it."

"Hastings Halt is a lovely house. Been in his family for donkey's years, set on a dominating hill with gardens running down to the sea. I am sure you will be happy there."

Not wanting to pursue this dangerous assumption, Miranda smiled vaguely. Lord Alvaney spoke as if the marriage were a settled affair. What had Rupert said to him? Obliging as he was, Miranda was not prepared to confide in him. His bright eyes spoke a question, but he was too tactful to ask it.

"Rupert is a fortunate man. All his friends are pleased that he is tying the noose," Lord Alvaney offered.

"Tying the noose. What an intimidating expression! I hope matrimony will not be so confining," Miranda responded laughing.

"Maladroit of me. Just a cant saying. You will be good for him. He needs settling."

If Miranda thought that sounded as if Rupert were a broody hen, she was wise enough not to demur. They finished the dance quite pleased with each other.

Lady Cowper, chatting with Lord Palmerston in the sitting-out corner, noticed the couple. "Alvaney seems quite taken with Miss Houghton. That should increase her standing enormously," she offered.

"Yes, and I believe that was his intention," Lord Palmerston agreed shrewdly. "He has heard the rumors and is rallying around. Hastings must have a vindicative enemy to spread such gossip about his fiancée, but they seem to be coping well. That girl has wit and intelligence as well as beauty. I met her at Kenwood and was impressed, but then I expected Hastings would not be caught by an adventuress."

"The best of men can be gulled by a winsome face and figure, but I trust you are right," Lady Cowper said and abandoned the subject to discuss their own scandalous affairs.

While Miranda was enjoying herself on the dance floor, Rupert had escorted Chloe Castleton to an obscure corner of the upstairs sitting room. Closing the door, he turned to her, his mouth grim and his eyes promising no evasion.

"If I thought you were the author of these letters which are causing Miranda such unhappiness, I would be very angry, Chloe. And my anger could force me to punish you in a manner you might find distasteful."

"How can you be so unkind, Rupert." She looked at him soulfully, as if such reprisal were beyond her imagination. Seeing that he was not moved by her denial and fearing he really might retaliate himself, she rushed into an inconsidered speech.

"I don't believe you are in love with that silly chit. What can she offer you? She has neither an impeccable reputation nor a noble family behind her. And there is probably a great deal of truth in the gossip. Your friends are worried about you, Rupert, for contracting such a misalliance." She tempered her protest with a cloying smile.

"You are among them, I suppose," he mocked.

"Of course. And I am shocked to think you would accuse me of such rancorous tactics. Unhappy as you have made me, I still care deeply for you, Rupert, and would do nothing to spoil your future—no matter how much I deplore your choice."

"If you are lying, Chloe, I will find it out and you will

never again be received, even in the few houses that now admit you. I have your unequivocal word that you did not write those letters?" he asked, his voice demanding a true response.

"Of course, Rupert. You or Miss Houghton may have an enemy, but be assured it is not Chloe Castleton. I would never behave so."

Rupert tended to believe her. It was not that he thought her incapable of this attempt to destroy Miranda's reputation and make him look a fool, but that he knew she valued her precarious toehold in society. He had the power to banish her from the scene, a prerogative she could not overlook.

"You would be wise to leave London for awhile," he suggested, and Chloe realized it was a demand.

"I cannot afford to visit the Continent now," she wailed. "And why should I go, just because you entertain these ridiculous suspicions?"

"If they are ridiculous, you have nothing to fear; but, in any case, your presence upsets Miranda and I will not have that. I will send you a draft which should cover your expenses. And see that you use it to travel abroad. You should do quite well in the watering holes of Germany, several easy targets for your charms there."

Chloe, not averse to increasing her fortunes, might have continued to protest, but she sensed that Rupert would not be impressed. Much as she wanted revenge for his callous dismissal of her, she had a practical streak; the chance to settle her debts and perhaps find a generous protector tipped the balance.

"You malign me, Rupert, but I cannot resist your generous offer. You believe that if you banish me this current scandal will vanish. You are wrong. But you are so confident you can arrange affairs to your taste whenever you wish that you deserve to be trapped by a light skirt. Someday, I vow, you will come back to me and admit you made a mistake."

"Not till hell freezes over, my dear. Take my money and

get out of town. That is your only option," Rupert warned, thoroughly angered by her insinuations. Then, turning on his heel, he left the room without even the courtesy of a farewell.

Enraged, Chloe reddened at his insult, but she was not so foolish as to disobey him. In truth, she had managed the business well, and Rupert's discomfiture soothed her vanity. She almost wished she had written the letters.

Returning to the ballroom, Rupert noticed Miranda dancing a country set with Randolph Cary. Propping himself against a wall with an aspect so forbidding that not even the most devoted gossip dared approach him, he watched Miranda as she tripped daintily through the steps. He believed Chloe had not written the letters; but, in any event, he had settled her once and for all. If these rumors and the attacks on him continued once she left London, he would have to look elsewhere for the culprit. A suspicion of the perpetrator, so outrageous as to be laughable, was beginning to form in his mind. He would confront Horace Howland, but somehow the thwarted professor did not seem the answer.

Could it all be a hum? No, those letters were a nasty fact, and now the highwayman accosting him and the shot in Marcus's wood had to be taken seriously. Someone was out to harm him—first through Miranda and, if that were not successful, with other more fatal weapons. Well, he was on his guard now and it would be a bold adversary who would chance his fate.

Of more importance was his marriage. The sooner that transpired the better. But how was he to persuade Miranda of the notion, she who neither trusted him, nor believed his offer serious. If she did not love him, he was digging a pit for himself; but he could not convince himself that she felt nothing for him. Rupert, accustomed to having his way and stimulated by a challenge, knew the toughest battle of his life lay ahead.

Chapter Sixteen

Although not completely convinced by Rupert's report of his interview with Chloe Castleton and his assurance she was not the author of the letters, Miranda did feel happier over Rupert's evident disdain for his former *chère amie*. And the news that she would be leaving London was especially gratifying. Miranda noticed, too, that the temporary furor caused by the letters appeared to have abated. Perhaps this was due to another new scandal, even more shocking.

Jane Ellenborough, married for several years to a much older husband, was conducting a flagrant affair with a Swedish diplomat and had just been delivered of a son by her lover. Her husband had agreed to a divorce; and the account of the trial in the House of Lords, faithfully reported in the *Times,* was avidly pursued by the *ton.* The marriage was finally dissolved by Act of Parliament, the only recourse for noble couples. Miranda applauded Joseph Hume, M. P., who wrote quite boldly in the *Times*, "Can anyone overlook the gross neglect on Lord Ellenborough's part that has led to the unhappy events?. . . In this country a woman is punished severely for faults which in a husband are overlooked." Miranda hoped Jane would find happiness in Sweden married to a more loving husband. She would never be accepted in London society again.

The days following the Rutland Ball saw no repeat of the attacks on Rupert, and Miranda believed the enemy, whoever it was, was disappointed by his efforts and had abandoned the attempt to harm Rupert. She was more concerned with her own decision over whether or not she should marry Rupert. She could not imagine following Lady Ellenborough's path if neglected by her husband, but the thought of a loveless marriage was abhorrent and she doubted Rupert had any but the most casual affection for her. No doubt he was piqued because she had not eagerly accepted his offer, but still his attitude remained perplexing. On the one hand, he was attentive, squiring her to parties, constant in his compliments, but certainly neither pressing nor behaving like a man whose heart would be affected if she eventually refused him. Unfortunately, her own heart was not so armored. She knew she was falling fathoms deep in love, no matter how she tried to reject these inchoate, unwelcome emotions.

Another worry was Randolph Cary's unwillingness to accept that she was tied to Rupert. He had become much more adamant in his professions of admiration, and she would have to deal with him before Rupert took some compelling action. The season had about a month to run, then most of London society would repair to its country estates or to Brighton; if she refused Rupert, she would have to return to Oxford and the complaints and anger of her parents. And if Horace Howland declined to renew his suit, no doubt her father would press some other unattractive husband upon her, for she could not remain unmarried for ever. She was amazed that Adrian Houghton had not tried to interfere before this.

Her relief at this strange lack of parental concern was short-lived. Several days after the ball, her father turned up unexpectedly in Mount Street, disgruntled and determined to exert his authority.

"Since you have not seen fit to let your natural guardians know how you were going on, it behooved me to interrupt my work and come to London to make the necessary inquiries," he informed her pompously, bestowing a chilly kiss of greeting.

"I am sorry, Father. How is everything at home? Mother and Robbie well?" she asked, hoping to distract him.

"Quite well, considering that your mother is extremely worried about you. I have come to see this Lord Hastings for myself, since he does not deem it necessary to seek your father's consent for this dubious match." On his dignity, Adrian Houghton was not to be appeased, although he was genuinely impressed with Lady Worthington and her establishment.

"Now that you have met Lady Worthington, you can appreciate my lines have fallen in very pleasant places," Miranda soothed. She sensed that her father was irritated not by the engagement, but because he had not been consulted. She understood his attitude, even had some sympathy for it, but she would not be cowed by his criticism; nor would she allow him to find fault with Rupert.

"Howland tells me this man is a veritable libertine, not at all the proper husband for an innocent, respectable girl," Adrian complained.

"And Professor Howland is? His views are not to be considered; he is animated by spite and was very malicious when he called on me here. I hope he realizes that any marriage between us is out of the question," Miranda said firmly.

"Don't be impertinent, Miranda. You will be guided by me in the matter of your marriage. I do not say that this Lord Hastings is unacceptable but that he is arrogant and inconsiderate. And have you thought what your life with him would be like?"

Since Miranda had done little else but think of this in the past few days, she wondered if her father had any respect for her common sense. "Yes, Father, I have. And I think it behooves you to hold your fire until you have met Rupert. Where are you staying in London?" she asked, changing the subject. His tirades did not move her. After seeing that he had not considered her welfare when his own was in danger, she had little respect for his assumption of paternal solicitude now.

"At Grillon's, and I can tell you it is ruinously expensive," he reported with asperity.

"Well, I will inform Rupert. You can expect him to call on you, if that will be satisfactory, but for heaven's sake, Father, don't be pettish with him."

"Pettish, what kind of remark is that? I will receive him, and I think I know how to act without instructions from my wayward daughter."

Seeing that she would achieve little by trying to gain his sympathy or understanding, much less profit by any selfish advice he might offer, Miranda bid him goodbye with relief. She hardly needed to add this to her problems. She accepted that her father's arrival was no testimony of his affection for her but only an attempt to learn what he could gain from her good fortune. His egotism had been affronted, and he demanded reparation. But he was in for an unhappy surprise when Rupert confronted him. Miranda smiled wryly. She had every faith that Rupert would puncture her father's pomposity and deflate his arrogance. But was that any solution? She would not be chivied by any of the men in her life to make a decision which might endanger her own self-respect or cause her unhappiness. Marriage to escape from home too often led to an even more grievous situation. Look at Lady Ellenborough.

When Rupert appeared to take her riding on the new mare he had bought for her, she greeted him with reserve. How would he take this business of her father's arrival? If she suggested he treat Adrian Houghton gently, he might laugh at her advice and in his lordly way pronounce that she could leave it safely in his hands. But he must realize her father could prevent the match. Somehow she sensed that Adrian

Houghton would be no competition for Rupert. Insisting her father might refuse permission would only postpone a declaration on her part. If Rupert believed she wanted to marry him, marry they would, whether Adrian Houghton approved or not. Well, whatever the outcome, Rupert must hear of her father's appearance.

"You are looking distrait today, my love," Rupert said as he helped her onto Merry, the chestnut mare, whose disposition matched her name. Miranda had become quite proficient, under Rupert's direction, in handling the horse he had selected.

"Well, I have several things on my mind, but wait till we ride out of these streets and I will tell you," she answered, still not certain of her prowess along the heavily traveled thoroughfares they had to cross before reaching the park.

Rupert watched her approvingly, touched by her intense concentration on reins and posture. He was pleased she had taken to riding with such enthusiasm and had a firm seat and good hands. Life in the country was insupportable if one did not ride. At last they reached the safety of the bridle lanes in Hyde Park and enjoyed a brief canter before pulling up and walking the horses.

"Now, what is troubling you, Miranda? Have I transgressed in some way that impels you to call me to account?" Rupert asked.

"This is quite serious, Rupert. My father is in town, staying at Grillon's and came around this morning to ring a peal over me complaining about your high-handed attitude in announcing our engagement without his consent."

"From my one, rather stormy interview with your august parent, I gather he does not suffer any opposition to his own wishes," he said.

"You might say that," Miranda grinned cheekily and added, "I do wish I could have been present when you stormed into our Oxford house, convinced the Houghton's

170

hussy of a daughter had lured your poor innocent nephew into a distressing elopement."

Not at all abashed, Rupert admitted, "Yes, well, it was a bit precipitate, perhaps, but I must say your father is quite as arrogant as I am. Wouldn't you agree? And since you seem to be able to handle—or should I say circumvent?—him, I wonder if this augurs well for our own union," he mused.

"Oh, I think so. I would not like to be under your thumb any more than under Father's. It's bad for your character, you know," she riposted.

"The professor has my sympathy, dealing with such a tempestuous daughter. I must asked him how he coped—after, of course, I have gained his consent to marry you."

"Really, Rupert, aren't you taking a good deal for granted?" Miranda asked, suddenly irritated by his treating the business of their marriage as a lighthearted jape.

He lifted an eyebrow and an amused smile crossed his face. If he were irritated by her intransigence, he did not reveal it. "Not at all. I could enlist your father's aid in the venture, but somehow I don't think that would sit well with you. I fail to see any rivals in serious contention, and you did say in the inn at Cheltenham that you intended to contract a respectable match before the season was done. I might remind you that you have only a month left in which to accomplish this. I would not for a moment suggest that you are not capable of luring your next victim within that time; but, aside from the ubiquitous Cary, I see no serious contender," he explained in that sarcastic tone that raised her hackles.

"Randolph Cary has already proposed. I could have him if I wished," Miranda responded, sulking. She did not like Rupert's reference to Cheltenham nor his playful analysis of her prospects. If he would drop that jeering manner and confess he felt some attachment to her, she would accept his offer. But her natural distrust of him and her wariness when faced with his jibes made her reluctant to let down her guard. What could be more humiliating than for him to realize she cared for him? He would take advantage of any tender emotions, she believed, and she would not give him the chance to make mock of her.

The mention of Cary had not pleased Rupert, although he did not evidence his displeasure. "I would suppose the thought of crossing the water to live among savages and puritans is not to your liking," he observed. "Otherwise Cary would appear to be just the ticket—amenable, easily dominated, and apparently besotted." He calculated his rival's assets coldly as if without prejudice.

Miranda, swallowing her anger and disappointment, did not rise to his bait. "Whatever I decide I think you had best call on Father and make your intentions known, if they are honorable."

"I am mean to tease you, Miranda; but it is irresistible, I fear. I will not only call upon your father but invite him to dine with me this evening and visit Crockford's. He will be fascinated, since I gather he likes a flutter now and then, and might enjoy hazard. I doubt that game has reached Oxford yet."

Miranda, who had heard a great deal about the famous gambling club, an exclusive house in St. James's Street where membership was greatly prized and even the Duke of Wellington played, realized this was a rare invitation. But not one she thought suitable.

"Father is very unlucky. That was what caused all the trouble in the first place. He is a fool with cards."

"Ah, but this is dice. And don't worry, I will keep an eye on him and not let him chance any great sum."

"I suppose when you gamble you win. It would be just your luck," Miranda retorted angrily. Unquestionably, Rupert needed a set down or two; he breezed through life without ever encountering any rebuffs—or so it seemed. Rupert could have told her he was currently experiencing some formidable obstacles to his heart's desire, but his pride prevented him from begging for her approval or her assent to his offer.

"No, I lose occasionally, but I have a financial interest in Crockford's and the old fishmonger likes to keep me sweet," he explained.

"I might have known. And why a fishmonger, which is surely a strange trade for a gambling proprietor?" Miranda was intrigued in spite of herself.

"That's how he began. When still a young man, after a twenty-four hour stint at the tables, he won one hundred thousand pounds from a series of gentlemen. With these funds he built his club in St. James Street. Cleverly he lured Monsieur Ude, the foremost chef in England, to prepare the cuisine; and not only hazard, but faro, *jeu d'enfer,* and blind hookey are available to those who want to indulge. Crockford's is the *sine qua non* of gambling clubs, very exclusive and elegant," he explained.

"Father will love it, alas. I fear he is a dreadful snob," Miranda confessed ruefully.

"Well, we must use that to our advantage," Rupert said, not one whit taken aback by this uncomplimentary view of his future father-in-law.

Their horses were becoming restive during this prolonged conversation, and Apollo began to snort and toss his head.

"Shall we let the horses have their heads," Rupert suggested, thinking enough had been said about Adrian Houghton's foibles. Spurring Apollo he galloped down the track, leaving Miranda to follow more sedately but happy to banish her worries in the exercise.

They returned to Mount Street in good spirits, much improved by their outing, to be greeted by Lady Worthington in somewhat of a tizzy.

"How unfortunate you were out when your grandfather called, Miranda," she informed them when they entered the morning room. Rupert had been invited for luncheon and apologized for his riding gear. Miranda, who wanted to change from her habit, looked puzzled at this unexpected information.

"My grandfather?" she queried on a note of surprise.

"The Earl of Moresdale, a very distinguished gentleman. He saw the announcement of your engagement in the *Gazette* and appears eager to make your acquaintance," Charlotte said smugly. She was discernibly impressed by this news that Miranda was so well connected.

"Well, if that isn't the end. He has ignored me all my life and, now that he thinks I have made a suitable alliance, he is prepared to make overtures. Well, I have no intention of meeting him," Miranda fumed.

Rupert smiled, thinking that his fiancée could not easily be tempted to betray her loyalties by a long overdue rapproachment from her crotchety relative. "Is that wise, Miranda? Perhaps your mother would like to be reconciled to her father."

"Then let him contact her. It's the outside of enough that he should want to see us after all these years, and only because of my engagement to a tulip of the *ton,*" she announced bitterly.

"I do think you might see the earl," Charlotte urged, overset by Miranda's forthright condemnation of one of the ranking members of the nobility.

"Do you honestly see me as a tulip of the *ton,* Miranda? What a disgusting appelation," Rupert mocked to distract her.

"Not at all, I am only repeating what is common gossip," Miranda riposted, unwilling to compliment her fiancé.

"Set down again. You are so refreshing to my conceit. However, I should think twice about seeing the earl. Perhaps you should ask your father what he believes would be the best course of action," Rupert proposed ironically.

"Well, right now I mean to change these clothes. Whatever

the noble lord wants with me is of little moment. He can wait," Miranda said abruptly and excused herself.

"Really, Rupert, you should not encourage Miranda to be so independent. I greatly fear she is not a biddable girl," Charlotte mourned when her charge had left the room.

"Not at all. That's part of her charm. She is not impressed with the earl and will give him a cool reception; and I, for one, cannot blame her. But, Charlotte, I want to talk to you about the wedding. I am thinking of a September date," he said to turn her mind away from an analysis of Miranda's character. And perhaps, by assuming the marriage was a settled affair, quiet his own concern.

Charlotte, delighted with the thought that Miranda would be off her hands so soon, entered enthusiastically into his plans, and they discussed the approaching nuptials in a rare charity with one another.

Chapter Seventeen

Adrian Houghton tried not to show it, but he was impressed, both with Rupert Hastings and Crockford's. He had intended to act very much on his dignity when his daughter's fiancé appeared at Grillon's, but he found himself unable to persevere under Rupert's charm, which could be formidable when he chose to exert it.

"I realize it was extremely maladroit of me not to call upon you and Mrs. Houghton in Oxford and request your permission to marry Miranda. I fear that I was hesitant because our previous meeting had been so unfortunate," Rupert explained smoothly when he met his future father-in-law.

"Yes, well, I think we were both intemperate in our behavior. That could be excused in view of the gravity of the situation, Miranda eloping with your nephew," Adrian replied pompously. Having glided over the necessity for that elopement and his part in it, he appeared prepared to accept Rupert's apology and his invitation. No mention was made of Horace Howland or the effrontery of Rupert's methods in preventing Miranda's escape from her home.

Adrian Houghton was a snob, one of the reasons he had been attracted to his wife in the first instance. He could not believe that her father, the Earl of Moresdale, would turn his back on his daughter. That humiliation still rankled, only mitgated by Miranda's attachment of a viscount. His sensitivities were soothed by the knowledge that Rupert would now sponsor him, not only at Crockford's but to other exclusive salons from which he had always been excluded.

Although a gambling salon, Crockford's was also a club where only the most exalted members of society were welcomed. The former fishmonger who ran the club knew that admittance to his sanctum would be prized only if it were limited. And he also sensed that he would have to furbish his club, at its prestigious address in St. James Street, with the most luxurious appointments, refreshments, and croupiers. The amount of money won and lost in his gilded salon was prodigious. Professor Houghton could not repress a thrill of satisfaction as he noted the fashionable faces at play. Under Crockford's glittering chandliers gathered figures of great note: "Golden" Ball Hughes, Count Esterhazy, the Dukes of Spencer, Queensberry, and Wellington himself. Young officers of the Household Brigade and the Guards—in stiff white neckcloths and blue coats with brass buttons and diamond studs—conducted themselves with propriety as they lost ruinous sums while displaying stoic, well-bred faces. Conversation was brilliant as most of the politicians, wits, and social lions frequented Crockford's to chance their luck.

Hazard, although illegal, had replaced faro, piquet, macoa, and *jeu d'enfer,* as the most popular game. As he watched, Houghton saw one young tulip lose ten thousand pounds on one throw of the dice without any sign of dismay. Rupert initiated him into the rules of hazard and kept a careful eye on his guest to see that he did not plunge too deeply. After a few throws, Adrian emerged two hundred pounds richer, and Rupert suggested that they repair to the supper table to enjoy some of the delicacies for which Crockford's was famous. Here they met the ubiquitous Alvaney sampling some lobster and Rupert made the introduction, mentioning that Adrian was his future father-in-law, a description at which the professor made no demur.

"I see young Cary from the American ministry is here tonight. Is he a member?" Rupert asked Alvaney, having spied Cary earlier at the hazard table.

"No. He's the guest of young Fitzwilliam. Rather unusual the way that young man has been accepted everywhere," Alvaney commented pointedly.

"Yes, he's quite popular with the ladies," Rupert replied.

"Your fiancée among them, I gather." Alvaney could not resist twitting Rupert. He had found Miranda a delightful departure from the usual run of debutantes and wondered if Rupert were jealous. Quite a turn-up if Lord Hastings found himself hoist with his own petard.

"Cary. Is he a friend of Miranda's?" Adrian asked, worried. His daughter was moving in circles which surprised him even while her acceptance by society gratified him. Now that he had accepted Rupert as her husband-to-be he wanted no hindrance to the match. Volatile as Miranda was, she easily could decide she preferred this American. Adrian noticed he was a handsome man with an assurance and bearing not expected in a colonial.

"Of both of us, sir. He has been very attentive in squiring Miranda when I was unavailable. They share a taste for history," Rupert explained dryly. If he found the professor's snobbery amusing, he hid it well. Alvaney raised a wry eyebrow, but nothing more was said about Randolph Cary.

The evening proceeded along lines carefully laid out by Rupert to afford Adrian Houghton the maximum enjoyment. About two o'clock in the morning, Rupert decided it was time to take their leave. He observed thankfully that Cary had left some time earlier, for he did want to introduce Carey to Miranda's father. Retrieving their hats and gloves from a minion, Rupert requested that his carriage be called. They walked outside, eager for a breath of fresh air after the close atmosphere of the club. Heavy clouds hung over London, obscuring the stars and making visibility beyond the flickering flambeaux on the doorsteps of Crockford's difficult. Rupert, waiting impatiently, could see no sign of his carriage or coachman. Excusing himself, he begged Adrian to remain where he was while he went to rout out the dilatory vehicle. Adrian, bemused by his successful and thoroughly fascinating evening, agreed, and Rupert walked into the mist. As his footsteps echoed eerily in the dark night, a carriage pulled up to the entrance. A liveried footman climbed down and opened the door of the coach. Adrian stepped up and entered the open door. The coach sped away.

Rupert, meanwhile, had not been successful in finding his missing carriage, and he returned to Crockford's cursing his coachman's carelessness, especially as a thin rain was now falling. Not seeing Adrian, he wondered if his guest had decided to walk back to Grillon's. Surely he would not be so rude. Perhaps he had gone to find a hackney. Rupert paced up and down, and then as a footman came out of the club he asked him if he had noticed his guest. The man looked puzzled.

"I thought you had left some time ago, my lord. Your carriage was called."

"It never came, and I left Mr. Houghton here on the doorstep. He seems to have disappeared."

"I have not been outside since you left, my lord," the man stated, wondering if Lord Hastings had taken one too many drams.

"Well, he may have decided to walk. I am sure I will find him. But if my coachman appears, tell him I have gone home after waiting an undue time," Rupert said angrily. This was too much. He stalked into the rain, irritated.

Some hours later as dawn was breaking, a disheveled Adrian Houghton limped into Grillon's, considerably upset. A servant on duty through the long night, although accustomed to his guests arriving in the early hours after a riotous time on the town, thought the professor looked more than bosky.

"Can I help you, sir?" he asked politely.

"Yes, you can get me breakfast and a bath. I have been abducted by rogues and then abandoned in Hyde Park beyond the toll. What is London coming to that such a business could happen? It's damnable," Adrian fumed, climbing slowly upstairs.

The servant, fearing his guest had encountered a roving band of cutthroats, hurried after him. "I am so sorry, sir. But let me help you. 'Tis true London is a nest of thieves and robbers and little is done to apprehend them." Cajoling and sympathizing, he escorted Adrian to his room and fussed over him, ordering the bath and promising a hearty meal as soon as possible. Adrian subsided wearily into a chair, bemused and aching in every bone. The strange abduction had turned out to be a case of mistaken identity. The masked men inside the coach had examined him briefly and then, amid muttered oaths, had asked him about Lord Hastings.

"We've nobbed the wrong toff, here. This cove is too old," one grumbled. Adrian could make out little of his captors, masked and heavily muffled in cloaks as they were. But he had managed to convince them that he was not Lord Hastings and insisted they release him. He had not expected to be dumped into the deserted park and left to find his own way back to Grillon's. Well, he would have some sharp remarks to make to Lord Hastings. The fellow had enemies, that was clear. Adrian wondered what he had done to inspire such a criminal assault. Probably a gambling debt or some other heinous affair. He did not see the irony of castigating Rupert for following a path he himself had not disdained. His embarrassment, anger, and exhaustion prevented him from recalling the events of the kidnapping with any clarity. After a hearty breakfast and a soothing bath, he fell into bed seeking a healing sleep but with every intention of challenging Rupert when he was himself again.

Rupert, upon returning home to Grosvenor Square, discovered his coachman, sleeping in the mews behind the mansion. Bleary-eyed and barely dressed, the man had a strange tale to relate.

"You had told me to return about one o'clock, my lord, and I did so. But a smart gentleman gave me a message, saying it was from you. He told me I was not to wait, that he would be driving you home. So I tooled up the horses and away we went. I never suspected nothin'," he apologized.

Rupert sighed, having an idea at what had transpired. Evidently his foes had not abandoned their efforts, but the victim this time had been the luckless Professor Houghton. He only hoped they had discovered their error before any harm had come to Miranda's father. He smiled grimly. They seemed to be an inefficient lot, missing their target at every encounter. Well, he would pursue the matter in the morning, or rather later this morning. Rupert trudged off to bed, worried but not alarmed. He would have to take measures to apprehend these fiends. The whole affair was mysterious and worrying. Who could hate him so much as to want to remove him permanently?

Just before noon, Rupert made inquiries at Grillon's but learned his quarry had left shortly before his arrival. Surmising that Adrian had gone around to Mount Street to complain about his brutal treatment to Miranda, he followed, partially relieved. At least the professor had suffered no serious harm if he were out and about this morning.

Radleigh, welcoming him, informed him that Mr. Houghton had arrived a few moments before and was closeted with Miranda and Peter in the drawing room. Lady Worthington was not at home, for which Rupert was grateful. Charlotte's wails and complaints would have been insupport-

181

able. He entered the morning room to hear Adrian ringing a peal over an appalled and mystified Miranda.

"Good morning, my dear. I see your father has suffered no lasting harm from the deplorable incident last night," he declared swiftly, giving Peter a small nod.

"It's the outside of enough, Uncle. Some varlets abducted Mr. Houghton last night right outside Crockford's. Disgusting," Peter exclaimed.

"So I understand. My apologies, sir, that you have suffered such a fate. It's certain the rogues thought they were kidnapping me. Careless of them," he drawled, determined to treat the matter casually. No point in exacerbating Adrian Houghton's temper.

"Yes, that's all very well, but why would anyone want to do such a thing? You must have been up to some nasty jape for them to revenge themselves in that fashion." Adrian's consequence was plainly damaged and he needed to take out his anger on the man he believed responsible for his nasty experience.

Miranda, who had not spoken during these exchanges, frowned. Her concern was not for her father. He had suffered no lasting harm. Rupert was in danger, and she realized with a start that she cared terribly whether or not he would escape the fate his enemies had planned for him. Rupert was convinced Chloe Castleton was not a factor. That left only Horace Howland.

"Could Horace have instigated this scheme?" she asked, interrupting a low-voiced observation by Peter.

"Horace! Now really, Miranda. You are placing too high a value on your charms. Granted he was disappointed and humiliated by your refusal to marry him, but he would never go to these lengths—abduction, and from what I understand, an attempt at assassination." Her father protested, "Horace is an honorable man."

"I don't believe it's honorable to coerce a girl to marry you

182

because your father owes him money," Miranda said to the point.

"It was not like that," Adrian blustered, reddening under his daughter's attack.

"Somehow, I don't think that Horace is our culprit," Rupert interceded, hoping to defuse the conflagration. He found Adrian Houghton's pomposity and refusal to accept any criticism pathetic, but he could see how such behavior in a father could be trying, especially for a girl like Miranda who failed to accept human weaknesses with charity. Her strength of character and notions of how to behave endeared her to Rupert, but clearly she and her father looked at life from widely opposed viewpoints.

Miranda gave him a speaking look and he knew she was thinking of Chloe Castleton, but Rupert was not prepared to discuss that lady before Adrian Houghton.

"Well, all I can say, Uncle, is that someone is out to cause you harm and you had best beware," Peter offered, although he himself was not inclined to take the threats seriously.

"I intend to, Peter. But now I suggest you take Professor Houghton into the library and give him some wine. I want to talk to Miranda."

If Adrian Houghton wanted to protest at this high-handed manner of dispensing with him, he decided—on looking at Rupert's grim countenance—it might be wiser to accept his proffered suggestion. Peter, grinning, agreed politely and shepherded the professor from the room, after saying that no doubt he would see them both at luncheon. "Mother will not be back," he promised as an added inducement.

Miranda, who had not abandoned her belief that Chloe Castleton was somehow involved in these threats against Rupert, barely waited until Peter and her father had left before setting to.

"I know you would not want to mention your mistress before Father, not at all the thing when you are supposed to be

183

courting his daughter, but what proof do you have she is not the instigator of all these troubles?" she asked Rupert, determined to make him see where the danger lay.

"Because she left London several days ago, right after I told her she had no other option left open to her. And somehow I can't see Chloe hiring thugs, planning an abduction, and mistaking Houghton for me," he argued without heat. "She's not a clever woman, but her well-being is her first concern. She realized that I had it in my power to make her life very uncomfortable."

"And is that what you wanted to do?" Miranda asked, not appeased.

"Stop raking me up, you little shrew. Forget Chloe. I want to talk to you about a wedding date. Your father, somewhat reluctantly, has agreed to our marriage. I want to settle matters before he changes his mind and introduces Horace or some other sapskull as a husband," he teased. Then, seeing that she had raised her defenses, he took her in his arms looking down at her with an expression she had never seen before in his dark eyes.

"I intend to marry you, Miranda, and I don't think you are averse to the idea. You have some maggot in your head that my reasons are far from admirable. You know you must marry someone, what better than a doting husband who can give you everything your heart desires?"

Except love, Miranda thought to herself. Rupert had not said one word about his feeling for her. He had decided to marry; she was available and the engagement announced. Nothing was more practical than to acquire a grateful and amenable girl who would answer all his requirements. But she was not willing to fulfill that role. She opened her mouth to protest, but he quickly silenced her with a drugging kiss, moving his hands with arousing familiarity over her acquiescent body. She could not prevent her response as her mouth opened under his and she was lost to the warmth and passion he could so easily evoke. Her hand stole around his neck and she melted against him, powerless to prevent giving him the reaction he demanded.

"You may think I am despicable, but you cannot deny we share this overwhelming need," he murmured, gazing at her with fiery desire. "We will be wed in September and then go off to Italy, a romantic and inspiring site to reassure you that our life will be all that you want." He wanted to tell her how desperately he needed her, that there was more than just a physical craving which was threatening to weaken all his resolution, but somehow he could not expose himself to her mockery. She would not believe him.

"I do not seem to have any choice," she conceded, distracted by the kisses which were undermining all her arguments. Not for the world would she tell him how much she wanted to be his wife—and not for the worldly reasons he suggested.

"No, you don't; so enjoy it. We will make a famous pair," he said with satisfaction having now attained his goal, although he knew a passing frustration that she would not admit to caring for him. He could not resist reminding her of what they did share. "From the beginning your response to me has promised we would suit. In bed you will be a passionate partner and, whatever follows, we have that to rely on."

"I have no doubt you are an expert lover, but physical affinity is a rather shaky basis for marriage." Miranda hated the idea that Rupert wanted her in his bed and cared little for any other aspect of their union.

"Without it, marriage is an arid affair. Don't worry, Miranda. You will discover it will all work out for the best. Believe me, you will not regret becoming Lady Hastings."

"If you live to speak the vows," she responded sharply, remembering they had come to no conclusion about the threats against Rupert.

"Oh, I will. Have no doubts about that. Now come, let us

inform your father that we will be wed in September. We will let him decide the arrangements. I will send my man of business to discuss settlements with him, and that will cheer him immensely for I will not be niggardly."

Struck by her morose expression Rupert implored, "Do try to look happy, Miranda. It will be your marriage, not your funeral."

"I just hope it won't be yours," she replied tartly and then gasped as he kissed her fiercely only to let her go with a pat on her backside.

Chapter Eighteen

Having gone upstairs to change from her riding clothes, Miranda wondered why she had given in so passionately to Rupert. Normally he would have mocked her, insisting there was nothing of the dominated female in Miranda's make-up. Despite her show of reluctance, she knew in her heart she was only surrendering to her own desires. She wanted to marry Rupert because she loved him, with all his faults or perhaps because of them. Life with him might not fulfill her dreams of a loving and sharing companionship, but to contemplate marriage with anyone else was unthinkable. And perhaps he would come to feel for her the deep affection she felt for him. Passion she distrusted, although she knew he inspired that emotion in her; but without friendship and respect, the arousal he evoked whenever he touched her would not be enough. Well, she had made her decision and she would abide by it, no matter what the future boded for good or ill.

She might have decided to marry Rupert, but that did not mean she would behave in a grateful missish fashion, aware that she had captured one of the most eligible *partis* on the London scene. She would not be dominated by his strong will, and she would insist he discover who was threatening him, and the reason for the attempted violence before they spoke the vows. Rupert discounted Chloe, and her father scoffed at the notion that Horace had either the will or the wits to take revenge on Rupert. That left some other adversary, a much more dangerous foe who had hidden his motives as well as his identity. How could they root out this stranger? Was it someone in Rupert's past? If so, he had better examine his transgressions, she decided firmly. She would not marry a man under the threat of death.

Joining the three men at the luncheon table, demurely gowned in a soft-peach muslin gown, Miranda was not surprised to see they were all in the best of spirits. No doubt her father's good humor could be traced to the generous settlement Rupert had promised. He had faults, but lack of generosity was not among them. Peter's amiability was more difficult to fathom. Could it be that he was relieved Miranda was marrying his uncle? Was he afraid that when the season ended she would hold him to his promise to marry her himself? Perhaps he had discovered that he really cared for Maria Henderson, and now he would be free to follow his heart. She hoped that was true, although she thought Peter too callow to wed anyone yet.

As for Rupert, his smugness could be laid to his satisfaction that once again he had triumphed. She wished she had the fortitude to refuse him just so that he would realize he could not always stampede through life taking what he wanted. But she had neither the strength nor the wish to thwart her own desires in order to score off him. Let him enjoy his victory for now. Later she would prove she was not a docile doll eager to obey his every dictate.

They lingered over the meal, discussing a date and location for the wedding, and Rupert insisted that time must be spared for Miranda to travel to his Wiltshire estates to look over her future home. All appeared to be marching well when Radleigh interrupted to announce a caller, "The Earl of Moresdale."

Although the earl had asked to see Miss Houghton, Rupert,

Peter, and certainly Adrian Houghton were each curious about the reclusive and irascible peer who had seen fit to seek out his granddaughter after years of neglect.

Miranda confided to Rupert as they trooped into the drawing room, "I must admit I am reluctant to see him. After all these years he has the effrontery to contact me! And he won't be pleased to see father. I really can't imagine what he hopes from this interview."

"Perhaps to give you his blessing now that you have contracted such an eligible alliance," Rupert said wryly, noting his fiancée's stubborn chin and sparkling eye. Whatever the earl expected, it was surely not this obstinate girl. The meeting should prove stormy, Rupert thought with unholy enjoyment.

"Just so. And if that is his reason, he will receive short shrift from me," Miranda promised, following Radleigh into the drawing room trailed by her three escorts.

The earl was standing by the tall windows overlooking the street and turned to greet the group, his eyes going immediately to Miranda. A tall, stooping man with thining white hair and thin features scored with harsh marks of either temper or pain, he was not an aimiable-looking man. His watery blue eyes raked over Miranda, giving her insult.

"Good afternoon. I take it you are my granddaughter. And who are these gentlemen? I did not ask to see them," he complained in a querulous voice.

"How do you do, sir? Yes, I am Miranda Houghton and this is Lord Hastings." She indicated Rupert, who stood at her side, and then introduced her father, who stared at the earl with an impassive face. "And Peter Worthington, whose mother is my hostess." She waited, offering no further explanation.

"I had hoped to see you alone," the earl replied rudely.

"Why, after all these years?" she asked, having no other question or commentary.

"Your grandmother is ill and she wants to make peace with your mother and father before she dies," he answered with a certain pathos.

But Miranda had hardened her heart. "I cannot see that any good would come of such a meeting. You and Lady Moresdale treated my mother and father in the most deplorable way; and now, because you are old and sick and probably lonely, you want to make reparation. Well, we don't need your sufferance," she said, not at all impressed.

"Can we not at least sit down and discuss it?" the earl pleaded, taken aback by this fierce girl who granted no mercy.

"Yes, of course. Miranda, it can do no harm to hear your grandfather. Have you no sympathy for his request?" Adrian Houghton interfered, although not surprisingly. It was to his advantage to placate the earl.

Miranda shrugged and seated herself on a settee, Rupert beside her. Observing her closed expression, Rupert felt some compunction, a fellow feeling for the old man who had surely not expected such a valiant spirit nor such immediate rejection.

"Have you any excuse for your wicked treatment of my mother just because she failed to marry a man you had chosen for her and followed her heart instead?" Miranda asked with a directness that the earl found patently startling.

"I was brought up to believe that children obeyed their parents and were guided by them when it came to selecting a life partner," the earl explained mildly.

"Guided, not forced," Miranda answered tersely with a telling look at her father, who reddened and turned away.

"We have been a bit obdurate, and I gather that Professor Houghton has made your mother a good husband." The earl obviously thought nothing of the sort but was prepared to make placating noises in pursuit of his goal.

"That is not the point. You had no right to coerce her.

Even if her choice was not to your taste and the marriage turned out unhappily, it was her decision to make. Why should she acquiesce to your desires for a match that satisfied your antiquated notions of propriety and ignored her own wishes?" Miranda refused to see any sense to her grandfather's arguments.

"But surely you are doing just what you decry in your mother," the earl offered slyly, intimating that Miranda was marrying for prestige and wealth rather than any softer emotion.

"Not at all. I am quite besotted with Lord Hastings," Miranda blurted out in her fury.

"Thank you, my dear. That does reassure me," Rupert interposed with irony.

"Anyway, the decision is not mine alone. If Father and Mother are generous enough to grant your request and meet with you after your despicable behavior, it is not for me to criticize them," Miranda conceded grudgingly. She did not like this haughty ill-tempered peer who, because he feared a lonely death, wanted to make tardy amends for his transgressions.

"I say, Miranda, you are being rather harsh," Peter interrupted, enthralled by this discussion of long-ago family differences.

"Yes, Miranda. If your mother can forgive her father—and, as you know, she is not of a vengeful disposition, I cannot see why you are so adamant." Adrian Houghton, not one to refuse a suggestion that might increase his own well-being, was appalled at Miranda's treatment of the earl.

"You may do what you wish, of course, Father, but I am not inclined to accept the earl's belated regrets."

"Since you refused my own guidance in the matter of a husband, I feel some sympathy for the earl's explanation," Adrian said boldly, but he should have known better.

"The situations are not parallel. And when it came to it, you were quite pleased to accept Rupert."

"Why do I feel I am a cardboard figure in this discussion, a man of no consequence? Really, Miranda, you treat me shockingly," Rupert grinned, enjoying the duel between his betrothed and the earl. The old man had not counted on such a rebellious granddaughter, expecting her to be overwhelmed by his magnaminity in tendering his apologies for a twenty-year rejection. There was not a whit to choose between them for obstinancy.

Then Miranda in a sudden *volte-face,* surrendered.

"Really, Rupert, you are ridiculous. Well, what does it matter? It does not concern me. If Mother and Father accept the earl's change of heart, then who am I to cavil? They must do as they want," she yielded, prepared to wash her hands of the whole unsavory business.

"Thank you, my dear," the earl said softly. "Do I take it, sir," he continued, turning to Adrian, "that you will bring Eleanor to her childhood home? My wife is unfit to travel."

"I suppose so. She will have to decide. Although I have been grievously wronged, I hold not a grudge against you, sir. And I am prepared to do the handsome thing and forgive you," Adrian said pompously, much to Miranda's disgust.

She stood up. "Then I shall leave you to discuss matters. Come, Peter and Rupert, we will leave them alone." Marshalling her escorts, she marched to the door and only then turning to bid her relatives a curt farewell.

"Really, Miranda, you quite frighten me. I hope you will deal more gently with my sins once you become Lady Hastings," Rupert observed as they walked across the hall.

"That depends on what they are. And it is not a matter for amusement, Rupert. The earl is a mean, ill-tempered old man who should pay for his neglect, not be welcomed as some kind of prodigal," Miranda was not chastened.

"Perhaps, but as a miserable sinner myself, I can only hope for your charity," Rupert replied soulfully.

Miranda laughed, her good temper restored. "You are not a bit like the earl, thank goodness."

"That's a generous assessment. Now, I must leave you as I have grave affairs to discuss with my solicitor. He's a tedious man but it's necessary for this business of our marriage. I will see you this evening. I believe we are going to the theatre," Rupert replied. And, paying no heed to a round-eyed Peter who was fascinated by Miranda's jousting with his usually arrogant uncle, he kissed her soundly and called for Radleigh, who was hovering nearby with his hat and and gloves. Before she could demur, he had taken his leave, and Peter and Miranda repaired to the morning room to discuss less controversial topics.

Rupert cared not one whit for the Earl of Moresdale's approval of Miranda's marriage, but he realized that his sister would be pleased at the connection. Charlotte had an inordinate concern for her social standing and one of the reasons she had signified her displeasure with Miranda had been because she felt the girl was little more than an adventuress. She should have known her brother well enough to understand that he gave no thought to the matter. His own standing was secure; and therefore, his wife, whoever she should be, would be equally accepted. However, if it made Miranda's lot easier, he was pleased to receive the earl's blessing.

Still, it was a warning that his volatile fiancée could not be easily coerced into a charitable view of a man's transgressions. He would have to walk carefully with her, but somehow that prospect did not depress him. There had been too many Chloes in his life, and he did not regret abandoning his pursuit of such light-minded women. That showed, he mused ruefully, how far gone he was. No doubt he would be an exemplar of the old saw that rakes made the most uxorious of husbands. He only wished that Miranda's confession to the earl that she was besotted with him were true. He was not at all convinced that she viewed him as little more than a sensible alliance. Well, he was still determined to change her mind.

Arriving at the office of his solicitor—a crusty, dyspeptic elderly gentleman, he was prepared for a long-winded discussion of settlements and boring legal demands. To his surprise, Robert Reith, the senior partner of Reith, Snyder and Reith, had some unusual news for him. Receiving Rupert with every sign of pleasure, Mr. Reith managed to convey that difficult decisions awaited his client's attention. Robert Reith had been privy to some dark secrets in the lives of his many distinguished clients, and the Hastings family was no exception.

After the formalities were observed, he eyed Rupert gravely, bringing his hands together and peering myopically over his high shirt points.

"Before we discuss the marriage settlements, there is another matter to attend to. Pursuant to your instructions, I have ascertained that this American, Mr. Cary, may have some claim upon you and the estate," he pontificated.

Rupert, rarely overset, found his worst suspicions confirmed. "How could that be, Reith? What has Cary to do with the Hastings?"

"You may recall that your grandfather had a younger brother, somewhat of an embarrassment to your great-grandfather and to the whole family. He was an inveterate gambler, libertine, and drunkard, I fear. Numerous times old Lord Hastings rescued him when he was in danger of succumbing to his sins. But finally, young Harry went too far. He forged his father's name on a draft from Child's Bank. Lord Hastings honored the draft but only under the condition that Harry leave the country. The young man emigrated to America, where he did not mend his ways, I regret to say. He married a young woman of dubious ancestry who served in a pub, and their son in turn behaved no better. The result of that union may have been Mr. Cary. My investigations have yet to confirm that fact, but if it is true, Cary would be your heir until you produce a son of your own," Reith concluded carefully, making no judgment on the follies of the noble family he served.

Rupert showed no surprise. "I wondered if that might be the case, although it seemed rather improbable. But if what you report is true, it might explain some of the attempts on my life. Naturally, if he is the heir, he would not want me to marry and produce a son."

"Exactly. It will take some time to verify this information, due to the distance from the colonies and the lamentable lack of reliable records. During the War for Independence, many proofs were lost or destroyed, but we have a basis to dispute his claim if he makes one. I find it remarkable that he has attained such a distinguished post within the American ministry. The Adamses are one of the most straitlaced and respectable of colonial families, with an irreproachable background. How could this young man have infiltrated the diplomatic corps so easily? Also he appears to have collected a suitable competence, with no hint of where the money came from. It's very puzzling." Reith, like most men of the law, did not like mysteries, particularly if they involved his clients.

"I wonder why he has not yet made a claim on the estate?" Rupert mused. "Why not just wait a suitable period until my demise and then produce his demands—insist on being hailed as the new Lord Hastings. You know, he gives the impression of being honest, aimiable, and completely respectable—necessary, I suppose, to play the role if he is to be believed."

"Do you think these recent attempts on your life can be traced to this young man?" Reith asked, as if murder were not unusual in noble families—as indeed his experience had shown it was not.

"Perhaps. It explains what has until now seemed quite enigmatic. I have enemies, no doubt, but not men prepared to go to these desperate lengths." If Rupert were appalled by these revelations he did not appear unduly afraid or even disturbed.

Reith, accustomed to the arrogance of the current Lord Hastings, might have expected such a reaction and his only reply was an noncommittal grunt. "Anything is possible, but murder is a bit drastic."

"But final. If I die before producing an heir, then he cops the lot," Rupert concluded succinctly.

"A regrettable conclusion but a sound one. Of course, you cannot have him apprehended without some proof of your suspicions," Reith warned, knowing that Rupert was capable of outrageous action quite outside the law.

"Now that I am on guard, I think Mr. Cary will find it more difficult to achieve his aims. And you must bestir yourself to arrange this marriage settlement. We have decided on September 16 as the date, which does not leave a great deal of time."

"Do be prudent, Lord Hastings," Reith warned, knowing Rupert's penchant for taking matters into his own hands, regardless of the risks involved. He distrusted his client's casual acceptance of his danger and he knew it would do little good to protest that perhaps an accomodation might be made to draw Cary's fangs. A settlement might dissipate the young man's ambitions, but he doubted Rupert would allow such a tame solution to the problem.

"Oh, I will, Reith. Never fear, I will handle Mr. Cary to my satisfaction. Now let us get down to more important matters. Not only the settlement must be decided, and a generous one to be sure, but would you arrange to have the family jewels retrieved from the bank, cleaned, and reset where appropriate? They will adorn the future Lady Hastings admirably," he ordered coolly, weary of discussing Cary and his fate.

"Yes, of course, my lord. And may I tender my sincere congratulations on your upcoming nuptials." Reith understood that Rupert would neither confide his plans for Cary nor entertain any suggestions as to how he might deal with that gentleman. Reith had long experience of the Hastings family, and he thought Mr. Cary had best beware, although, of course, he did not voice his thoughts and fears. Reith and Rupert parted with expressions of esteem on both sides, but as Rupert left the office, Reith wondered what would be the result of his disclosures.

Chapter Nineteen

The announcement that the marriage of Lord Rupert Hastings and Miss Miranda Houghton would be solemnized September 16 in St. Margaret's, Westminster, duly appeared in the *Gazette* a few days after Rupert's interview with Robert Reith. The Earl of Moresdale had signified that he would open his Berkeley Square house, whose tenants providentially had given up their lease, to host the reception following the ceremony. His wife evidently felt well enough to come to London, probably made energetic by the prospect of reconciling with her daughter and son-in-law. The family arrangements appeared satisfactory. Even Charlotte was pleased.

Rupert, however, was wary. Would the approach of the wedding force his enemy out into the open, inspire him to try once again to remove the obstacle to his own succession to the Hastings title and estate? Rupert had not yet mentioned to Miranda his suspicions that Randolph Cary was the culprit. She might think jealousy impelled him. He doubted if she would accept Cary's guilt without proof and corroboration was not available. Short of his own demise at Cary's hands, what could he offer? Somehow he could not imagine the affable and charming Cary commiting such a crime and the idea of Cary, who professed to care for Miranda, attempting to smear her through those odious letters was improbable. If he were the instigator of that scurrilous attempt to discredit Miranda and force Rupert to break the engagement, his acting was worthy of Drury Lane. Well, the next few weeks should settle the matter.

And tonight, Rupert vowed to take steps to discover more of the man he believed wanted to kill him. He was escorting Miranda to a diplomatic reception at Lord and Lady Castlereagh's St. James Square house this evening with only one object in mind, to have a quiet word with John Quincy Adams about Cary. Normally he found such receptions dreary, but he had a purpose for attending this one.

Miranda, despite her preoccupation with the dramatic decision she had taken to marry Rupert, had not abandoned her concerns about the murderous attacks upon him. She had decided, as he had, that the letters, which had failed to achieve the end their writer had hoped, were aimed at him. He had failed to cast her off and now the date was set. Would the attacks resume? She recognized that Rupert had come to some decision about the perpetrator but was unwilling to confide in her. Would tonight's reception answer some of his questions, and would someone he suspected be there? Determined to learn what he had discovered, she confronted him with her worries.

"I wish you would share what you know with me," she said, unable to read his expression in the shrouded twilight that darkened the carriage.

Rupert sighed. He might have known he could not fob her off with some specious excuse. "My dear, if this uncanny ability of yours to read my mind is an omen for our future life together, it quite terrifies me. Can I have no secrets?" he jested. She looked so young, so expectant, so beautiful, in an apricot, figured-silk gown which showed off her creamy skin and her sparkling eyes that he forgot for a moment the danger which threatened him. He drew her close and kissed her, but she responded with less than her usual ardor.

Looking up at him, she broke the caress and insisted "That's all very well, but do not change the subject. You have some ploy in mind. I can tell."

"You won't like it," he answered ruefully, realizing he must tell her something of his suspicions.

"I don't like the thought of your being shot, garroted, bludgeoned, or killed either," she responded huffily. "I have become very fond of you," she admitted reluctantly, not eager to give him the satisfaction of knowing how he could arouse her.

"Fond. How tame. I must see if I can't improve on that tepid feeling." And, ignoring her protests, he proceeded to show her just how far from tepid were the responses he could evoke.

Gasping for breath, blushing, and confused, she finally drew away. "You must stop this. I will be completely disheveled when we reach the Castlereagh's. And you have not answered my question."

"You distracted me," he pouted. Then, seeing her set chin and the darkening storm in her eyes, he surrendered. "All right. My solicitor, Robert Reith, thinks the attacks on me are the work of some long-lost heir who will benefit by my removal."

"Long-lost heir! I thought you had no relations but Lady Worthington and Peter, and surely *he* entertains no evil intentions toward you," she protested, shocked by Rupert's bald announcement.

"Certainly not Peter. No, this mysterious heir can be traced back to my uncle who emigrated to the colonies under a cloud, married, and probably produced a son, who—if he can prove his claim—would be my natural heir until *I* have a son. I understand he was an incredible dissolute."

"Dissolute. It must run in the family," she responded caustically.

"Really, Miranda, when will you abandon this picture of

me as a ranging libertine up to all sorts of japes? No, if it is true and this cousin exists and is in London, he might have decided to remove me and claim the title and estates," he ended with a serious tone to his voice which quite alarmed her.

"But surely he would be the first to be suspected," she replied, not convinced.

"Oh, I think he would be too clever to submit his claim the moment I am in the tomb. No doubt he would wait a suitable interval and, with expressions of regret, come forth to lay his affidavits before Reith, my solicitor."

"You have a fair idea of who it might be," Miranda concluded shrewdly.

"Possibly. But I will accuse no one until I have proof. Let's forget it for now. We are almost at the door, and I wish you would take that frantic expression off your face. Our noble hosts will suspect me of bullying you."

"And you do," Miranda agreed, not at all mollified, but so busy turning over the disturbing news in her mind she barely heeded him. Before she could argue further, the carriage drew to a stop and the footman appeared to let down the steps.

"Don't be surprised at Lady Castlereagh, Miranda. She is a true eccentric, not at all like her elegant husband. Overdressed, fat, and capable of the most *outré* behavior, like wearing her husband's Order of the Garter in her hair. She fusses over him, but he treats her with the utmost courtesy, probably because she never produced a child and he knows it is a continual sorrow."

"This emphasis on heirs is a curse of the *ton*," Miranda replied sharply as they entered the hall of the ornate mansion.

Making her courtesies to Lady Castlereagh, Miranda could barely repress a giggle. She was indeed a ridiculous figure. Her voluminous purple-satin gown and matching turban lavishly adorned with jewels struck a bizarre note. Especially as her urbane and fastidious husband, apparently impervious to her costume, looked every inch the impeccable peer.

The Egyptian-styled drawing room was crowded with guests as they entered, but they were signaled out immediately by the Egertons, who asked them about their approaching nuptials. Several other notable members of the *ton* also gathered around, and they were soon the center of interest. Although Miranda enjoyed being the object of such gratifying and kind approval, evidence that the letters had been discounted, she had not forgotten the conversation in the coach. Somewhere in this fashionable crowd was the man Rupert thought responsible for the threats on his life. He must be a consummate actor to hide his real motives, she thought, even as she parried a jocular remark from Lord Alvaney.

After a while, Rupert, seeing that she was safely under the aegis of Francey Egerton, excused himself and sought out the reason for his attending this dreadful squeeze.

John Quincy Adams, the son of America's second president, was a prim puritan but an excellent diplomat who spoke several languages. Educated in the courts of Europe, he was not a really likable man but rather an estimable one. He stood surveying the company with an air of aloofness. He did not enjoy such occasions. His preference was for solitary study, scientific experiment, and poetry. His one indulgence was the theatre, proving his was a personality of irreconcilable tastes. He had failed to marry his first love and settled for a southern belle, Louisa Johnson, a nervous and gloomy woman, and completely inappropriate as the wife of a diplomat. She had not accompanied him this evening, preferring to remain in the ministry and nurse her neuroses.

As Rupert approached America's minister to the Court of St. James, he noticed that Adams had attracted the attention of the Iron Duke. Wellington disliked revolutionaries of all types, and Rupert wondered why he would speak with Adams for the duke viewed Americans especially as colonial upstarts. Rupert had no hesitation in breaking in on their conversation.

Wellington hailed him with measured enthusiasm. "Ah, Hastings, I hear you are to be married shortly. Has to come to us all, my boy. Do you know Mr. Adams, America's minister?" he asked politely.

"We have met," Adams replied tersely.

"Hastings was on my staff in the Peninsula, a doughty fighter and a good strategist," Wellington explained kindly.

"Thank you, sir. I sometimes miss those days."

"Well, you are now about to enter the marital arena," Wellington quipped. "I think your wife will be an ornament to society. You are a fortunate chap." Knowing that the Duchess and Wellington were far from compatible, Rupert did not overlook the element of envy in his former chief's congratulations.

"Marriage can be a man's best refuge," Adams interposed priggishly.

"Yes, indeed. Oh, there is Sidmouth. Must have a word with him," Wellington said. Having done his duty, he was now eager to be gone. Rupert made no effort to detain him. Since they were in a sheltered alcove removed from the press of guests, he was anxious to quizz Adams about Cary but did not want the Iron Duke to overhear. As soon as Wellington had left them, he wasted no time in coming to the point.

"I wanted to ask you, Mr. Adams, about a member of your staff."

Adams, always quick to take affront, did not like the tone of this arrogant peer. The English could be oblivious to the niceties of diplomatic conversation when it suited them, he thought.

"I do hope no one has given offense, my lord," he answered stiffly.

"On the contrary. We have been seeing quite a bit of young Cary, an estimable young man I am sure. But I wondered

203

about his background. He has managed to be received everywhere," Rupert challenged boldly.

"I see no reason why he should not be," Adams replied severely. He did not like this implication against a member of his staff.

But Rupert was not deterred. "Not at all. I am sure he is a credit to the ministry. I only wondered because my fiancée sees quite a lot of him. They enjoy sight-seeing together."

"Mr. Cary was recommended by his Cary and Carter relatives, all of the most highly regarded families in Virginia. We like to have a representative group of our fellow citizens in our ministries. Since I am myself from New England, I have to rely on my southern colleagues to propose suitable candidates. Mr. Cary does his work well and is a great aid in helping us understand English society," Mr. Adams clarified in a tight voice.

He resented exceedingly being quizzed by a member of that society, and one of the reasons he left much of this sort of thing to young sprigs like Cary was because he found it distasteful to defend himself and his country to the nobility. Despite his long years in European courts he remained a puritan and a republican, not at all impressed by the decadent life around him. He hoped to return home soon and take a position in the Cabinet, much more to his liking.

Rupert, well-aware of Adams' view of the Prince Regent and the sophisticated courtiers who surrounded him, wondered if there was much more to be gained from Adams.

"And do you now understand English society, Mr. Adams?" Rupert questioned, unable to resist twitting the minister.

"Well enough, Lord Hastings," Adams replied shortly.

"I wonder. Our former colonies judge us quite harshly, I think. Deservedly so, perhaps, but it is daunting nonetheless. Still, you have reassured me about Cary."

Adams remained silent and Rupert, seeing no more was to

be gleaned, bade him a polite farewell. Frustrated by his abortive questioning of the American minister, he sought out Miranda and was not pleased to see her talking animatedly with the object of his investigation. He crossed the room toward them.

"Ah, good evening, Cary. I have been chatting with your chief, an uncommunicative type," Rupert complained as he joined them.

"He's really a good sort, but not as jovial as Virginians. I was just telling Miranda I wish she could visit my home. Southern hospitality is lavish, not at all restrained as in the cool North, where the citizens are a bit aloof. I think the climate freezes our New England compatriots," Cary explained cheerfully.

"And where in Virginia is your home?" Rupert asked, determined to find some clue to Cary's background.

"In the Tidewater. My parents have a small tobacco plantation, but quite a charming house," Cary answered, apparently eager to confide.

"They are both alive, then. You are fortunate. My parents have been dead many years and I have few relatives, only Lady Worthington, my sister, and her son Peter."

Miranda, who had remained silent during this exchange as she was a bit puzzled by Rupert's insistent probing, now turned to Cary with a smile. "Are you ever homesick?"

"Sometimes, but you all have been so kind to me. I wonder why my fellow countrymen find so many of the English standoffish. That has not been my experience at all," Cary said in that ingratiating manner which was beginning to rub Rupert's sensibilities.

"Ah, but your charm melts the heart of the most reserved matron and the haughtiest gentleman," Rupert answered with an implication Miranda found patronizing.

"We are delighted you are here, Randolph," she affirmed, irked by Rupert's attitude.

"Yes, indeed, Cary, and I hope you will still be here for our wedding next month," Rupert beamed. The American made no response to that remark except a pleasant acknowledgement. If he were indeed the man who planned Rupert's demise, he was a clever dissembler, more than able to parry Rupert's thrusts. How in the world was he to force Cary into the open? Surely the man, if he had drastic action in mind, could not delay much longer. His earlier failed attempts must be frustrating, and the next time he needed to succeed if his plan were to be accomplished. If Rupert had doubts about the agreeable American, this conversation had not vanquished them. He was still convinced that Cary had designs on his life.

As if bored with this sparring, he turned to Miranda and suggested they leave. "I find these crushes wearisome, and since, unlike Cary, I have no duty to perform, I believe we can make our polite *adieux* without causing comment."

Miranda, wondering if Rupert had suddenly come to dislike Cary, acceded and they paid their respects to the Castlereaghs and departed.

In the carriage on the way back to Mount Street, she asked him, "Are you annoyed with Randolph for some reason, Rupert?"

"Not at all, my dear, just a bit mystified by his reticence," Rupert replied, not ready to voice his suspicions to Miranda. She was too acute and already sensed that he had reservations about Cary.

"I find him very open and confiding. I suppose, though, he finds it difficult to explain his Virginia life to us. It's so different from ours."

"I am sure it is that," Rupert agreed dryly. "Let us forget the young man. He is becoming a thorn in my side."

Miranda, realizing that Rupert would not be pressed further, turned the conversation to the plans for the wedding. With an effort Rupert followed her lead, but she felt his mind

206

was elsewhere. Could he be regretting his decision to marry her? Perhaps he had hoped she would be persuaded by Cary that she was making a grievous mistake and the fact that the young American had not pushed his own desire to wed her disappointed him. But, after all, Rupert has been the one to insist on marriage. She felt a hollow, sinking feeling in her stomach. She might love this complex man, but she was neither sure he felt any such emotion for her nor convinced he was not trying to find an excuse to jilt her. Of course, a gentleman could not cry off. Was he just doing the polite thing and hoping to force her into breaking the engagement? It had begun for the most cynical of reasons, and they had not intended for it to end at the altar. Events had rather pushed them into this alliance. Confused and unhappy, Miranda turned to Rupert.

"It's not too late to cancel the wedding, my lord, if that is your wish," she said stiffly.

"Oh, dear, when you call me *my lord* in that menacing way, I know I have offended again. Believe me, Miranda, I have no intention of letting you escape. You have promised to marry me on September 16 with all suitable ceremony and I will hold you to it."

"I wonder why," she questioned, "when you appear to find the prospect daunting."

"What I find daunting is your refusal to believe I think marriage between us would be of benefit to us both. And then there is this strong affinity. You are a bit of a minx, Miranda. And there is but one answer to that."

As the carriage turned into Mount Street and swerved to avoid an oncoming vehicle, he took her in his arms and proceeded to quiet her doubts in the only way he knew. As she surrendered to his arousing hands and mouth, she abandoned all efforts to protest the wisdom of their marriage. As long as he could make her respond in this reckless fashion, she could not fight him—no matter how much she tried to hold on to her resolution.

Alas, she thought, she would be that poor specimen, a girl madly in love with a husband who entertained only the most physical desire for her. And she had not the courage to refuse him. It certainly did not bode well for their future together.

Chapter Twenty

Rupert might have believed his questioning of John Quincy Adams had produced few answers, but he would have been surprised that his probing had raised some questions in the minister's mind. The day after the Castlereagh reception, Adams called Cary into his office.

"Yes, sir, you wished to see me?" Cary appeared ever-obliging.

"Have you done something to offend Lord Hastings?" Adams queried his second secretary bluntly. "I don't care for the man myself, but he is not without influence with members of the government, Wellington and Palmerston for example. He asked me some impertient questions about you."

"On the contrary, I thought we were friends," Cary replied, giving Adams a limpid look.

"Could you perhaps have been too assiduous to his fiancée? She is a very attractive girl and I can understand you would find her appealing, but it would not do to irritate Hastings with your attentions. As you know, I am trying to sort out some rather vexing trade matters between our two countries. It will not help our relationship, tenuous at best, if one of my staff causes problems."

"Miss Houghton is a friend, nothing more. She was already engaged when I met her or perhaps I might have pursued her—with only the most honorable intentions. But that was never a possibility," Cary explained guilelessly.

"Well, I would walk warily with Hastings. He seems suspicious of you for some reason."

"I regret exceedingly if I have caused you any embarrassment, Mr. Adams. You have always been kind to me, encouraging and regarding my work here with approval. I assure you I have no fell designs on Miss Houghton." Cary faced his chief, candor glowing from his youthful face.

"You Virginians are much too charming; but although that is an asset which has served you well, it can also be misinterpreted. It might be best if you put some distance between yourself and Hastings and his fiancée."

Cary, eager to disclaim any accusation of philandering, agreed quickly. "Of course, sir. I understand. I would do nothing to endanger your negotiations."

"That is all, Cary. I would not have badgered you if I were not worried about these trade talks." Adams dismissed him, feeling his warning had been taken.

Cary smiled ingratiatingly and took his leave; but once outside Adams' office, a calculating cast darkened his blue eyes. Damn it, he had almost queered his pitch. If he were sent home now, it would be disastrous, as close to his goal as he was. He must act decisively and resolve his dilemma, or all his plans would be foiled. And he had come too far to turn back now. Shaking off a sensation of impending doom, he pondered his next move. He had considered every angle of his deception and, until today, had believed all was marching well. If Adams' suspicions were aroused and he contacted his Virginia friends, it might cause trouble. He could wait no longer. He must act and this time succeed. Frowning with unusual ferocity, Cary retreated to his own office and brooded over the next step in the intricate plot to achieve his long-held desires.

For the next few days Miranda's uneasiness about her up-coming nuptials and Rupert's impatience with Reith's investigation of Cary's duplicity were tempered by the rush of festivities honoring the couple. Rupert came in for some good-natured teasing from his contemporaries and Miranda for some ill-concealed jealousy from young women who envied her good fortune. She wondered bitterly if they realized how insecure and apprehensive she felt. But she knew that for many of them the capture of a husband was the vital task, unsullied by worries of how the marriage would develop. Miranda had not enjoyed the advantage of living in a household where her parents loved and respected one another. She had watched her mother defer to her father, apologize, and cajole, all the while fearing his displeasure whether she were at fault or not. Rupert's forceful personality might offer similar dangers, but Miranda had no intention of following her mother's path. How foolish women were, victims of their affections completely at the mercy of the men they chose, while the men had other pursuits—business, property, clubs, and, alas, other women.

Miranda was not prepared to play the role of a subservient wife, content to let her husband go his heedless way. She craved a loving companion, a partner in life's journey, and she doubted very much that Rupert had the qualities to conform to such an ideal. Unfortunately, like thousands of other foolish girls, she had fallen in love, and that prevented her from using what common sense she had. Reviewing her options, Miranda decried her inability to refuse this man. It would serve him right if she cried off at the last moment and left him standing at the altar. But she knew she would never have the courage to refuse a chance at happiness, even if it were only the slimmest of chances.

On Rupert's part, he had determined to make Miranda admit she cared for him before the vows were spoken. The danger represented by Cary, if he were indeed the unknown attacker, receded somewhat as the day of the wedding drew near. But Rupert was not convinced that the villain had abandoned his plotting. Why didn't the man just confront Rupert with proof of his paternity and make a claim on the Hastings? Surely he realized Rupert would not ignore his right to a settlement? Not particularly blessed with a charitable view of his fellow man, still Rupert found it surprising that the man would go to such lengths to achieve his ambition. On the surface he appeared to have a respectable competence, a satisfying career, and a position of some prominence. Why would he take a chance on sacrificing all that in order to become Lord Hastings, especially if it involved murder? Having always been used to privilege, it was difficult for Rupert to understand such unholy desires.

Well, somehow he must resolve the problem of Cary, and he felt that he could not enlist Miranda's aid in view of her own feeling for the young man. His decision not to confide in her was a detriment to their relationship, and he feared she suspected his reserve meant his commitment to her was less strong than it should have been. What a coil! He must sort out this Cary business before the vows were spoken.

They had not seen much of the young man lately, which Rupert thought a boon for he did not quite know how he would behave if he should encounter him. So it was with annoyance that he noticed Cary at White's, where he had gone to lunch with Marcus. Cary obviously did not share his uneasiness for he greeted Rupert with his usual affability. He crossed the room to the pair as they were finishing their Stilton and a bottle of port.

"Good afternoon, Rupert and Sir Marcus. I have been meaning to contact both of you. I want to repay the generous hospitality so many of my friends here have offered and thought a picnic in Richmond Park might be suitable. Would

212

you be agreeable?" Cary asked them accepting their invitation to join them in a glass and settling into a chair at the table.

"I am not fond of dining *al fresco,* but I suppose Miranda might enjoy it," Rupert admitted grudgingly. He questioned what lay behind this gambit. Giving his attention to Cary, whose guileless face appeared to hide no evil intent, he found it difficult to believe this candid young man could be plotting his death.

Sir Marcus accepted happily and then engaged Cary in a discussion of an upcoming race at Newmarket. "Have you placed a bet on the favorite?" he asked, drawing him into an animated analysis of the horses while Rupert brooded, unable to accept that his suspicions had any basis in fact. Marcus, puzzled over his friend's reluctance to accept Cary's friendly overtures, valiantly covered Rupert's silence with his own spate of gossip. Could Rupert have taken Cary in dislike because of his attentions to Miranda? This was a conundrum, but Marcus employed his usual tact.

"Tell me, Cary, how do you find relations between our two countries now? Has the recent unpleasantness been relegated to the past? Do your compatriots still resent their former masters?" Rupert asked, determined to goad Cary into some honest opinion. The man was too unctuous by half—always obliging, never expressing any irritation or awareness that his country's one-time enemies might not regard him kindly.

"Well, there remains some resentment over the impressment of our seamen and a residue of dislike from the war, but that is mostly confined to the common folk. Our statesmen and merchants regard England as a bastion against the autocrats of Europe. No, I can honestly say relations are pleasant," he answered fulsomely.

"Yes, many of America's most prominent men have English connections. That would incline them to view us favorably," Rupert interjected. Would Cary acknowledge the allusion?

He did not. Instead, he rose, renewing his offer of the picnic. "I will arrange a charming *fête de compagne,* I think, and let you both know the date shortly. You have all been so hospitable I must make my long deferred return," he insisted, and, bowing, exited their company.

Marcus turned a searching eye on his friend. "What's going on, Rupert? Have you become annoyed with young Cary for some reason?"

"Yes, a very good reason. I think he is behind those attacks upon me," Rupert said bluntly, needing to confide in his friend and knowing he could rely on his discretion.

Marcus could not believe his ears. "Why would you suspect him? A nicer young man I have yet to meet. Surely he is not so enamoured with Miranda he would descend to such despicable behavior?" He thought Rupert had maggots in his head. None of their acquaintances was less likely to be a murderer than Randolph Cary.

"Reith thinks he might be, due to some suspicion about his background. What do we really know about him, after all? Just that he is a gentleman with an engaging manner and a position at the American ministry," Rupert argued.

"Surely Adams would not employ a charleton," Marcus objected.

"Not wittingly, despite his scorn of the English; but Reith believes Cary may be the Hastings' long-lost heir. The whole thing reeks of a gothic novel. Still, there is reason to suspect him. Naturally, if he is the unknown inheritor, he will not want me to marry. He tried to detach Miranda with his winning ways, and when that failed I suspect he decided to remove me before I could marry and have a son." Rupert spoke with a conviction that assured Marcus he was quite serious.

"Have you investigated the possibility of his having a claim? I know if it were proven you would do something for him. And why in heaven's name would he want to kill you?"

"Because he wants to be Lord Hastings, not just some

hanger-on. I doubt his modest estate in Virginia can compete with Hastings Halt. If he has inveigled his way into our circle in order to rid himself of any obstacle to owning the Hastings' assets, he would act cleverly. And I think he is a champion dissembler. What at first appears to be a pleasant, charming personality could well hide a villain of the worst type. I no longer trust him but can think of no way to force his hand," Rupert said in perplexity.

Seeing that his friend was troubled, Marcus refrained from further argument. But he had the utmost doubts.

"So you think he tried to shoot you in my woods and as you crossed Hampstead Heath? Have you tried to discover his whereabouts during those two episodes?"

"No, and I doubt I could find any conclusive evidence. Reith is trying to track his antecedents in America, but that takes time and I am not sure I can afford the delay. My wedding is but three weeks away. Surely he will try to take some action before the vows are said."

"You know I can't believe this tale; it is so outrageous, and there is no hint of any villainy in his manner. He would have to be an incredible actor to deceive us all." Marcus, shocked by these revelations, had to discount such a bizarre state of affairs. He prided himself on his judgment of men and could not accept that he had been so mistaken. All along he had felt Rupert, for all his reputation as an experienced charmer of women, had suffered real jealousy over Cary's attentions to Miranda. Could he have lost his usual imperturbability and his good sense in the face of this most turbulent of passions?

"I know it sounds most improbable, Marcus, but I am beginning to surmise it is the only answer. What puzzles me is how I can deal with it. Should I confront him with what I suspect? I tried to draw Adams out about Cary, but he has accepted him in good faith and would not be influenced by any aspersions on the young man's character. He probably assumes me an arrogant peer jealous of Cary's attractions. Not

215

so amazing, as I think you are inclined that way yourself, old fellow," Rupert suggested, not unaware of the tenor of Marcus' ruminations.

"If this is at all true, how can you confront him? He will only deny it and you will feel a veritable fool without having accomplished much. Perhaps he has decided, in view of two aborted attempts, to abandon his vile intentions—if indeed he were the culprit."

"You know, Marcus, it is not that I lack courage or that I fear for my life, it is the duplicity of it all that vexes me. Why wouldn't the fool declare himself and put forth his claim? He must be eaten up with ambition, and I am damned if I know how to counter his ploys or what to expect next. Not a condition for a happy bridegroom."

"Have you told Miranda of your suspicions?" Marcus queried with import.

"No, and I won't. What would be gained even if she believed me? She would worry about what would happen to me, at least I hope she would. And besides, she likes Cary. She might think I was behaving like a jealous lover, a pitiable picture."

Since this was what Marcus had thought, he could not disagree although now his opinion had altered. "Whatever you are, Rupert, you are not pitiable. I think you must flush this man into the open and give him the opportunity to work his nasty designs. Forewarned, you can take precautions."

"Rather like beating a game preserve, what?" Rupert observed dryly.

"No, rather more like anticipating your enemy's move and countering it. You had enough experience of that on the peninsula—with some success as I remember."

"Thank you, Marcus. You restore my faith. I will give it some thought, but somehow I fear he is several steps ahead of me. Rather a grim prospect. But enough of these wretched surmises. You are a good chap to listen to my meanderings.

216

Now let's forget it and have a game of *piquet*. I will beat you, and that will bolster my confidence."

Marcus laughed hollowly, but agreed. Not for one moment did he think Rupert would forget the threat that loomed over him, even if it seemed the wildest scheme. Marcus determined he would keep his own watch upon events, prepared to come to Rupert's aid if any further attacks threatened him, although he found the whole affair too incredible.

What bothered him most was Rupert's indecisiveness. Not like the chap to hesitate, usually he was too rash. The marriage must be behind it all. For the first time in his life Rupert must be genuinely in love, and now he saw the chance of happiness slipping from his grasp. Under a threat of death, how could he plan for the future or enjoy the felicity he deserved? In the past Rupert had not always behaved with propriety nor treated women as kindly as he might, but then never before had his emotions been involved. He was obviously deeply in love with Miranda, even if he had not admitted it to himself or Marcus, and this was clouding his normal ability to direct events.

Love was the devil, and other strong men had bowed before its demands. Marcus had faith that Rupert would come about, decide his destiny, and handle Cary. If that young man had another vile plot in his mind, he would find a formidable adversary in Rupert—and in Marcus himself.

Chapter Twenty-One

Miranda's mother and her brother, Robbie, arrived in London for the reunion with the Moresdales in their Berkeley Square mansion, encouraged by a complacent Adrian. Miranda was invited to join them until the wedding and, concluding that her mother needed her support and that Lady Worthington would be pleased to see her go, agreed.

When she explained the necessity, stressing the long overdue reconciliation to her hostess, she was surprised at Lady Worthington's reluctance to see her depart.

"I know at first I was not so overly welcoming, Miranda, and I regret that exceedingly. My brother is apt to set my back up with his various japes, and I thought there was something havey-cavey in this engagement," she admitted with engaging candor.

And so there was, Miranda corroborated silently. Before she could attempt any explanation, Lady Worthington hurried into her own excuses. "In the weeks you have been here I have been both relieved and delighted that all has worked out so well. There is little doubt in my mind that you are just the bride for my scapegrace brother and I think he truly cares for you. Whether he will be a good husband is another matter as he's too fond of having his own way with little consideration for others. But I am sure you can handle any disgressions firmly," she said, if not completely convinced.

Miranda smiled, following the direction of Charlotte's deliberation. "I am quite stubborn myself, a fault my parents have often complained of, and quite as strong-willed as Rupert. No doubt there will be fireworks," she admitted.

"Good," Lady Worthington approved, remembering her own contests with Rupert in which she had inevitably come out the loser. "And, Miranda, since we will now be sisters, you must call me Charlotte," she concluded nobly.

"Thank you, Charlotte. I appreciate your kindness to me. You have done all and more than anyone could ask of a chaperone and patronness. Without your acceptance I know that my introduction to society would have been a disaster, and your championship after that horrid affair of the letters was more than generous."

"I wonder who the author was. Have you no ideas on the subject?" Charlotte asked, eager to avoid anymore references to her original distrust of Miranda.

"Well, at first I thought it might be Mrs. Castleton, but Rupert appears to discount that theory. And then I suspected Horace Howland; but my father assures me that although Horace may be pettish and egotistical, he would never descend to such calumny. Too frightened of Rupert's revenge, I imagine. I can only conclude it must be the person who has attacked Rupert on two occasions."

Charlotte, who had not known of the attempts on her brother's life, looked aghast. "I knew he was hiding some grave matter from me. Is he in danger?"

Since Miranda thought it most unfair for Charlotte to be kept in ignorance of what was, after all, a family problem, she explained about the lost heir. As she expected, Charlotte rose in indignation, feeling that the information cast a slur on her beloved Peter.

"Does Rupert think that Peter, fearing he will not continue to enjoy Rupert's benevolence, was at the bottom of all this?"

"Not at all. We never considered Peter capable of such villainy for a moment. No, it is someone who has hidden his real identity in order to accomplish his evil ends."

"Oh, dear. This is most worrying. You know Rupert can be the most exasperating of men, but I am truly fond of him and would hate for him to be injured or worse."

"I know, Charlotte," Miranda consoled gently, her opinion of her sister-in-law much improved by this honest expression of her feelings for her brother.

Miranda's departure from the Mount Street house was deplored by Peter, who believed he was losing an ally against his mother's onerous demands. That feeling, however, was tempered by his relief that the mock engagement had turned out to be real. Like his mother, he had every faith that Miranda would handle Rupert gracefully and firmly. His surprise was that his uncle appeared to welcome these heretofore detested restraints on his freedom. But then Miranda was a Trojan, an unusual girl, much too mettlesome for him, but perfect for Rupert. Peter grinned when he thought of the ructions ahead.

The situation in Berkeley Square, although not entirely one of unalloyed cheerfulness, had settled into a benign acceptance of the *status quo*. Lord Moresdale, having made the first overture, was not inclined to go much further; but his wife—a gentle, ailing woman, rather like her daughter—was happy beyond belief to be reconciled with the Houghtons. For once, Adrian, sensing he could easily cause the truce to be upset, behaved with an unusual want of pomposity and selfishness, trying within his limits to tread carefully.

If Miranda's marriage was an occasion of gratification to the Moresdales, the presence of Robbie, their grandson, was a source of sublime happiness. A spirited boy and a handsome one, he was worthy of his grandparents' pride. He had the enviable ability to take life as he found it, with little sensitivity to slights and an abiding interest in all aspects of his existence. He highly endorsed Miranda's choice and regarded Rupert with awe, despite that gentleman's attempts to get on a more relaxed footing with him.

"I say, Miranda, Rupert is a great gun, you know, a member of the Four-in-Hand Club and a top-of-the-trees rider. And he has promised to take me to see the Bournemouth Bruiser fight next hols. Of course I could go before, if you were not to be away on your honeymoon," he complained as if this necessity was a ridiculous sop to tradition.

"Sorry about that, Robbie. But I am glad you approve." Miranda smiled at her brother and ruffled his hair in a gesture of sisterly affection. They had always been the best of friends, and if he had disapproved of Rupert, it would have caused her real pain. Not that she would have cancelled the vows. She realized every day, as the ceremony grew nearer, how much she wanted to become Rupert's wife. Not that she was yet prepared to admit such a lowering abject feeling to his lordship.

For the last few days she had seen very little of her fiancé, who had repaired to his estates to apprise his servants of the wedding and make preparations to receive his bride when they returned from the wedding journey. This weekend the Houghtons and the Moresdales would be Rupert's guests at Hastings Halt, and she would get her first glimpse of her future home. In the meantime she was occupied with her trousseau and listening to her mother's worries about this fashionable wedding.

On emerging from Mme. Berthe's salon one afternoon with her mother and waiting for their carriage to come down Bond Street, she met Randolph Cary, her first sight of him in some time. She introduced him to her mother, before whom he bowed deeply. He smiled and made a flattering remark about the resemblance between Miranda and her parent.

"I think Lord Hastings may have mentioned that I am planning a picnic in Richmond Park soon. I hope you and your family will do me the honor of accepting my invitation," he said with gallantry.

"We are going down to the country for the weekend to visit Rupert's estates. He is there now making preparations for the descent of all our relations, but I am sure when he returns, if there is time before the ceremony, we will be delighted to accept."

"Yes, indeed, Mr. Cary," Eleanor Houghton agreed, approving of this genial young man with such charming manners. She wondered for a fleeting moment why Miranda had preferred the rather formidable Rupert to this very agreeable and handsome American. It was obvious he admired her daughter exceedingly.

They parted with expressions of approval on both sides, and, as Miranda and her mother rode down Bond Street toward Berkeley Square, Eleanor Houghton professed herself quite taken with Cary.

"What a delightful man! And an American, so polished and yet unassuming. Have you known him long?" she asked.

"Since I first came to London. He squired me about a great deal, sight-seeing, but always with the utmost propriety. I was already engaged to Rupert, you understand," Miranda explained wryly, having a very good idea of the direction of her mother's thoughts.

"And did Lord Hastings approve?" Mrs. Houghton knew that, whether he did nor not, her daughter would have followed her own inclinations.

"Oh, yes. He liked Randolph, how could one not? But I think he has rather gone off him lately. I don't know why." Miranda spoke idly, but realized with her words that indeed Rupert did seem to have abandoned his initial approval of the young American. In the beginning he had been amused rather than annoyed by Cary's conspicuous interest in Miranda.

222

Lately that reaction had changed. Miranda could only hope, echoing her mother's musings, that jealousy was at the root of his altered attitude. Hope she might; but, knowing Rupert, she doubted that such an emotion was one he had ever suffered. She rather enjoyed the image of Rupert pricked by love's arrow. It was such a ridiculous picture, she almost laughed out loud.

"In some ways he appears a very suitable *parti,* this Mr. Cary," Mrs. Houghton suggested.

"Perhaps, but I have made my choice," Miranda insisted. Then acknowledging her mother's concern, she added, "I know Rupert appears arrogant, formidable, and even cynical at times. Indeed, he is all of those things. But I do care for him. You cannot imagine how much, not that I am prepared to admit that to him just yet," she concluded wryly.

"If you believe you and Rupert can be happy together, it does not matter how your relationship appears to others, even your parents. Certainly you are not without faults yourself," Mrs. Houghton offered briskly. "However, we were wrong to try and persuade you to accept Horace Howland—and not just from a worldly point of view. He could never adjust to a girl with your spirit and independence. I blame myself for not being more courageous, but I was so worried about Adrian. In truth, Horace is quite an old maid," she admitted. Returning to the real issue, she added, "Marriage is a gamble, but entering into it without love would be unsupportable."

Her spirits restored by her mother's frank admissions, Miranda abandoned her own doubts. Whatever the outcome, she was committed to Rupert. There would be shoals ahead, but her mother's words had reassured her. Grateful yet reluctant to discuss her own chaotic emotions, she turned the conversation to the wedding plans.

* * *

Miranda's first view of Hastings Halt overwhelmed her. The great Palladian house, designed by Inigo Jones on the site of an earlier, less impressive, Elizabethan moated-castle, lay on a slight rise reached by a long avenue lined with lime trees. At first glance Miranda's heart sank. How could she ever preside over such an imposing house? And also play hostess to the distinguished guests who were accustomed to the most sophisticated and elegant of entertainments? Her apprehension, added to the welter of emotions the upcoming marriage to Rupert inspired, clouded her first impressions; and her welcome to Rupert was more angry than affectionate. She might love him, but at times she disliked him. Here she was with stiff grandparents, a sycophantic father, and a shrinking-violet mother, each of them with private motives for encouraging this alliance. What about her own fears and expectations? Every time she implied to Rupert that she was filled with doubts, he ridiculed her reservations with his usual condescension.

With uncharacteristic geniality, he came out onto the steps at the approach of the carriage to welcome his guests. Miranda, watching him play the urbane host, wanted to give him a resounding whack. Had he so little sensitivity that he did not realize that Hastings Halt overwhelmed her? She averted her face when it appeared he might give her a warm greeting and scowled at him, her irritation getting the best of her. Rupert, not as unaware as she supposed, cocked his head appraisingly, and murmured into her ear, "Now what wild idea are you entertaining and what sin have I committed to earn such scorn?"

"It's all this," Miranda complained. Her hand trembled as she indicated the scurrying servants unloading luggage, the broad facade of the house, and the general formality of her arrival at the grand habitation that was to become her home and domain. Lord Hastings had drawn together inside the entrance hall a veritable battery of servants, eager to anticipate every wish of the guests.

The Moresdales, well-accustomed to such ways, paid little heed to the retinue, and Adrian Houghton, preening, tried unsuccessfully to hide his awe. His wife, tired from the journey, gratefully accepted Rupert's offer to have the housekeeper take her directly to her room. Lady Moresdale also professed a need for a period of respite. Miranda, dazed by the feverish activity, was relieved to see Charlotte advancing across the wide marble hall to join Rupert.

"Charlotte, how nice to see you." Miranda's greeting to her former hostess was far more effusive than to her fiancé, a disparity not unremarked by Rupert. Whenever he absented himself from Miranda for any length of time, her defenses went up and he had to persuade her that this marriage was not the dubious prospect she feared.

How long would it be before she did not need his reassurance that all would be well and, if not blissful, at least bearable? He sensed that her initial opinion of him as Peter's wicked ogre of an uncle had never been completely eradicated. Well, he had made his choice and bullied her into accepting him, so what else could he expect? The unhappy idea that she might never really trust and love him for a moment darkened his wish that she might enjoy this first view of her future home and come to feel for it what he did. Rupert truly loved his estates—although he would never be so gauche as to admit it—and he wanted Miranda to share his pride and respect for the house, his tenants, and the vast acreage which he oversaw with scrupulous attention. He never thought of Hastings Halt as just a rent roll to support his London life. But he would not plead for her affection either for himself or his home.

Whatever Miranda's shortcomings in terms of effusive regard, her father more than made up for them. His enthusiastic praise was an embarrassment to her, although Rupert accepted each tribute with polite gentility. She was happy to escape with Charlotte to view her own bedroom, leaving the gentlemen alone. She turned as they mounted the broad marble stairs and looked down on the company, startled to see Rupert watching her somewhat mournfully. Aware of her glance, he bowed and shot her a meaningful glance. Although she made no acknowledgment, her heart lifted and she felt reassured.

The visit which had begun so inauspiciously for Miranda surprisingly became a relaxed and pleasant experience. Intimidated by the regal housekeeper, Mrs. Clemson, she found that lady anxious to please and proud to escort her about the house, introducing her to the kitchen larders, linen closets, and still rooms.

"May I say on behalf of the staff and myself, Miss Houghton, how happy we are to welcome Lord Hastings' bride-to-be. We have all hoped he would wed and are delighted he chose such a charming and attractive girl," Mrs. Clemson said in her queenly manner.

"Thank you, Mrs. Clemson. I do hope I will suit and that you will all help me to adjust to my responsibilities here," Miranda replied, realizing that she must enlist Mrs. Clemson's aid and win her approval if her life at Hastings Halt was to progress smoothly. She needed Mrs. Clemson to teach her the ways of this great *ménage*.

"You will find it not so imposing once you have become accustomed to it, Miss Houghton." Like all well-trained upper servants, Mrs. Clemson had taken Miranda's measure at once. The girl was a lady, granddaughter of an earl, but not accustomed to the high position she would be expected to assume with ease and style. Lord Hastings was a fair master but a strict one. His households had to be run competently and smoothly. Her sympathies engaged, Mrs. Clemson decided she would cooperate with her new and inexperienced mistress and see to it she learned her responsibilities quickly.

Miranda, grateful for Mrs. Clemson's welcome, realized she had gained an ally. She had a shrewd suspicion of the housekeeper's assessment of her and agreed with it. But if Mrs. Clemson liked her and decided to ease her path, perhaps life as Lady Hastings would not be too difficult. Miranda, who had no trouble exerting her charm when she felt like it, only wished that Rupert could be as simply won over. She had not banished her doubts about his ability to become a faithful and devoted husband, able to forego his former libertine ways to lead a tame benedict's existence. The picture of Rupert as a doting husband and father was so fatuous she laughed at the thought, and Mrs. Clemson wondered briefly what Miss Houghton found so amusing in her recounting of the two hundred linen sheets she superintended as they inspected the well-stocked linen room.

That evening Miranda confided to Rupert that perhaps she might settle well at Hastings Halt.

"Thank you, my dear. You must not feel intimidated by Mrs. Clemson, who is something of a Gorgon and terrifies the younger staff. She has a searching eye but a kind heart and has been with the family since she was a tweeny."

"I felt rather like a tweeny myself when we met, but now we have a firm understanding," Miranda admitted with a twinkle.

"I have every faith that you will be an ornament to Hastings Halt," Rupert replied, knowing that would cause Miranda's mercurial temper to rise. He could never resist teasing her, enjoying her spirited response. She might not yet know it, but she was a passionate girl and the delights that promised soothed Rupert's sometimes uneasy feeling that she would never admit she loved him.

"I do intend to be not an ornament but a partner in this no-doubt turbulent union," Miranda riposted quickly.

"Turbulent. Oh dear, the vows not yet spoken and already

you are planning battles," he sighed soulfully. But laughter lurked in his dark eyes.

Miranda ignored that sally; and, since dinner was just then announced, she marched into the vast dining room, her back rigidly militant but her eyes sparkling. Just before they were seated, a footman brought Rupert a note. Answering a question from her grandfather, who was seated on her right, she missed the exchange and Rupert's frown when he opened the letter. Pocketing the missive, he made no mention of it and turned to Lady Moresdale seated on his left with a decorous remark about the ceremony. Charlotte was presiding as her brother's hostess and Miranda envied the smooth way she conducted her duties. Would she herself ever attain such composure? Miranda was delighted that she and Charlotte had settled their differences. She would not like to be at odds with Rupert's sister. Looking at the *soignée* Lady Worthington, gowned in a brilliant-emerald silk dress, cut simply and showing off Charlotte's smooth shoulders and diamond necklace, she wondered why such an attractive matron had not married again. Surely it was not from lack of offers.

Dinner proceeded quite happily. Rupert's French chef, imported from his London house, had extended himself. Turtle soup was followed by a well-dressed turbot and a saddle of lamb with *petits pois*. Miranda ate with a hearty appetite. She had no patience with girls who picked at their food, and she sighed extravagantly when finally the meal concluded with an imposing spun-sugar concoction. Only then did she notice that Rupert had remained remarkably silent throughout the meal.

"Is something bothering you, Rupert? I cannot believe you are unhappy over this family gathering. Actually I am amazed and pleased that it has all gone off so well. Even Robbie is on his best behavior," she exclaimed, for her brother had viewed this formal dinner gloomily when told he must be present.

"Just an annoying problem posed by an old retainer, a man that served with me in the war and lost a leg," Rupert explained. "Too vexing, but I will deal with it." Rupert's answer was indifferent, and Miranda forgot all about his confidence when the ladies repaired to the drawing room, leaving the gentlemen to their port.

Her grandmother indicated she wanted to talk to her, and Miranda found the old lady full of regret for the lost years. It took her some time to quiet her anxieties, but eventually she felt she had some success.

"You and grandfather have made mother so happy with this reconciliation. I know it was an aching pain for many years. Now we can really be a family and enjoy each other's company," Miranda assured Lady Moresdale cheerfully.

"We have you to thank, my dear. I do wish I had some of your spirit and ability to stand up to my husband as I am sure you will with your masterful Lord Hastings. I must admit he terrifies me."

"Oh, he's not *that* domineering. I find our exchanges quite a tonic, and I do care most dreadfully for him," Miranda admitted, relieved to confide in this timid old lady whose own marriage must have proved difficult at times. She was such a reticent soul, and the Earl at first glance seemed quite as intimidating as Rupert—but without his sense of humor.

"When you return from your wedding trip, you must bring Lord Hastings to visit us in Derby," Lady Moresdale invited, much heartened by her granddaughter's confidences. "And I hope young Robbie might spend some time with us, too. Such a dear boy."

They settled down to talk about Robbie, his school, his interests and his future, for Miranda was a great champion of that young man and was pleased to see that his grandparents shared her affection for him.

The evening ended early in deference to the Moresdales' age and Miranda had no further talk with Rupert. He bade her goodnight under the vigilant eyes of her family and promised that the following day they would ride over the estate. She drifted off to bed in charity with everyone, delighted that no storms had arisen to spoil the even tenor of the gathering. All seemed set for pleasant days ahead and in her relaxed mood she was able to view her coming marriage with hope and a determination to win Rupert's love as she had his admiration.

Chapter Twenty-Two

Miranda snuggled against her pillows, viewing her breakfast tray with pleasure. Sinful indulgence that it was, she accepted that one of the virtues of becoming Lady Hastings would include having her morning meal in bed. She remembered with distaste less enjoyable repasts at her family's Oxford table: Her father's complaints about the consistency of his eggs, his directives as to how Eleanor should arrange the household, and strictures to Miranda on her behavior. Not the best way to begin the day, which had usually included a host of tiresome chores. How different this was. And then she noticed a note propped up against her cup of chocolate, her name inscribed on the envelope in Rupert's distinctive hand.

Miranda, my dear,
    I regret we must delay our ride until later today as I have some business to conduct which cannot be postponed. Marcus is arriving today, and I would appreciate you greeting him in my absence. Try not to get into trouble and think kindly of your obedient servant,
                                    R.

Not exactly a lover's missive, but Miranda appreciated his thought of her. Would he always be so considerate? And she had forgotten that Marcus was expected to spend a few days and contribute his own brand of bluff friendliness to the company. Probably a good idea, as too much intimacy among her relatives might lead to dispute. Marcus was among her favorites—so obliging, so resolute, and so tolerant of life's vicissitudes. She was glad he was coming. Mention of Marcus distracted her from her musings about Rupert's errand. Rising, she dressed with the aid of her abigail, eager to face the day's events.

Late in the morning, just before luncheon, Marcus appeared, having ridden his curricle down from London. With his usual *sang froid* he accepted Rupert's absence, made his addresses to the company, and won Robbie's immediate respect as a veteran of the Peninsula. By the time they had finished luncheon, Miranda was beginning to wonder at Rupert's absence. She took Marcus aside, intending to confide in him about this summons from the one-legged veteran.

"Do you know of this man who has asked for Rupert's help?" she asked.

"I believe so, a surly devil but a valiant fighter. He lost his leg at Salamanca. Rupert saw to his being shipped home and established him as the landlord of the Pig and Whistle, a pub nearby. Of course, the whole village is owned by Rupert. The fellow—Jack Smithers is his name—appeared to think that was only his due. Now he is probably demanding Rupert extricate him from some scrape."

"Well, it must be a serious matter. I know Rupert expected to be back long before this. Do you think he may have met with an accident?" she asked, not liking the sound of this man.

"Not to worry, Miranda. Rupert is well able to take care of himself. But if you wish, I will ride down to the pub and investigate," Marcus said, not understanding her concern but willing to make allowances.

"I will go with you," Miranda said stubbornly. "You must

remember that Rupert has suffered some brutal attacks. I thought his unknown enemy had decided to abandon his aim, but perhaps he has not."

Marcus, reminded of the shot in his woods, frowned. At the time he had believed the incident the result of a stray poacher's bullet, but now Miranda told him again of the highwaymen on Hampstead Heath and of her father's abduction, which she believed was meant for Rupert. He could have met with another such assault. Marcus protested that he was capable of handling whatever lay ahead without Miranda's assistance, but she insisted on accompanying him. Although he discounted her alarm, he kindly consented, seeing she would brook no refusal.

"And I will tell Peter, in case we need reinforcements. If we do not return, he can notify the authorities," she announced with a determination that would not be shaken. She had become convinced that this errand had been a spurious excuse to lure Rupert away from his home and into peril. She would not remain fretting at Hastings Halt waiting for Marcus to discover Rupert's whereabouts. Her sense of tragedy loomed too great.

Hurrying to change into riding clothes, she begged Marcus to wait for her. Clemson, Rupert's butler, informed her that Peter was in the library, trying to catch up on some reading, and she interrupted him abruptly.

"I say, Miranda, aren't you being a bit silly? Rupert is on his home ground; he can take care of himself. You are imagining horrors that have no foundation, I am sure," Peter counseled when informed of her concerns.

"Rupert has been attacked twice and almost abducted once by a distant, unknown heir. He told me that much, and I think he was hiding some clue as to the identity of the villain."

"You sound like a page from one of Mrs. Radcliffe's gothic novels," Peter objected. Then, seeing that she would not be soothed, he added, "But you and Marcus embark on your rescue mission, and I promise if you are not back with Rupert within a few hours, I will ride out with reinforcements. But I warn you, Rupert will laugh at you for your ridiculous fears."

"And I will laugh with you. But, Peter, I simply have this feeling that all is not right." And before he could object further, she darted from the library, leaving Peter confused and now apprehensive himself. He hadn't realized just how seriously Miranda viewed these attacks, and Marcus, who had been present during one of them, must have found some cause to agree with her. How horrible if Rupert could have come to harm just when his life promised happiness! Miranda would be devastated, for Peter was convinced she was deeply in love with his uncle. He abandoned his books and walked to the window, watching as Marcus and Miranda mounted their horses and rode down the drive. Could there be any truth in Miranda's wild surmises?

Rupert, irritated at the interruption of his plans for the day, had nonetheless ridden off soon after an early breakfast to answer Smithers' appeal. His mind was thoroughly occupied with thoughts of Miranda. He had hoped that on this morning's expedition he might introduce her to the tenants and view the estate and in so doing produce an intimacy so far denied to him. He had determined to force some acknowledgment of her feelings about him from her under these benign auspices. And he had decided to confide in her about Cary— his suspicions that the young man could be behind the attempts on his life and the wicked motive which impelled the American.

He cursed Smithers. The man had held a grudge ever since the war, holding Rupert responsible for his injury although it had been French bullets which had cost him his leg. Rupert had done what he could to satisfy the man's demands, but he was not prepared to go further. Jack Smithers had been a trial since his youth, terrorizing the neighborhood with his viciousness, and war had done nothing to temper those actions. Rupert would make it plain to him he was tired of his complaints and not willing to make any further redress for what Smithers considered his wrongs. The man was a radical, a troublemaker, and a greedy extortionist as well. Rupert's patience was exhausted. His villagers were a conservative—mostly contented—lot, holding no resentment toward their generous landlord. Only Smithers cherished a vengeful thirst, but Rupert could deal with him, banish the man if need be.

He rode into the courtyard of the Pig and Whistle, noting its generally disheveled air. Obviously Smithers was not up to his job—probably imbibing too generously of his tavern's potions. Rupert called for a stableboy and, when no one answered his summons, stabled his horse himself in the grubby quarters behind the main building. On entering the low-raftered inn, he found Smithers behind the bar, quaffing ale from a pewter tankard.

"Rather early in the day to indulge, isn't it, Smithers?" he queried disapprovingly. "And what is the reason for this urgent summons?" His tone was far from encouraging. The place was a disgrace. It had been almost six months since he had last paid a visit to the Pig and Whistle, and conditions had deteriorated badly during that time. Either Smithers improved in his management and tempered his drinking or he would have to go. Whatever Rupert's sympathy for the man's plight, he would not countenance this sty on his doorstep.

"Ah, your lordship. Just in time to join me. I was sampling the latest shipment. Have a draft," Smithers whined, his eyes shifting beneath Rupert's searching stare.

Seeing that the man would not get down to business before he had consented to share a pint, Rupert nodded. Smithers poured the ale and handed it to him, watching slyly. Rupert downed it hurriedly, intent on learning the reason for this

235

summons, and that was the last he remembered. Whatever powerful drug was in the ale, it felled him almost at once, and he sank to the ground insensible. Smithers chuckled coldly and gazed down with satisfaction on Rupert's recumbent form. Leaving Rupert, he went to the back of the tavern and called to the man hiding there.

"He's all yours, guv'ner. And now I want the gold. I'll have to leave here right quick or the constables will be on me tail," he grunted.

"You won't be going anywhere, Smithers," the man said and shot him neatly through the heart.

Some hours later Marcus and Miranda rode into the yard of the Pig and Whistle. They were struck by the ominous silence surrounding the thatched, isolated tavern some half-a-mile from its nearest neighbors. Miranda, her fears confirmed, searched the lot for a familiar form.

"Where is Rupert's horse?" she asked. "We can't have passed him on the road. Something terrible has happened; I can feel it."

Marcus, himself infected with Miranda's worry and remembering the previous attacks on his friend, could not discount her concern. "There must be some explanation. Let us go in and see what the landlord can tell us."

But Jack Smithers was beyond telling anyone anything as they soon discovered. Marcus, taking one look, tried to shield Miranda from the gruesome discovery, but she saw the body outstretched on the floor before he could turn her away.

"I knew it. Rupert has been abducted." she cried, averting her eyes from the sight of the dead man. "Where can he be?"

"I have no idea. Whoever committed this murder must also be responsible for Rupert's absence. Perhaps he tried to interfere. But come, Miranda, don't despair. He is not here, and he might have escaped," Marcus reassured her. But he himself was not convinced of the truth of his words. He bent down and examined the body to make certain the man was beyond help and saw the bullet wound in his bloodied chest.

Miranda looked about wildly. "We must search this place. Obviously there is no one about, but Rupert may be wounded somewhere in the building."

"Yes, of course, but we must also summon the constable. This is a serious matter and should be investigated," Marcus insisted, taking charge. "Sit down here while I make a survey of the other rooms. There cannot be many places to hide. Will you be all right, not faint or feel sick?"

Accustomed to seeing dead soldiers, Marcus was not as appalled as Miranda who had never before encountered violent death. She had never, till now, even seen a corpse. Determinedly she shook off her nausea, her worry about Rupert overshadowing whatever shrinking she may have felt from the sight on the floor.

"Never mind me, Marcus." she said bravely. "We must find Rupert."

Marcus hesitated. He was reluctant to leave her while he searched the rest of the tavern, but he had no choice. Placing a chair for Miranda as far from the body as possible, he lowered her into it. "Will you be all right for a while?" he asked, noting her pallor.

"Yes, of course, Marcus. Do hurry," she urged.

Marcus, who had been in many dangerous corners during the war, somehow felt this eerie tavern and this murdered man were far worse, here in this bucolic spot far from any foreign battlefield. What had happened to Rupert and was he involved in this death? Loyally Marcus discounted any suggestion that Rupert might have killed the man or, if he had, that it was anything more than self-defense. He looked behind the scarred bar and saw little but dirt and bottles. Giving another glance at Miranda, who waved him on, he made a rapid search of the ground floor and the first storey. The tavern was small and the barroom had only two doors, one onto the road and another to the back courtyard.

Mounting the stairs, he feared the worst. Obviously the landlord lived above the taproom in a squalid bedroom with grey linen tossed carelessly on a rough wooden bed. Little else filled the room but a wardrobe. Marcus opened that gingerly, but it was empty save for a few grubby garments and a spare pair of muddy boots. Disgusted by the filth and seediness, he still missed nothing. Who would have patronized such a place? Returning downstairs, he glanced at Miranda, who was holding onto her composure with difficulty.

"The place is empty. There should be at least a potboy about. Obviously the villagers did not frequent this tavern often. Quite understandable as it's a nasty place with little to recommend it. I will have to go for help. Can you stay here alone or will you be afraid?" he asked, uncertain what to do about Miranda. "Perhaps it would be best for you to wait outside. I should not be long."

Miranda summoned a small smile. "I am not so fainthearted, Marcus. That poor man cannot harm me, and you say there is no one else on the premises. I will wait here, but do be quick. It's a frightful place full of menace."

Thankful that Miranda was not wailing and fainting as many females in her position would do, Marcus gave her a comforting pat, still hesitant to leave her but not knowing what else to do. "You could come with me," he suggested, turning away to throw a dingy blanket which he had brought from the upper storey over the body.

"I don't think I could mount my horse. I'm shaking too much. Sorry to be such a ninny," she apologized, rather ashamed of her timidity. "It's dreadful here, but I must stay. Rupert might return."

Reluctantly, Marcus decided to seek help, although he felt some compunction at abandoning her. What if the assassin returned? "I wish I had a gun."

238

"Even if you left it with me, I would be too terrified to shoot it." Miranda admitted. "But there is a knife on the bar. It's rusty and foul, but better than nothing. I will take that." Miranda gathering courage, suited action to words, and picked up the knife, used—no doubt—to cut bread or open kegs. Grasping it firmly beside her, she sat down again and motioned for Marcus to be gone. With one last worried look, he left her and hurried to his horse.

Alone, Miranda's fears subsided as she began to think about what happened in this awful tavern. Her eyes roamed around the room, ignoring the blanketed figure. A fugitive light streamed in the open door, and she noticed it shone on a small object some feet from the man's head.

Steeling herself, but clasping the knife, she stooped down and picked it up. What was this? Some blue worsted threads clung to the shiny silver button. It must have come off the attacker's coat. Inspecting it closely, turning it about in her hand, she saw that the button had the raised figure of an eagle on it. Putting the knife absently in her pocket, she pondered this discovery. She had seen this button before, and then she realized where. Randolph Cary had worn a coat with just such a button. She gasped. Had he been here? How could that be?

Holding the button tightly in her damp hand, she returned to her seat, overwhelmed. It could only mean that Cary had come to this tavern, and she was certain his motives could not have been honest. No decent man would visit such a den. Confused and distraught, her head awhirl, she could not fathom what it all meant.

Had Cary deceived them all? Was he playing some wicked game that involved Rupert? Her fright vanished before the dreadful suspicion which now consumed her. The button testified to his presence. There could not be two such buttons, for the eagle was a symbol of his heritage. Englishmen did not wear the American emblem. He had been here and possibly killed the tavern keeper. But why? Did the man pose some threat to him? Obviously Cary was not the ingenuous charming young man they had all thought. Her head bent, she examined the button, totally bemused, concentrating so on the terrible pictures forming in her mind she was deaf to her surroundings.

"I believe that belongs to me, Miranda. How unfortunate that you found it." A soft voice interrupted her jumbled thoughts. Startled, she looked up, surprised, as if she had conjured him up from her deepest fears.

"Randolph, what are you doing here? Did you kill that man?" she asked simply, prepared to hear any explanation no matter how preposterous, although the first dreadful notion of what Cary had done now appeared confirmed. "Where is Rupert?" she asked, noticing for the first time the hard expression in Cary's usually guileless blue eyes.

"Alive for the moment, but not for long. And I am afraid you, too, will have to be sacrificed. I am sorry you became involved. If you had broken your engagement, you would not be in any danger; but I should have known you would push your charming little nose into this business. Did you come here alone to rescue your fiancé?" he asked.

"Of course not, and my protector will return any moment with the authorities. They will want to question you," she declared resolutely, summoning up reserves of courage she did not know she had. Cary seemed all the more dangerous because of his previous amiability.

"You are bamming me, Miranda. I could dispatch you here to join that stupid man on the floor, but that would be cruel. I will not deny you one last reunion with your lover," he sneered and, taking a gun from his pocket, he waved it before her. Then, reaching down, he wrested the button from her hand and jerked her to her feet. "I think you are lying, but if not, there is little time to waste." And he dragged her unresisting frame to the back door of the tavern.

Chapter Twenty-Three

As Miranda stumbled down the rough path behind the Pig and Whistle, pushed from behind by Randolph Cary, she was comforted by the feel of the knife hidden in her riding habit pocket. She had little else to console her. Shocked and frightened by the realization that Cary had completely deceived them with the handsome facade of an agreeable young man, she faced the knowledge that he meant to kill her. There was the small chance that Marcus would return in time to rescue the two of them; but no matter how firmly she clung to this hope, she felt her spirits sinking. And what had happened to Rupert? She could not believe he had been lured to that wretched inn and then allowed himself to be captured by Cary. All these confused thoughts rattled in her head as Cary prodded and dragged her down a rutted lane, hidden by close-packed yews and prickly shrubs. Breathless, scratched by brambles, and feeling a stitch rapidly developing in her side, Miranda finally stumbled, gasping.

"Stop. I cannot go on," she cried. Then, facing her abductor, she gave him a fierce glare. "If you intend to shoot me, you might as well do it now because I refuse to be manhandled in this fashion." She should have been overcome by fear; but, whatever her initial fright, anger was now replacing her first reaction. How dare Cary attempt this murderous plot against Rupert?

Cary stopped because Miranda had jolted him for not only resisting his attempts to pull her along, but for her courage in facing him with such resolution. He hesitated a moment, admiration replacing the cruelty which had darkened his face. He looked as he always had—affable, open, charming; but Miranda shuddered. In a way she preferred the new ruthless countenance to the mask he had worn so cleverly, the pretense that had hidden his hateful motives.

"You know, Miranda, I regret exceedingly that you have become a pawn in this game I am playing. I sincerely admire you," he said in the gentle voice she had always found so captivating.

"You have an odd way of showing it, dragging me along this miserable lane and scaring the life out of me with threats as to your intentions. Let me tell you, Randolph, if you have harmed Rupert, you will not escape justice. You have behaved intemperately if you think you can engineer the disappearance of Rupert and me without any questions being raised. She suspected that such was Cary's egoism that humiliating him by jeering at his behavior would throw him off guard. The danger in taking such an attitude, if it occurred to her, did not prevent her from continuing.

"Be careful, Miranda. Do not try me too much," Cary warned, that ugly expression returning to his face.

"Why not? You have already warned me that you mean to kill me, so what would be the point in my cringing and wailing for mercy? I doubt very much if that would change your mind, which appears to be firmly settled on acting in this savage manner. I suppose you colonials are so used to violence living cheek by jowl with red Indians that it's all I could expect." She goaded him, determined to make him lose control. She prayed she would be able to gain enough time so that Marcus could come to their rescue.

Cary stared at her in amazement. Really she was a foolish chit, daring him when he had her in his power. She was asking for whatever she suffered.

"Stop this foolish bravado and get along or I will shoot you right here," he threatened and poked at her with the gun.

With a withering look, she reached down and brushed away the gun. "I doubt if you would because the noise of the shot might easily alert the searchers. And make no mistake, Mr. Cary, there will be pursuit and you will be taken," she promised with more assurance than she felt.

Cary glowered but only grunted and pushed harder against her side with the gun. Miranda drew herself up and looked him in the eye without a trace of fear. Then, surprisingly, she shrugged her shoulders. "Since I wish to know what has happened to Rupert, I will go along with you; but remove that wicked weapon from my person and allow me to walk sensibly."

She wondered at her temerity in challenging this madman. He had to be crazy or he would not undertake so dubious and murderous a scheme, she decided. There was little doubt this effort to remove Rupert was not his first. Right now Cary might think she was unafraid, but the sound of her beating heart echoed loudly in her ears and she feared he would sense her true terror. Her defiance had shaken him, and he looked unsure for the first time since she had met him in the tavern. She turned away and walked sedately up the path, knowing he was following and expecting either a blow or a shot at any minute. But only silence and growing shadows greeted her. Even the birds were quiet. They had now entered a deeper part of the grove, at least a half-a-mile from the Pig and Whistle, and she could smell the sea.

They proceeded single file for about ten minutes, but Miranda heard Cary's heavy breathing behind her and suspected he might lose whatever vestiges of control he had at any moment. Her appearance had surprised him and he was

243

having difficulty altering his plans to deal with her. Even if she could escape his vigilant eye, she was not about to make the attempt until she had discovered what had happened to Rupert. Suddenly, Cary grasped her arm and turned her from the path.

"We go down here. Be careful. It's quite treacherous," he warned, returning to the pretense of the careful, polite young man who had originally charmed her. What an actor the man was. Then before she could argue, he led her under a huge yew and behind a rock into a dank and brooding cave.

"An old smugglers' haunt," he explained, as if detailing the history of the Elgin Marbles. Just inside the cave, so dark she could see little, a man loomed up and she barely suppressed a scream.

"Ah, Bert, any trouble with our lordship?" Cary asked. The man, whom Miranda could now see, looked liked a rough burly type. Not a person with any sense of charity or mercy, she thought. He was dressed in heavy boots and a seaman's jersey, much-stained. His grizzled, brown hair tumbled over a low forehead. But it was the look in the hard, hot eyes which startled her the most. Not a man to challenge, although his openness made him somehow not as frightening as Cary. Whatever Bert's vices, they were written large on his face and he made no pretense of being other than he was, a brutal villain.

Cary confirmed her impression. "No use appealing to Bert," he told her. "He was impressed into the navy and suffered under the lash. He hates the British and quite enjoys having an arrogant lord under his thumb."

"I hope he will enjoy the results of his disastrous alliance with you, Mr. Cary," Miranda said defiantly. "And just where is Rupert? What have you done to him, you and this brute?" She saw she was chancing her fate provoking Cary in this way, and Bert did not appear to appreciate her bravado either.

"What's this mort doin', guv'ner? I have no truck with killin' doxies," he grumbled.

"Be quiet, Bert. Do you want to lose your head? We will have to kill them both, but right now I am more concerned with her horse. It's still at the tavern. You will have to retrieve it and put it with the other," he ordered.

"I ain't going back there with that dead cove on the floor. Someone will have found him, and there'll be a terrible to do. Like walking into a nest of hornets, 'twill be. And then there'll be those that come looking for her. She didn't come to that den by herself, whatever line she spun you," Bert argued with a shrewdness that surprised Miranda.

"Quite right, Bert. Don't stick your head in a noose for this one. You had best get out of here while you can. You will be accused as an accessory to a murder. He shot that tavern keeper you know," Miranda interposed as if her chief motive were to save Bert from the punishment he deserved.

"Pay no attention to her, Bert. She's lying. She came alone to rescue his lordship. She's a firebrand, that one. Stand outside and keep an eye peeled. I have a few words to say to these fine folk before they meet their end."

"Shoot him now and let's cut the cackle. I don't like the feel of this business." Bert shifted his feet nervously.

"Wait for me outside. I won't be long." Cary's pale blue eyes burned with a light that Miranda sensed even if she could not see. She felt he was rapidly approaching a crisis, and that did not bode well for her. Then, as Bert ducked out of the cave with a mutter, Miranda heard a groan and turned an inquiring eye on Cary. "That's Rupert. What have you done?" Without waiting for a reply, she hurried further into the cave. Slumped against the mossy stone wall toward the back of the cave, Rupert held his head in his hands and groaned once more. Ignoring Cary, Miranda rushed to his side.

"What's wrong, Rupert? Are you hurt?" she asked, putting a gentle hand on his face. He blinked blearily at her.

"Miranda, what the devil are you doing here? What has happened to me? The last I remember was drinking some foul brew with Smithers." He shook his head as if to clear it. "He must have drugged me."

Cary, angry at losing command of the situation, derided him. "At my instigation, my lord," he said with a scornful bow.

Rupert, making an effort, staggered to his feet and faced his adversary. "I might have suspected. Cary, by all that's holy, and, if I am not mistaken, the long-lost heir."

Miranda, beginning to grasp the source of the duel between the two, interrupted. "Yes," she cried. "He shot Smithers and left him lying on the tavern floor, where I found him."

Rupert threw an arm around her, more for support than a loving embrace. "And I suppose you thought you could tackle this villain on your own?"

"I didn't intend any such thing, but I found a silver button on the floor and recognized it as Randolph's." I was about to go for help when he arrived and carried me off as well," she said calmly. However furious and frightened she felt, she would not give Cary the satisfaction of seeing her cringe. She felt it would be only prudent not to mention Marcus, for Cary believed she had been alone. Perhaps they could stall him until help arrived, although she had doubts that Marcus could find this hideaway. Still, Rupert was alive although he was not in any condition to challenge their captor.

"Were you concerned when I did not return, Miranda, and decided to come to my rescue?" Rupert sighed, moved by her valiant effort but afraid all she had done was stumble into danger. "It's my fault. I had a good idea Cary was responsible for those earlier attacks. I should have taken precautions. And now you have walked into a mess which I would have done a great deal to prevent. Thank you, Miranda," he said softly.

He looked into her face with an expression which made her heart lurch, and she almost forgot Cary, who watched with cynical contempt.

"Touching, this reunion, but only temporary." he said sarcastically.

Rupert, his head throbbing but clearing rapidly, eyed him with disgust. "And what do you intend now, two more murders?"

"Of course. You will not escape this time. I have planned this for months and, with my goal so close, I have every intention of accomplishing it," Cary answered smugly.

"And as soon as the corpses are discovered you mean to claim the title and estates." Rupert spoke in a bored tone which might have deceived Cary, but not so Miranda, who realized he was afraid, not for himself, but for her. This knowledge heartened her, and she remembered the knife in her pocket. Could she distract Cary and charge him?

"I would not be so precipitate," Cary responded, proud of his scheme. "I am prepared to wait for some time before putting my claim to the test. I have all the necessary documents to prove that I am your rightful heir," he explained complacently. "Really, I have been very clever about the whole business. Unfortunately Miranda interfered and I cannot afford to let her live."

"Nor could you afford to let her marry me and produce a son. I quite understand. So I suppose you were the author of those letters which attacked her virtue. Rather shabby, don't you think?" Rupert flashed Cary a look of utter contempt. His natural arrogance was fast returning, and Miranda prayed he would not attempt some impossible course of action. But Rupert had been in tight corners before and was not yet willing to surrender hope of extricating Miranda and himself from their desperate plight.

"Suppose you tell us about this spurious claim. I understood you were the son of some colonials," he observed, knitting his brows in a frown that questioned the validity of his heir's suit.

Cary, irritated that his victims refused to cower and plead for mercy, waved the gun at them, but seemed eager to explain.

"The Carys adopted me. My mother, a tavern wench, married your drunken cousin and then died at my birth. The Carys, who had just lost a baby, were eager to take me on, and my graceless father had no objection. But I have the documents, marriage lines, and birth certificate to prove I am the only surviving heir, after yourself, to the Hastings title and estates."

"And your father?" Rupert asked coldly, as if the existence of such a man were doubtful. If Cary could be sufficiently needled, Rupert might be able to take advantage of his loss of temper.

"Alas, he died when I was a lad." Cary grinned spitefully.

"Or you might have been forced to attend to the matter yourself," Rupert suggested.

"Exactly. But we are wasting time. I understand you will do all you can to avoid your ultimate fate, but my patience is not inexhaustible," he finished with brutal candor.

Miranda moved closer within Rupert's arm and could not repress a shudder. But she had not lost her spirit. Pleading with this monster would do little good even if she could force herself to behave so cravenly.

"You know, Randolph, you are the veriest fool. Of course you will be suspected. And what do you plan to do with our bodies—leave them here to moulder away? That will avail you little. I believe the authorities will insist on proof of Rupert's death before awarding you the estate. It can be as much as seven years, if I am not mistaken."

Cary, unnerved by Miranda's calm demeanor and Rupert's unwavering stare, flushed. "That's enough," he growled. "Kiss your fiancé farewell, Miranda. If you had agreed to break your engagement, and agreed to marry me, I would not be forced to this pass."

"The thought never occurred to me. I must have had a sense that you were a counterfeit. And you are the fool; for if you had faced Rupert honestly, he might have honored your claim and given you a share of the estate."

"I had no idea you thought me capable of such generosity, my dear. Your faith warms me," Rupert intervened.

"A share! Why would I settle for a share when, with a little forethought, I could have the whole thing?" Cary cocked his gun.

"A little forethought and three murders. But I suppose they would not trouble you," Miranda rejoined with repugnance.

"Brave words, but I will shut your silly mouth," Cary said and stepped closer, as Miranda had intended he should. When he was within a few feet, she drew the knife from her pocket and threw it swiftly at his right arm. He yelped with surprise and pain and dropped the gun, which Rupert, bending over unsteadily, quickly retrieved. Holding the weapon with practiced skill, he faced his enemy.

"And now where are all your plans?" he asked.

Cary, furious at the failure of his months of waiting, seeing the prize slip from his grasp, bellowed with rage and launched himself recklessly at Rupert. Lord Hastings did not hesitate but fired, hitting Cary in his left shoulder. The pretender fell to the ground, blood pouring from the wound; and then, providentially, Miranda heard scuffling outside the cave. Leaving Rupert's side, she ran to the entrance to see Marcus, Peter, and a posse of hearty men securing the cursing Bert.

"Oh, Marcus, Peter, how glad I am to see you. Rupert has been drugged, and Cary planned to murder us both. You can't imagine . . ." Her voice trailed off, and to her shame she slid into a faint.

* * *

When consciousness returned, she was aware of a splitting headache and an uneasy sense of tragedy. What had happened? She was being held securely by Peter before him on a horse, and they were riding slowly down a strange road.

"Peter," she muttered, "Where is Rupert?"

"Just behind us with Marcus. He was not up to carrying you, or riding, I fear. That murdering swine gave him a powerful potion. I am surprised he recovered." Peter's voice was tranquil, but he was appalled by how narrowly Miranda and Rupert had escaped death.

"And Cary?" she asked faintly, afraid he might not have been apprehended.

"The constable has him secure. At any rate, he is in no condition to put up a fight. Rupert winged him neatly after you pricked him with that little knife. Lucky one of the villagers remembered that cave. Otherwise it would have taken considerably longer to find you." Peter was cheerful and a bit regretful. He had hated missing the most exciting part of the business.

"Pricked him! I'll have you know it was a noble thrust and routed him completely," Miranda protested, her spirits returning at this aspersion of her desperate action.

"Now, don't get your hackles up. It is bad for you and I was only teasing. You are a brave girl and deserve a huge reward for your courage. Rupert is very proud of you, although angry that you put yourself in such a horrid situation."

"Hah. He would be dead if I hadn't."

"I am sure you are right, but it is all over now. I never suspected that American of such villainy. What an actor the man is, charming us all while behind that affable veneer, a greedy murderous b—" Peter restrained himself just in time from uttering the scandalous word.

Miranda giggled weakly. "Unfortunately not a bastard, Pe-

250

ter, or we would not have been attacked." Then, a wave of giddiness overcoming her, she subsided. Her eyes closed without warning.

When she awoke sometime later, she was in her bed at Hastings Halt; and as her eyes fluttered open, her first sight was of Rupert sitting quietly by her bed, his hand in hers.

"So, my girl, you have decided to return to us. If I were not so relieved, I would turn you over my knee and give you a justly deserved spanking. How dare you put yourself in danger like that, rushing recklessly to my rescue?" he fumed.

But Miranda, now rapidly recovering her wits, would not allow such ingratitude. "You would be dead if I hadn't," she reproved firmly.

Rupert smiled. "Are you going to spend our married life rescuing me from my follies?" he demanded sternly. But his ardent eyes belied his fierce tone. "Oh, Miranda, I cannot spare you, so take care in the future. Promise me. If I lost you now, I could not go on." And, heedless of her condition, he took her into a hard embrace, his mouth stifling her protests with a kiss which warmed her cold arms and quivering lips.

"I love you, you little termagant; and even if you feel only the most lukewarm affection for me, I will never let you go," Rupert warned and continued to caress her, leaving her in no doubt as to his sincerity.

"My affection is not lukewarm. It's raging hot. I love you terribly, Rupert," she sighed, relieved that at last she had wrung from him the admission she craved.

"Yes, love me terribly, because that is what I feel for you," he agreed and kissed her again, his hands wandering possessively over her body. Then, recollecting what she had endured, he drew reluctantly away.

"That's quite enough. You are looking flushed and your heart is pounding. You should be resting and recovering from your ordeal. I want a relaxed and carefree bride in two weeks, not a wilting flower," he teased to relieve the tension.

"Two weeks," she sighed, giving him a provocative look. "However will we wait?"

"We won't," he said abruptly and took her back into his arms.

Epilogue

"What a beautiful city," Miranda exclaimed, gazing from the balcony of their *palazzo* onto the Grand Canal in the faint shimmering pink glow of Venice at dawn.

"Not as beautiful as you, Lady Hastings," Rupert murmured from the vast baroque bed behind her. She turned at his voice.

"Come, look, Rupert. I know you have seen it all before, but to me it is magic."

"I am captivated by the magic you possess, my lovely. What a passionate young woman you are. You have quite exhausted me," he teased.

Miranda blushed. "It is just that you are such a skilled lover, my lord. I am reaping the benefit of your misspent youth and all those earlier conquests, like the luscious Mrs. Castleton."

Rupert groaned. "I cannot win, and just when I thought that bestowing all my worldly goods upon you might have softened your unjust criticisms of my past."

"Not criticism." Miranda crossed to the bed and sat on the side, keeping a safe distance from her lord. "Really, Rupert, this has been the most wonderful wedding trip. Promise me we will return to Venice, to Italy, again." She put out a hand and smoothed back an errant lock of hair from his forehead.

"I promise, you witch," he said. Then, as if fearing emotion would get out of hand, he taunted her. "If you had not run off with poor Peter and charmed that villain Cary, I would never have realized what a siren you are. Before I knew it, you had me firmly in your clutches, all the time resenting what you were coming to feel for me."

"I quite disliked you for a long time," she admitted ruefully. Then, recovering her resilence, she countered, "But then you thought I was the most blatant adventuress. Still, you gave me my season and enabled me to attach an eligible husband. Very noble of you."

"Yes, although you might have taken Cary and then still become Lady Hastings," Rupert replied sardonically.

"Don't suggest such a horrid fate, Rupert. Even now I cannot believe Randolph Cary's treachery. We were all so kind to him, and I know you would have helped him if he had been honest with you about his claim."

"Perhaps, but under that charming facade, I soon sensed another motive. What a shock for that prig Adams to discover he had been harboring a murderer under his wing." Rupert smiled reminiscently, remembering John Quincy Adams' horror when Cary's villainy had been revealed.

"Well, Cary has been hanged, and a good thing, too," Miranda said firmly, not at all tolerant about his end.

"Vengeance, thy name is woman," Rupert sighed. "The female is always the most dangerous, and I would do well to remember it. But for now, I think I will bask in this unusual tenderness you show. Come back to bed."

"We must be up and about. I want to ride in a *gondola* and visit St. Mark's and San Giorgia Maggiore," she insisted, though not entirely unwilling to be persuaded against this plan.

"Later. Now we must think about the heir. Who knows, another dubious chap may turn up at any moment claiming my title," he mocked. And then, he pulled her down beside him and all thoughts of *gondolas*, St. Mark's, and Palladian churches were forgotten. Rupert was doing his best to provide the much-wanted son, and Miranda was in no condition to deny him.

A Memorable Collection of Regency Romances
BY ANTHEA MALCOLM AND VALERIE KING

THE COUNTERFEIT HEART   (3425, $3.95/$4.95)
by Anthea Malcolm

Nicola Crawford was hardly surprised when her cousin's betrothed disappeared on some mysterious quest. Anyone engaged to such an unromantic, but handsome man was bound to run off sooner or later. Nicola could never entrust her heart to such a conventional, but so deucedly handsome man. . . .

THE COURTING OF PHILIPPA   (2714, $3.95/$4.95)
by Anthea Malcolm

Miss Philippa was a very successful author of romantic novels. Thus she was chagrined to be snubbed by the handsome writer Henry Ashton whose own books she admired. And when she learned he considered love stories completely beneath his notice, she vowed to teach him a thing or two about the subject of love. . . .

THE WIDOW'S GAMBIT   (2357, $3.50/$4.50)
by Anthea Malcolm

The eldest of the orphaned Neville sisters needed a chaperone for a London season. So the ever-resourceful Livia added several years to her age, invented a deceased husband, and became the respectable Widow Royce. She was certain she'd never regret abandoning her girlhood until she met dashing Nicholas Warwick. . . .

A DARING WAGER   (2558, $3.95/$4.95)
by Valerie King

Ellie Dearborne's penchant for gaming had finally led her to ruin. It seemed like such a lark, wagering her devious cousin George that she would obtain the snuffboxes of three of society's most dashing peers in one month's time. She could easily succeed, too, were it not for that exasperating Lord Ravenworth. . . .

THE WILLFUL WIDOW   (3323, $3.95/$4.95)
by Valerie King

The lovely young widow, Mrs. Henrietta Harte, was not all inclined to pursue the sort of romantic folly the persistent King Brandish had in mind. She had to concentrate on marrying off her penniless sisters and managing her spendthrift mama. Surely Mr. Brandish could fit in with her plans somehow . . .

SHE DEFIED CONVENTION

be the lesser of two evils! To esca
ateful suitor, Miranda Houghton
off with Peter Worthington instea
a thoughtful husband, even if he
en route to their marital destin
Peter's guardian, the arrestingl
ings. Though his haughty manne
had to admit that his rakish cha
entional proposal sound most in

HE COURTED SCANDAL

duty to protect his ward from th
ch as the auburn-haired Miranda
g for the little baggage himself. O
ould only be a useful ploy to esca
s; in return, he would sponsor Mi
was well—until the dashing pee
and tender stirring in his own ja

eluctant Pro

04232

0 71268 00399 7

ISBN 0-8217-4232-9